Lyle —
Anything
is possible!

[signature]
5.17.2006

Gaia's Revolt
The Day Tomorrow Never Came

Gaia's Revolt
The Day Tomorrow Never Came

Patricia Griffin

Gaia's Dreams Publishing
Orlando

ACKNOWLEDGMENTS

Many thanks to all those along the way that generously provided this wanderer a place to sit and scribble for hours. Much of this book was conjured at, and I'd like to give a special thanks to, The Coffee House of Thornton Park, Bear Rock Café, and Firehouse Subs #195.

The above trademarks are used under permission of the establishments' owners with the sole purpose of acknowledging the referenced establishments, and in no way are meant to imply an endorsement by said establishments. The statements, views, and opinions presented in this book are either the product of the author's imagination or are used fictionally, and are not endorsed by, nor do they necessarily reflect, the opinions of The Coffee House of Thornton Park, Bear Rock Café, or Firehouse Subs.

This book is a work of fiction. Names, characters, places, and incidents either are the product of the author's imagination or are used fictionally, and any resemblance to actual persons, living or dead, business establishments, events, or locales is entirely coincidental.

Published by Gaia's Dreams Publishing

Copyright © 2006 by Patricia S. Shao

All rights reserved. No part of this book may be reproduced in any form, except for the inclusion of brief quotations in review, without permission in writing from the author/publisher.

http://www.gaiasdreams.com

Book Design by Storm

LCCN 2006923425
ISBN 0-9779033-0-3

Printed in the United States of America
First Edition: May 2006

To my companions along the way that have inspired, supported, and influenced me during this journey and many past, may we go down many more roads together.

And the earth proclaimed...
Take only that you may give,
For only by giving may you live,
Balance will always pervade...

A circle has no beginning and no ending,
It has all beginnings and all endings,
Each journey, each path, a circle is made,
The earth entrusted her meaning...

But the snake spoke with its silver tongue,
Of paths and messages only it could see and learn,
And veiled itself in tradition and fear...

While the messenger entered the circle too near,
Potential revealed a path seemingly limitless,
Compelled is She, Compassion as boundless...

But the grieving child is infected with madness,
And casts aside all knowledge and independence,
The silver tongue feeds and darkness enfolds...

Strange bedfellows they make,
The child and the snake,
The circle, the messenger,
Both reel from attack...

A connection is made and a pattern revealed,
The messenger and fellows, knowledge they now wield,
As one journey does end, so another begins...

A bread crumb, a gift, the messenger finds,
Her children she blesses with abilities new,
But their path they must uncover and no harm must they do....

As the serpent and company do plot and scheme,
From inside weakness builds along the seam,
The circle they do wish to break,
Yet the mother reveals herself to the snake....

Deception is a double edged sword,
The serpent refuses to see,
When the clock is ticking and the lies are told,
Its use must eventually, the innocent set free...

Empowered with knowledge of frailty and fault,
The fellows prepare, the snake they will halt...

Of peace and of blood,
They will challenge in battle,
The messenger falls, the foundation rattles...

The mother cares not for the road,
Taken more or less,
Only for herself and her children,
The journey is the true test.

Gaia's Revolt
The Day Tomorrow Never Came

prelude

And the earth proclaimed...
Take only that you may give,
For only by giving may you live,
Balance will always pervade...

It didn't come suddenly. There had been plenty of warning of the impending cataclysm, from Nostradamus to Edgar Cayce and beyond, for ages psychics and prophets endured disparagement as they desperately tried to prepare society, and more recently, Gaia – the earth herself – had cast out a warning of her impending change. For over a year before the Cataclysm, the number of natural disasters had inexplicably risen – just as the prophets and psychics had predicted. California and Japan were being rocked to their foundations by earthquakes that broke both intensity and frequency records, sending the few residents that were concerned more with their lives than their property values fleeing to more stable ground. From the Virgin Islands up the eastern coast of America and across to Great Britain, massive hurricanes were pounding away all traces of civilization faster than the disaster crews could rebuild. And Canada and the Soviet Republic were frozen wastelands, in the middle of a severely harsh winter that refused to end despite the calendar indicating that their summer was approaching. Yes...society could have prepared itself.

1

A circle has no beginning and no ending,
It has all beginnings and all endings,
Each journey, each path, a circle is made,
The earth entrusted her meaning...

The crackles, pops, and hisses from the fire blended with the chirping, screeching, and howling of the night animals in a calming rhythm. But despite the crisp night air and this music of her solitude, Jez was unable to relax. With every breath she scanned the darkness for any signs of an approaching stranger. And she worried. It had been over three weeks since the world had been turned on its side, and Jezzelle still had not discovered any leads on the whereabouts of her sister Alzatia or their mother. She was certain that they had both survived the Great Cataclysm, her intuition told her that much. But she had yet to develop her innate psychic abilities enough to sense their location. Sometimes during her nightly meditations, Jez felt that she could sense their emotions, whether they were frightened or upset or at peace at that moment in time and she wondered if they could sense her too at these times. Did they feel her thinking about them? Did they know that she was desperately searching for them? It frustrated Jez that she could tell something was changing in the way her brain worked but she had no idea how to harness or direct it. She had always known that one day the secrets of the human mind would be revealed, she just didn't know if she had time to wait for the answers. She was thankful for the gifts that she had, after all, her intuition had saved her mother's and sister's lives, as well as her own.

Jezzelle had been on her way to work. Puk, her massive Heinz 57, was sitting contently in the passenger seat enjoying the rare sunny day by hanging his head out the window as she sped down the street. Suddenly Puk pulled his head in and began barking as he frantically scratched at the dash, and she had known. Without a second thought Jezzelle had turned around and gone home. She was not just a believer in the unconventional, free-thinking was at the core of her every action. Her mind refused to be satisfied by answers that only served to limit the possibilities because "God said so" or "it was scientifically impossible." To her, psychic predictions of an upcoming cataclysm deserved as much respect as scientists' theories on black holes, and she researched them all equally. So she had recognized the earth's signals of the past year and heeded the warning, keeping survival packs in both her car and house. Jezzelle had even gifted "hurricane" survival packs to her family and close friends who had agreed to keep the packs handy although they thought that much of the contents were overkill. Jez didn't bother to explain, she was just relieved that they would be prepared.

In the five minutes it had taken Jez to make it home, the Cataclysm had begun. The sky had grown dark and the winds howled from all directions. Within a few minutes the rains poured down from the sky so hard that it was impossible to see even a few inches away. The sounds of blaring horns, screeching tires, and crunching metal filled the air as car after car slammed into whatever was unfortunate enough to cross its path. The yelping and screeching of agitated family pets added to the message of doom carried on the winds as the emergency alert system buzzed from every radio and TV. Tornadoes appeared out of no where and lightning struck every few seconds, people were urged to remain home and find shelter, but despite all this chaos, the severity of the situation escaped most people until the earth started to move under their feet.

As Jez regained her mental focus she remembered her own family and called her mom, her hands were shaking so badly from her growing anxiety that she had to dial the number twice. Jez mouthed the words carefully in order to keep her voice from shaking, "Mom, is Dad there?"

"No honey, he's already left for work," her mom's voice was cheerful and comforting as always, "Why?" the wind and rain on the other end of the line created ironic background music to her mother's cheer.

"What about Al?" Jez asked, the panic seeping through her controlled enunciation.

Her mom's voice lost its cheer, "No she's not here either. Now what's this all about Jez? You sound really upset."

"It's time," her voice quivered.

"Time for what?" Jez's mom was caught off guard by the sound of fear in her own voice.

"What I warned you about..."

"Do you mean that end of the world thing? You can't be serious, I thought it was just a hurricane watch." And suddenly she accepted the reality she had known all along, "What am I supposed to do? What about your father? I have to go after him. And Al?" her mother cried between erratic breaths.

"It's going to be okay Mom. Yes, it's that end of the world thing but there's time. Now don't worry about Dad or Al, I'll get in touch with them in time. Mom, please just stay home and find a safe place..."

Her mother interrupted, her voice now full of apprehension, "Jez, what kind of safe place? Maybe I should go to the local shelter?"

Jez attempted to sound reassuring, "No, don't go anywhere. Just assume you're preparing for a tornado...Mom!..." The connection had been lost and Jezzelle knew that it would be futile to redial the number, the phone lines there were obviously down and there were others that she needed to warn. Her dad refused to carry a cell phone so there was no way of reaching him before he arrived at work, if he ever arrived. Even if she was able to warn him at work, there really would be no time for him to prepare and she was fairly certain that he wouldn't have the survival pack she had given him. For the brilliant professor that he was, sometimes he could be a damned fool! Jez cursed the stubbornness that accompanied his genius. She unconsciously knew that it was too late to help him and quickly dialed Al's cell number next.

"Hello, Jez," the caller ID had forewarned her sister.

"Yes, Al...It's me," she struggled to speak against her throat constricting with a new fear that only the familiarity of her sister could release, "It's time."

"For what? That shift?" Al anticipated her thought and her voice spilled with concern.

"What else? Please take care of yourself and I think Mom could use your help," Jez ended with a sob, relieved that she didn't have to explain herself to Al.

"OK, but if you're wrong about this," Al lovingly chided Jez, "I love you Sis...hugs and flowers."

Jez wept, "Love you..." ...static... and the signal was lost. Jez prayed that she had reached Al in time for her to make it to their mother's house before the roads washed out. *Time to follow your own advice Jez,* she swallowed the new lump growing in her throat and set to the task of surviving.

Although Jez regularly inspected and refreshed her survival pack and knew everything that she would require was there, she now felt the need to inspect everything one last time. The reality of the situation was fast setting in, but the fear and panic growing inside her were burgeoning at an even faster rate. She would not have been able to admit to this fear even if her terror stricken mind had been clear enough to comprehend it. The best she could do right now was to occupy herself with menial physical tasks, so she proceeded to hurriedly rifle through her survival pack. Batteryless flashlight/radio, Camelbak, water, water purification tablets, blankets, bed roll, ration bars, pillows, cell phone and photovoltaic charger...*I think that's everything.* She gathered up her survival pack, called Puk to her side, and made her way to her shelter. Her modest income as a scenic artist couldn't afford her a true "Panic Room", so she had previously determined that the large oak desk her father had given her would provide the sturdiest shelter within the house. Now she hunkered down under the desk with Puk, curling her petite frame loosely around him. Her make shift shelter reminded her of her secret hideout as a child, hiding from her sister Alzatia in the back of the closet. These memories, along with Puk's warmth, were the only thing keeping Jezzelle from losing her sanity as she felt the ground shifting under her. The earth screamed through the howling wind and creaking floorboards, and she could hear glass breaking and metal grinding. Sirens blared in the background as several well-meaning rescue vehicles went on what probably would be their final trips. Jez was horrified as she experienced so many people dying around her, feeling their collective terror as a thousand souls cried out at once. It was as if her consciousness was linked with the mind of every person in the city and she was filled with their pain, their fear, and their death as if it were her own. But still more terrifying was the familiarity of one soul that she sensed...it felt like her father. Jez struggled to shield herself and finally closed her mind to their cries, but it was too late to protect her from the effects of the trauma, she fought for each breath as her body quivered.

In a split second Jez lost the fine control she maintained over her fear. As the terror ripped through her like a razor, Jez's body and mind convulsed and her ability to reason was lost. Tears gushed from her eyes and the intensity of her sobs nearly caused her to hyperventilate and lose consciousness. Jez had never before been forced to face head on the distinct possibility of her own death. Now she was sure that she was going to die despite all the precautions she had taken. There was no way that this little desk would prevent her house from crushing her, she was so angry with herself for believing that she would be okay. It was so unfair that this should happen when she was following all the "rules". She recycled everything she could and conserved and reused everything else, she volunteered the majority of her free time to environmental causes, and gave everyone the benefit of the doubt and held no ill will toward anyone. Everything about her was fused with positive energy, so why were the powers that be allowing this to happen? This couldn't happen because if it did she was going to die! Jez put on her headphones, attempting to block out the screams – her screams.

It had been almost an entire day before Jezzelle had gained the courage to leave the safety of the oak desk. She still had trouble accepting that she was alive; to her it was a miracle, but she felt that there was no one left that gave a damn. Her despair fed her pessimism and she was sure that her house would collapse around her once she emerged from under the desk. Puk had ventured out only hours after the earth had settled and had returned wet and dirty, but otherwise unscathed, so she knew logically that it was relatively safe to go out. Notwithstanding this, Jez didn't really want to see how bad everything was. Or was it that she didn't want to say goodbye to her old world even though she had prepared and looked forward to the new one? Jez wondered if her negative perception could possibly get any worse, and based on the view from her desk she could only imagine the tremendous devastation.

Long ago anything breakable or precious to her had been packed in bubble wrap. Now everything she had not packed away was strewn about the floor. Pages from books fluttered in the breeze across the room which glittered with broken glass from windows and mirrors. The floor itself was twisted and buckled as if the earth had tried to free itself from the confines of the house's foundation. And in their struggle the bookshelves and lamps in the room had ended up in a strangely balanced pile in the middle of the floor where parts of the ceiling were hanging down, allowing the insulation from the attic to leak out. Even her oak desk had taken a beating and was now sitting at an odd angle – the symbiosis between the desk and the interior wall seemed to be the only thing keeping them both in place.

Remarkably, Jezzelle's condition was a striking contrast to the condition of the room. Aside from being shaken up, Jez was nearly unmarked, her makeup gone except for the eyeliner and concealer wedged in the fine wrinkles of her young looking face and her skin was coated with a fine layer of grime and sweat. Still, the mild wounds she had suffered were healing quickly. The thin cut across her forehead and her other numerous abrasions had already scabbed over and her bruises had started to fade from their original bright purple.

Jez grabbed her survival gear and a few personal belongings and set out, for the first time witnessing the true magnitude of the destruction that had taken place. As she clawed her way through the maze of debris, she soon discovered that everything was coated with a thick layer of soot and dust. The smog from fires burning out of control across the city seeped under her goggles and burned her eyes, forcing her to survey her surroundings through more tears. The neighboring houses lay in various degrees of ruin. Most roofs had either collapsed inward along crumbled walls or slid off the underlying building entirely, and the Spanish tile from one house littered the landscape like confetti. All but the sturdiest trees had lost their grip on the earth and lay wounded across roofs, cars, or whatever would provide the needed support. The man-made light posts and street signs fared no better, most lay bent and broken along the street. And the street itself was nothing more than a collection of large chunks of jagged, crumbling asphalt and concrete placed sporadically along randomly arranged trenches. Cars and trucks lay upturned or flipped where the earth had thrown them, and bodies, both human and animal, peered out from inside. Still more bodies and parts lay about the landscape or caught under some large piece of debris, and the resulting stench of rotting flesh had already started to permeate every molecule in the air. As Jez inhaled her first breaths of the smoke and death filled air she nearly choked, running to the closest bush where she knelt as all the despair and disgust burst forth from her belly. She heaved and sobbed in rhythm with the still moaning earth until she lay there entirely empty, physically and emotionally.

Jez sat up and wiped the tears from her eyes and the filth from her face and hands with a wet nap. She felt some how distanced from her body; it was as if she was watching the world through a two-way mirror and it made her dizzy, she had to get away from this place before she went completely mad.

She scrolled "I'm alive" across her front door with a large red Sharpie just in case someone came looking for her, and with a sense of finality, she reluctantly began walking "north" towards her family's last known location. Since north was no longer North according to her compass and her GPS had died searching for a signal, she decided to follow the remains of the old interstate north. The level of destruction seemed to increase as Jez walked toward the highway and she tried to close herself off from her senses but everywhere she looked she could see and smell the signs of death. Even more bodies littered the approaching landscape than in her neighborhood, making the stench even more unbearable. Jez battled the urge to be sick again while the urgency of her need to find her family increased with the vision of each lifeless body. She received no comfort from the fact that other survivors were wandering about the rubble or that the injured were receiving some level of basic medical attention. She tuned out the calls for help from the other survivors, she couldn't even help herself right now, so how could they expect her to help them. Jezzelle began to run with an overwhelming frenzy, she had to get away from the city and its surrounding death. Puk followed protectively by her side.

Jezzelle had been traveling north along the highway for three days now and she estimated that she had traveled about ninety miles, which left at least four hundred to go! Although she had been traveling twelve hours a day, she was covering a shorter distance with each hour that went by. Jez had kept herself in shape and ran various distance races on a regular basis, but now her body ached all over and the muscles in her calves felt as if they had turned into stone. Adding to her misery was the fact that her hands and knees were cut and bruised from having to climb over mountains of debris. Living in a relatively flat area, it hadn't occurred to Jez that she would have to do so much climbing, and she now regretted not taking up the sport. And she had thought she was so overly prepared! Jez consoled herself with the fact that she had finally made it past the city limits and was now surrounded by relative wilderness. She avoided walking directly beside the road and its certain carnage, so she only stumbled across the occasional body. Although she had desensitized herself to the gruesomeness of the dead through her baptism by the bush at her home, she still preferred to avoid any unnecessary contact. The sheer effort that she had to make in order to continue to survive day after day wore on Jez even more emotionally than the physical beating her body suffered. It seemed she had to fight these mental battles more and more often and she was having a difficult time finding a reason for her survival as she once again labored to force the doubts to the back of her mind.

The smell of fresh oranges snapped Jez out of her forlorn daze and the sight of an overturned produce truck provided the distraction she needed. The stench from the driver's corpse remained despite the fact that someone before her had already disposed of the body. But more importantly, the large truck created an insulating distance and most of the fruit was still good. She practically jumped into the piles of fruit she was so delighted with her find. The scent of the oranges was so overwhelming as she started to pick through the piles of fruit that she ate two of them right there. With her belly full, she packed as many oranges in her sack as she could carry. Still there was so much fruit left that the potential waste pained her, so she marked the location on her old highway map just in case she ran into anyone with whom she might share her discovery. Refreshed, Jezzelle walked on.

The long shadows cast by the setting sun signaled Jez it was time to make camp so she and Puk began to survey the area for signs of other travelers or anyone that might prove to be a threat. Once Jez was satisfied that they were the only ones in the area she selected a grassy knoll at the edge of the woods to settle down for the night. As she approached the tree line, she was greeted by the recognizable stench of death; it was a dead horse still wearing its saddle and bridle. Besides a sizeable bloodstain in the dirt, there was no sign of the former rider, who had obviously been caught off guard by the Cataclysm during a morning ride through the woods. Jez doubted that the rider or anyone disposing of him would be returning, so she salvaged the riding gear and set to the task of cremating the horse's remains. As if to lighten the gravity of building such a monumental pyre, Puk handed Jez the slobber soaked stick he had been chewing on.

By the time she had the cremation bonfire well established it was late in the evening and she was physically exhausted, but the smell of burning horse flesh was overwhelming. The fire was well contained in the ditch the horse had been caught in, so Jez decided that she would be close enough to monitor the bonfire as long as she could see its light, not smell it and she made her way through the dark to an alternate campsite.

As she drifted off to sleep, Jez made her plans for the next day. She figured that there should be a stable nearby and some of the horses must have survived the Cataclysm. After all, the dead one had to come from somewhere and she needed something to hope for. Jez was seriously beginning to wonder if she would be able to make it the rest of the way on foot and she desperately prayed she would be able to find a horse in the morning.

The sunlight sliced through the veil of clouds over the pasture causing the dew to sparkle with a rainbow and the scent of new grass and flowers to fill the air as the earth began to warm where Jez lay in the still of sleep sheltered under a large oak. Despite the protective branches of the great tree, a few rays of the sun penetrated its canopy and their warmth on Jez's tender sunburned nose roused her from sleep, but it was Puk's wet kiss that ultimately forced her to rise with the morning while it was still early and the heat of the day had not set in yet. Before the shift the weather had been plagued by cold fronts and storm clouds, warm sunny days were a rarity, but now the weather was tropical and Jezzelle's skin had taken on a bronze tone from the constant exposure to the sun.

    She was anxious to find the horses so Jez headed out before it got too hot. She reasoned that the rider could not have had time to travel far from the stable since the Cataclysm had hit early in the morning, therefore the stable must be close by. She followed the horse's tracks away from the highway, making a mental note of the landmarks to find her way back. Puk had already taken off, she assumed he was scouting the area ahead of her as always.

After hiking along the trail for roughly an hour she detected her objective. While the stable was still not visible, she could hear the neighing of horses nearby. She approached the pasture slowly and carefully, not wanting to startle the horses. It had been six days since the CAT, as she was now calling the Great Cataclysm, so she reasoned the horses should have had time to calm down. Jez assumed her appearance would serve to calm them down further since they were conditioned to the presence of humans; however, she was careful to approach them in a subservient, non-threatening manner. She could see three horses in the pasture, two males and a female. Although Jez thought one of the males might be a gelding, she was positive that the larger male with the pearlish gray coat and bright ivory mane and tail was a stallion and the dominant one in the small herd.

Jez remained kneeling silently at the edge of the pasture, captivated by the beauty of the horses and filled with a renewed determination, maybe she would make it home after all. Suddenly the stallion nickered loudly and shook his forceful head sending waves of sunlight through his mane. She watched him direct the others in what must be the direction of the stable; he had picked up on her scent despite the fact that there was no breeze to speak of. He was an incredibly sensitive and intelligent creature and Jez decided she would like the assistance and companionship of the gray stallion. She would take the mare and gelding along on her journey as well; she could use them as pack horses and, if necessary, trade them for supplies, although, she wouldn't split up his herd if she could avoid it.

Just as she was wondering how she was going to go about rounding up the horses, Puk appeared. He began herding the horses toward their camp near the highway just as if he had been doing it all his life. Jez laughed, it was the first time she had laughed since a movie she had seen last week...but that was a different lifetime, a different world. Just as last week she would have never attempted taking the horses since it would have been considered grand larceny, but today Jez's decisions were based purely on survival.

2

But the snake spoke with its silver tongue,
Of paths and messages only it could see and learn,
And veiled itself in tradition and fear...

With a loud snap, the thick oak support beams of the roof finally gave way, leaving the ceiling to crumble under the weight of the water. It had been just over eighteen hours since the CAT, but the old church could resist no longer. It was a testament to its strength that it had not crumbled to the ground during the CAT, for the wood and stone structure of the old church was no match for the will of nature. The high ceilings and thick stone walls had provided shelter to both the faithful and desperate for nearly one hundred years, but now the only thing that seemed to be holding the heavy stones in place was luck, or maybe it was the power of their faith. The grand carved steeple, which had been the tallest in the county at one time, crashed down into the chapel and shattered, shooting shards of stone and stained glass across the room. The hard wood floor glittered with the jagged bits of glass and stone and every gust of wind seemed to force another stone out of place. Did the old church sense that without the steeple as its anchor, the structure was too weak to stand in this new world? Suddenly the silence was broken by the explosion of another pipe bursting, the water quickly streaming through the church as it made its way to the world waiting outside.

Cold water and plaster splattered from the church's wounded ceiling and ran down the body of an old man slumped next to the altar. The bloodstains on his sermon robes began to fade with the ice cold water which rushed down to the floor with a powerful determination without regard to the obstacle he presented. The water mindlessly flowed into his mouth and nose and he coughed in reflex. The man stirred.

Sam Brown was a tall, wiry man whose steel blue eyes and silvery gray hair created the illusion of the perfect southern gentleman when he greeted his flock each day. He had come to the church fresh out of seminary school, nearly thirty-seven years ago. Sam had given his life to and grown old with his ministry. He had performed every marriage, baptism, and funeral service that had taken place since his arrival. Sam was the father of the entire town, never marrying nor having a family of his own, and he controlled the town as he would a child. Being the pastor of the only church in a small Carolina town gave him an almost unlimited control over the one hundred sixty-seven lives of the townsfolk since, as a Man of the Cloth, Sam's views were taken as those authorized by God's word. When Sam was not busy writing or conducting his sermons he occupied himself by monitoring the activities of his flock. He had no time for anything other than his control over the town; nothing happened in town – his town – without his knowledge and approval. This control over and prominence in the community were the only things that brought joy to his solitary life and Sam justified this satisfaction and joy by rationalizing that it was merely the joy of doing the Lord's work – after all, serving the Lord was supposed to be joyous.

Recently he had used this influence, along with the townsfolk's fear of the new century, to require attendance at daily sunrise sermons. Each morning he would purport to be guiding the townsfolk straight into the pearly gates, they need only follow his directions as given to him by God's words in the Holy Bible. He commanded the town to return to a simpler way of living – the modern world created too many distractions from God, whereas a life free of modern distractions was deemed a step closer to God. Televisions, stereos, video games, and the like were accorded to serve no useful purpose according to the Lord as he spoke through Sam Brown. Accordingly, any piece of technology that was used for leisure was viewed as taking time away from worship and was therefore deemed unnecessary and forbidden.

In their feverish need to comply with Sam's every word, the townsfolk overcompensated, interpreting his command to include anything and everything that used electricity. Almost instantaneously church members had amassed a mountain comprised of televisions, stereos, MP3 players, video games, washers and dryers, and every other possible appliance as their need to destroy these items as quickly as possible exploded into a panicked chaos. The mountain appeared to be throbbing and breathing, fed by the ever-increasing frenzy, as if at any moment it would erupt into some menacing life form that would destroy all mankind. Men, women, and children seemed to be running in circles as they went to and from their homes in an effort to rid themselves of every potential seed of damnation. Fights and arguments broke out as people encroached upon each other's efforts to destroy their forbidden belongings and neighbor accused neighbor of sabotaging his quest for salvation. The monster grew bigger. The few members of the congregation that dared to refuse to accept that evil was embodied in technology were helped to see the light by the rest of the congregation. In evidence of this, Sam watched proudly as Ethan Brown threw his vrBox to the ground despite the admonishments and protests from his parents. Sam smiled broadly as he further witnessed the growing chaos of his congregation gathering together to burn, pulverize, and bury the mountain of appliances. The frenzy he had created made his heart race and his mind soar. It was truly wondrous that God had given him such tremendous power to carry out His word. The monster was born.

Samuel raised his gaze from the Bible resting on the podium. His vision was filled with the smiling face of every member of his congregation. Every pew was full and yet still more people stood along the walls and in the corridors. Adoration permeated every piece of stained glass, floorboard, and wall of the church. Despite the howling winds outside, Sam could hear the collective breath released by every member of the church as they realized that he had finished reading the excerpt from the Bible; frenzied applause soon followed. The congregation was so entranced by Sam that they failed to hear the tremendous storm brewing outside the church. The claps of thunder and howling winds were no more than a soundtrack played to emphasize Sam's words. And now the noise from the congregation's thunderous applause caused the members to not hear the first moans and creaks of the church's tortured foundation. The swaying chandeliers and wobbling candlesticks went unnoticed by eyes fixed on the Lord's messenger.

SMASH...the seven-foot brass crucifix attached to the wall appeared to fly from behind the altar before crashing to the floor, just missing Sam.

Instantly, silence filled the room and suddenly everyone was aware of the screaming walls of the church and the howling winds and thunder. With infinite awareness a small child screamed and began to cry, and with that the congregation lost its collective composure. With the congregation on the edge of panic, Sam's need for power took control.

"All right, everyone calm yourself!" Sam commanded and obediently the congregation regained its composure and grew silent. "It seems that God has chosen to test us sooner rather than later. You have known for quite a while that God was preparing to serve judgment on this world. I have been readying you for this day. Now is the time that your faith must remain strong! Now we must pray for guidance and forgiveness. As long as our faith remains strong and we accept the Lord's commands there is nothing to fear. Everyone, now is the time to kneel and pray to God for forgiveness! Joshua, would you lead us off in prayer?"

With the spotlight now on him, Josh's thick chiseled face beamed with pride, the intricate facial muscles struggling to suppress a smile. His deep green eyes peered up at Sam from under his thick brow. Josh slouched his upper body forward in a subservient manner and lowered his voice to a respectful tone, "Ah would be honored ta, Pastor Sam," he whispered. Josh clasped his large callused hands tightly and began the prayer. He prayed for God's mercy and the strength to follow

God's will. He thanked the Lord for allowing them to hear His Word by sending Sam to guide them.

Everyone lovingly regarded Josh as a gentle giant, even though he was not so much tall as he was thick with only a slightly greater than average height, but his girth made him truly intimidating. Josh could have easily taunted even the largest football player or professional wrestler as years of hard work on his parents' farm had caused the once skinny little boy to swell into a thick and powerful man. But when it came to Sam, Josh was the one who was intimidated; he was no longer aware of his true size, idolizing and revering Sam as a small child would.

Josh had been raised alone on his parents' farm by his aunt ever since his parents' death nearly twenty years ago. He had been preoccupied with birthday wishes for bikes and dogs and skates when he had learned of the tragic auto accident taking his parents. Josh was devastated by their death and took full responsibility for the tragedy on himself. His selfish birthday wishes had been answered with an equal selfishness when the Lord had taken back both his parents. Filled with self-loathing and guilt, Josh avoided his aunt and spent all his time tending to the farm. He thought that it was his responsibility alone to keep his parents' farm in working order since he needed to atone for his guilt and he was now the "man of the house". Sam had known that it was not healthy for the boy to blame himself for the tragedy and push himself to the break so Sam had arranged for additional help on the farm in order that he might have some time to counsel the boy. Ever since then Sam had been like a father to Josh, who felt that Sam had not only saved his parents' farm from ruin, but had also saved him from being overcome by grief and guilt. As far as Josh was concerned, Sam Brown could do no wrong.

The church was now silent, the air filled only with the sound of the wind and the roaring of fires in the distance. An eerie calmness had settled over the church despite water streaming down the aisles tainted red with the congregations' blood. Some members had been trapped and crushed under the very pews at which they had prayed for their lives as the church rippled with the tides of the moving earth. Others had been struck down by falling wrought iron candelabrum whose flames had carried the flock's prayers to God only moments before.

    Sam attempted to steady himself by anchoring his grip tightly onto the altar as he stood up. He was shivering in his soaking wet blood stained robes and his head throbbed with a maddening rhythm. He searched with his free hand for the source of the pain, following the path created by the crusted blood in his hair. His right temple was bruised and swollen to the size of a golf ball, the skin ripped and bloody, throbbing in rhythm as the pressure in his head intensified and nearly caused him to blackout. Clouds of red and brown sharpened into images of the bodies of his slain followers as Sam's eyes went in and out of focus in time with the throbbing in his head. He fought off the confusion and fear stemmed by the pain and the blood and this vision by reminding himself over and over that God had saved him from certain death for a reason, he was but God's implement...God had a mission for Sam Brown.

Somewhere an old floorboard creaked, wood scrapped against wood. In the corner of his eye Sam thought he noticed a toppled pew shift slightly so he turned toward the pew and waited silently, only the sound of water trickling past him filled the silence. Sam tuned out the sound of the water and waited. Afraid to dare even the slightest breath, each second tortured Sam for an eternity as he waited for some sign that he had shown his flock down the right path. The fear and uncertainty peaked just below a boil, slowly eroding away his control and threatening to cloud his senses again. Sam closed his eyes and listened once more; it was there – a faint panting noise. Sam slowly crept toward the pew and the panting grew imperceptibly louder, but he knew it was there.

"Oh Dear Lord...Josh," Sam moaned as he carefully rushed to the man's side, navigating around the fallen pews and twisted floorboards. Only the man's panting breath reassured Sam that he was still alive once Sam was close enough to assess the situation.

Josh lay nearly paralyzed on his stomach, held down by the seat of the pew resting across his upper back. His face was scraped and bloody, so badly bruised from the debris falling from the crumbling ceiling that his eye was swollen shut. His arms were pinned under his body – still clasped in prayer – so he lay there blind and helpless to free himself.

The terror and desperation building in Josh had clouded his mind so much that he was completely unaware of Sam's struggle to lift the pew off him. Bracing his back against the wall, Sam used his legs to raise the pew and then stacked hymnbooks to hold it up. It wasn't until Sam had dragged Josh from under the pew that Josh finally became aware of Sam's presence, he then said a silent prayer thanking God for his mercy and begging forgiveness for his momentary lapse of faith.

With the precision and care of a nurse, Sam slowly rolled Josh over onto his back and wiped the debris and dried blood off his face with a damp piece of his own robe until Josh opened his good eye and gasped a sigh of relief.

"Josh, its Sam. Everything is going to be all right," Sam's words echoed as Josh blacked out.

Josh awoke to his own moans to find his arm throbbing with pain and bound in a makeshift splint. As the fog of sleep left him the sounds of the living filled his ears like the most beautiful hymn he had ever heard. Once again he thanked the Lord for his good fortune, noting that he was indeed alive and the swelling in his eye was gone. He carefully sat up in his cot and surveyed the combat like medical setup he was blessed to be convalescing in. Josh reflected on why God had passed such a harsh judgment on the world, and anxious to avoid any more of God's wrath, he decided that he could serve God better if he got up and pitched in despite his obvious pain and handicap.

As he searched for Sam, Josh credited Sam for the rescue of the many survivors he passed by while he made his way to the makeshift emergency room in front of the church. Before he could reach Sam, Betsy Carter, the local school nurse, put him to work, handing him a pail of cold water and rags to clean wounds of those lined up in the tent.

Sam approached carrying the Jones' boy and gave Josh a nod of approval, "Good to see you're up and pitching in."

"Thanks ta ya," Josh praised.

"No, thanks to God's mercy. Nothing I could have done would have helped if He did not wish to be merciful."

"Yer right as always. Thank Ya Lord!" enthusiasm saturated his words.

"Now watch Matthew here for me," Sam handed the young boy to Josh, "He won't seem to leave my side and I really should be helping bury the unfortunate. I don't think it's the kind of thing a child should be around, especially since his parents..."

"Ah understand. Come on Matt'ew; let's go play with the other kids. They've been ask'n about ya," Josh walked off with the boy in tow.

The pages made a solemn, faint thump as Sam closed his tattered Bible. The surviving members of the church had all turned out to say a final farewell to their fallen members and now they stood there silently in the aftermath of the stirring funeral services given by Sam. As they realized that Sam was finished speaking, the survivors released their sobs and cries, the sounds of their grief carrying along the field of the dead as a mysterious echo to Sam's eulogy.

After contemplating the grief of his flock, Sam stepped down off the dirt mound from which he had given the services and slowly walked over to the temporary church set up outside the ruins of the old church. As always, Josh followed on Sam's heals and seated himself in the front pew. Taking this as a signal that Sam intended to give a sermon, the congregation began to make their way back to the church, hurriedly pulling themselves together and wiping away their tears as they took their seats. Impatiently, Sam started his rally as soon as everyone was sitting quietly in the church.

"I realize that we have all lost many dear, close friends and loved ones. And the grief is hard to put aside. But put it aside is what we all must do.

God's mission depends on us to do just that. To permit ourselves to continue to grieve would be to put ourselves above God, and that we can not do! Now you all must realize that God has spared us in particular for a very specific reason. And I now give you that reason," Sam heralded his Bible overhead as if the answer might begin to flow directly from the book itself.

"I have contemplated long and hard on what the Lord could have had in mind when he placed such harsh judgment on the others, yet in the same breath spared us. And the Lord has helped me understand his wishes. Once you accept God's will, the reason that we were spared is simple, you see. We believed in Him and His word and we abided by His word without question. Those that perished had questioned the Lord's words or even failed to abide at all by those words. Now I know you are wondering what they questioned for they all attended every service I gave. However, even though they attended the services, they failed to heed all that was said in those services. It is not good enough to simply feign obedience and acceptance; the Lord knows what is truly in your heart. Josh, were you not the first one to get rid of your television and stereo?" Josh smiled at the recognition of his good deeds and nodded his head in affirmation.

Sam's gaze singled out a middle-aged couple sitting in the back with three young children, "And Marybeth and Jacob, did you not start teaching your children at home so that they would not have access to computers and all the filth that children can gain access to through them?" They smiled with pride as they stroked their children's hair. "Have you all not followed the Lord's words as I have given them to you with every ounce of your soul?" The entire congregation applauded in agreement.

"And if that is not enough evidence for you, then look at the other side, look at who felt God's wrath. Brian and Sandy Jones refused to destroy their stereo equipment; rather, they sold the unholy things and received an unholy bounty for them. Would you sell what appeared to be a piece of fruit to another even though you were aware that it was poison and not fruit?" the congregation mumbled abhorrence for such an act, "And what about Kevin and Stacy Brown and their infant daughter? They insisted that technology was not a distraction from God and refused to get rid of their television at all. In fact, they watched the lurid programs broadcast on their TV with their infant daughter in the room, and so they doomed themselves and her. They mocked the Lord every time they stepped foot in this church, acting as if they intended to follow the path that God had set out for them," outrage further filled the temperament of the room. "Now, Ethan, I know these words must seem harsh to you. But you're almost a full-grown man, so I think you can handle it. Besides, I know you recognize the sins of your parents because you followed the Lord's wishes and took it upon yourself to destroy your video games in spite of their protests. I think that you will agree with what I am saying once you've had time to think about it."

Ethan recoiled at such a hostile mention of his parents and sister. How could Pastor Sam use such words against his dead parents when just a few moments ago he had praised them and asked for the Lord to show them the way to heaven?

But Ethan knew better than to challenge Sam's words, especially in front of the congregation, so he nodded his head in agreement and forced a faint smile to part his lips – the same way he had forced himself to smash his vrBox when he realized that Sam was watching him carrying it away. "You're right Pastor Sam, as always," the words burned as they flowed off his tongue. If only his parents had listened to him when he had begged them to go with him to the local bomb shelter... If only he had not gone back for his prized video game system... His parents' only wish had been for him to get accepted into a good college so that he could escape this suffocating town and he had failed them because he wanted to take some stupid video game with him to the shelter! Now how would he ever break free from Sam Brown's control, especially with the surviving congregation being comprised mainly of Sam's most fanatical followers. They would never let him go because it would challenge the validity of Sam's preaching. If only...

3

While the messenger entered the circle too near,
Potential revealed a path seemingly limitless,
Compelled is She, Compassion as boundless...

Jez stood in the forest glen, making sure that she was out of the line of sight. After a deep inhalation she let out a long, loud warbling whistle. "One thousand-one...one thousand-two...one thous..." the sound of Trace's approaching hoof-steps pleasantly interrupted Jez's counting. "Yes, Trace, you're such a good boy!" she praised him and stroked his mane and brow ridge affectionately. He had passed her test with flying colors; it amazed her how strong the connection between them had grown in such a short period of time and he made his loyalty and adoration of her amply apparent. In slightly less than a week Trace had learned to come to Jez on command, and now he had proven that he could find her even when he couldn't see her.

Unfortunately, Jez's triumph with Trace was marred by the fact that the other two horses refused to follow anything but the simplest physical commands and she doubted that they would follow those simple commands if Trace had not bonded with her. Even her attempts to get them to respond to the names she had found etched on their stalls had failed; nevertheless, she continued to plead for their assistance and obedience. Sadly, they responded more to Puk's commands than to her pleas and she could almost feel their longing for their old stalls and masters. But now that Trace had successfully completed the limited training she was able to provide, she would at least be able to resume her journey. Jez was confident that Trace had no desire to escape her company, and she knew that Jade and Amber would not leave her without him no matter how homesick they might be.

After walking with Trace back to the campsite, Jez packed up her few belongings and readied the horses for travel. The riding gear she had salvaged fit nicely on Trace and she had also scrounged up a couple of bridles and leading reins for the other horses during her exploration of the stable. Now as she tethered Jade and Amber to Trace's saddle, Puk sensed her intentions, leaping about and barking nervously, anxious to be back on the road. Jez smiled as she felt a hum escape her lips, an old habit of contentment that Puk's enthusiasm had managed to re-energize. A "chronic hummer", that's what a close friend had once called her...she allowed herself to be transported by these old memories as she set off on Trace.

Her breath was slow and controlled as Jez concentrated on minimizing any extraneous movements and sounds and she hoped that Puk and the horses would continue to remain silent in the distance. She narrowed her eyes as she peered with precision through the scope on her rifle, her prey moved into range and Jez faded into the surrounding trees. She nearly hesitated too long as she reassured herself that she had no alternative but to fire. Smoothly and evenly she applied pressure to the trigger and the rifle exploded in her ear, but Jez controlled the backfire and her aim was true. She sobbed with relief and terror as the rabbit slumped to the ground and its mottled white and gray-brown coat turned red. She had never killed anything other than insects before, the closest she had come to hunting at all was fishing in her parents' backyard and even then she always threw her catch back – to the dismay of Patches, the family cat.

As hard as it had been for Jez to kill this rabbit, she still faced the task of skinning and gutting her kill. The very thought caused her stomach to churn so that she was on the verge of vomiting, but she fought the growing nausea by drawing on her survival instinct. She could not allow herself to be so upset by the essential tasks of killing and preparing game. Her supplies were getting dangerously low and if she didn't deviate from her daily ration of power bars, she had at most two weeks of food left. Not to mention that the very thought of her steady diet of ration bars was enough to make her nauseous all over again. It was all a mind game...*mind over matter*, she chanted. Jez reminded herself that being a part of this new world meant being able to provide for herself.

With a single sweeping motion, Jez slipped her rifle into the holster strapped across her back and went to fetch the rabbit, but then though better of it. The vet had once told her that Puk was part hunting dog and she wondered if his instincts might kick in now since she was hunting. With a sharp, short whistle she called her friend to her side.

"Fetch Boy!" Jez gestured to the fallen rabbit with a powerful thrust of her arm and Puk raced over to the rabbit. Once there he stopped and sniffed the carcass, hesitated for a moment – confused by the "food" scent of this new toy, then remembered her command. He carefully snatched up the soft toy in his mouth and ran back to Jez and waited for her to take the toy. Instead she pointed at the ground by her feet and he obediently dropped the toy there, and wagging his tail vigorously with self satisfaction as he looked up at her while he waited for his treat. Jez knelt down on her knees and roughed the fur between Puk's ears, "GOOD BOY! GOOD BOY Puk!!" She kissed his wet nozzle and gave him a powerful hug before picking up the rabbit and leading him back to camp where the horses were tied up.

The fire hissed and cracked as the juices dripped from the rabbit roasting on the spit. Despite her initial repulsion to killing and preparing her own meat, Jez's mouth watered at the scent of the roasting rabbit. It had been too long since the last time she had a hot meal! Jez's stomach cramped with a hunger intensified by the anticipation of the feast she would be having shortly; she had remembered to pack a few essential seasonings and had used them to marinate the rabbit meat and she had made a tasty stuffing out of some of her granola bars. If only she had a nice bottle of pinot... Jez chuckled, now that was being silly.

Until the roast was ready, she bid her time by going over her map, tracing her path on the worn map with her index finger. Although the creases and folds in the map made it difficult to decipher many of the city names, Jez was able to interpolate her location using her notes and the occasional mile markers that had survived along the highway. She remembered passing mile marker fourteen sometime the day before, so she estimated that she had traveled somewhere over two hundred and ten miles. Jez had hoped that she would be able to pick up her pace when she found the horses, unfortunately, her progress remained unimproved thanks to her struggles with the other two horses and, to her dismay, her rather rapid development of saddle sores. But Jez refused to give in to her growing desperation, her mother and sister needed her and she desperately needed them. She was sure that in a few days both her saddle sores and her horses' attitudes would be better. After all, her successful hunt today had proved to her that she could survive off the earth and that was a definite improvement.

Jez swished her fingers in a circular pattern through the fur on the freshly cured rabbit skin. The softness of the fur gave her a sense of comfort, reminding her of a baby's bedding. For a moment she was content and closed her eyes and thanked the rabbit for its sacrifice and asked for its forgiveness. Jez knew that she didn't have a choice, but that didn't get rid of her distaste for hunting. If only there was some way that she could survive on nuts and berries, but being on the road constantly just didn't leave her time to find and gather enough food to survive. Jez worried that her mother and sister had probably already run out of nutrition bars. How would they feed themselves? Al was a botanist, so she supposed that would make finding edible plants easier for them than it had been for her. Had Al thought to use her archery equipment for hunting? Useless questions! There was no way of knowing the answers short of finding her family. Jez forced herself to stop thinking such negative thoughts by packing up her gear. There were still a few hours of daylight left for traveling.

As the cremation fire engulfed the car, Jezzelle began to relax. It had been another long day, starting with her discovery of a carload of remains. Whenever she stumbled upon a body, Jez took it upon herself to preserve any possible means of future identification and cremate the rest. She had decided that this was part of her responsibility as a survivor since she still had not come across any sort of governmental effort to deal with the dead and the health threats they posed, even though the threat had become as blatantly apparent as the smell.

Jez had been traveling for less than an hour when the stench hit her first. A moment later she was able to see the source from her perch atop Trace, the overturned car was peering out of a rift across the highway. The view of the bodies through the windows made her think of Mother Theresa and Lenin, or was it Stalin, their bodies forever preserved behind glass. It had taken Jez the remainder of the day to dig a trench around the vehicle so that she could safely burn the car to cremate the bodies inside. It had been nearly two weeks since the CAT and Jez had no desire to remove the bodies from the car, no matter how much quicker it would make her task, it was bad enough that she had to smell them through the glass. Not surprisingly, today's excursion had left her completely exhausted and fairly nauseous so no sooner had she curled up in her sleeping bag, then she was sound asleep.

Through the silence and blackness of the night the lookout screamed down from the makeshift tower, "Looks like we've got another small fire over to the west near the highway."

"Fire-team One, Fire-team One...Report to tower for duty!" blared repeatedly from bullhorns across the settlement. Within minutes the settlement's lead councilperson quickly dispatched the small group of volunteer firefighters to investigate and contain the reported fire before it became a threat to the settlement.

Jez swiftly leapt out of her sleeping bag with her rifle drawn and cocked, her light sleep disturbed by the sound of approaching voices. It had been weeks since she had any contact with another living person, and now such a possibility put her on edge. How would she be able to tell whether they were looters or escaped convicts or some other threat to her? Her mind and heart raced as she attempted to remember all her self-defense training at one time. Puk sensed her unease and stood protectively by her side with his teeth bared.

To Jez's surprise, the voices continued moving well past her toward the cremation fire nearly thirty yards away. Now that the party was near the fire, it illuminated them enough so that Jez was able to monitor their actions. She could make out four figures, each wore a helmet of some sort and carried some long weapon or tool which they poked around the edge of the fire. It appeared to Jez that they were investigating the fire or were they looking for survivors? At any rate, they were apparently satisfied that the fire was well contained and there was nothing further they could do because they began heading back the way they had come from at a much slower pace than they had arrived at. Her curiosity piqued, Jez decided to follow them. She rationalized that she needed to determine if they represented a threat or not, so she quickly slipped on her shoes and ran to catch up to the group's trail with Puk running silently by her side. Dawn was creeping over the horizon when she and Puk finally found where the trail turned into a clearly worn path.

As they continued on down the path to approach the settlement Jez noticed a watch tower perched on the edge of the road. Fortunately, she had paid careful attention to make sure that she and Puk were always under cover, so they continued to creep along until they were just close enough to see and hear the goings on inside the settlement. As Jez studied the town's setup she questioned whether she had leapt back in time, the settlement looked and sounded like a frontier town of the 1800's. Children of all ages were playing in the streets, while the sound of hammering joined with their giggles and screams, filling the air with the music of the living as various buildings were being constructed by nearly every able hand. In a distant field, freshly washed clothing swung in the breeze from lines on which it had been hung to dry.

Despite the apparent normalcy, Jez was unsure whether she could safely approach the settlement. Wandering strangers were often reviled before the CAT, so she couldn't imagine a very warm reception now that there were food shortages and convicts running loose. Erring on the side of caution, she decided that she would approach the town alone after dark, that way if they did treat her as a threat, she wouldn't have to worry about her gear or the other horses and could ride off into the darkness before they could go after her. If the town proved to be honest and friendly she always could retrieve her gear and horses later.

As Jez and Trace approached the settlement she heard someone yell down from the tower; gently, she pulled back on Trace's reins and eased him to a stop. Just as she had predicted, the lookout had seen her approaching and announced her presence to the town, so she would just stay where she was and let them come to her. As she anxiously awaited their arrival, Jez readjusted her rifle and her grip on the reins; she would be ready to spur Trace into a gallop for a quick get away – if necessary. Confident of her ability to defend herself, Jez allowed herself to fantasize about interacting with actual living people again. The very thought made her stomach swirl and her palms sweat worse than any public speaking engagement she had ever experienced.

Trace shuffled his hooves with Jez's shared anxiety as the group of advancing men and women grew closer, but just before Jez was about to protest their proximity the group stopped. She swallowed against her anxiety before addressing the silence, "I'm Jez. I'm sorry but I had to stop here. You're the first people I've seen alive since *It* hit. I promise I don't want anything other than information."

An elderly woman stepped away from the group and held her hands out, palms up, apparently in an attempt to demonstrate that she was not a threat. "Well Sugar, Ah was just gonna ask ya about that vary same thang," the woman's Southern accent was underscored by her light-hearted voice, "Ya've got nothing ta fear from us. An Ah appreshate yer honesty. By the way, I'm Bess, the town's head councilman...urrr, Ah mean person." Bess proceeded to introduce the remainder of the council, "An may Ah ask why yer travel'en solo?"

"Oh, I'm on my way to Virginia. That's where my mom and sister live. I've been on the road for weeks now...I think. It's been kind of hard to distinguish one day from the next," Jez responded with less anxiety, even managing a weak smile. There was something reassuring about the woman and she found herself beginning to trust this Bess despite the reservations pounding in her rational, logical mind – there was something powerful growing inside her that could not be denied or ignored no matter how hard she tried. Recently Jez had been experiencing a lot of accurate "gut" feelings that went far beyond the simple intuition that she relied on for reassurance of her family's survival. Still, she found that believing in the existence of psychic phenomena was a lot easier than accepting that she was experiencing it herself. She had always felt that her intuition was stronger than most people's, however, Jez had never contemplated the possibility that it might develop into something more.

"Lordy darlin, how'd ya manage ta travel all that way with the mess that's out there? Now come here an let Miss Bess take care of ya. How's a hot bath sound?" Bess said in her most motherly as she made her way over to Jez.

Jez hesitated only a moment before she dismounted Trace and followed Bess into town. The offer of a hot bath was just too tempting to refuse, especially since she couldn't seem to suppress her growing trust of Bess. In fact, Jez was beginning to feel more at ease with each person she came in contact with. Everyone felt so familiar and she could feel the positive energy, suddenly she was sure that everything would be just fine, this new world wasn't such a bad place after all. She was sure that she would soon be friends with the entire town and in the short time it took for them to reach the main area of the settlement, Jez's reservations had been replaced by genuine trust. She even allowed Bess to make arrangements for some man, Bess assured her that he was a complete gentleman and honest to the bone, to fetch Puk and her horses while she was bathing and having her saddle sores tended to.

"Hey there Jez! I went ahead and rubbed down your horses. They're over at the livery," Zeke called to Jez as she was leaving the clinic. "That one stallion seems really distressed without you around, maybe you should let him know that you're okay. Come on, I'll walk you over there," he rattled on nervously as Puk cheerfully bounced between them before deciding to run off with some children.

"Thanks, Zeke?" Jez wasn't sure if she remembered his name correctly, "I'm sorry I hid my gear so far away, I didn't realize that anyone besides me would be going back for it all. Did Puk behave himself?"

"That's me," Zeke's voice still quivered with unease despite Jez's grateful smile, "So, I take it Puk is that massive dog that was guarding your camp. Almost scared me off at first, but then I remembered that whistle thing. Calmed him right down...anyway, you're welcome. I didn't mind anyway. It gave me a good excuse to take my horse out. With your stallion the only mature male around and her in heat, she needed a good long ride." He belatedly recognized the sexual innuendo and laughed nervously.

"So, Zeke, how did your town council get organized so quickly? I just can't get over the miracle of being able to take a hot bath! I mean, I took the highway here and didn't find even one open Motel 6," Jez attempted to put him at ease and avoid the awkward silence that was looming overhead by changing the subject.

"Well, I know that Bess was one of the first to start pulling everyone together...she's retired from FEMA or something like that a few years ago and she's a long time Red Cross volunteer. But other than that, I'm not really sure of what specifically went on those first few days. We're all really lucky that she just happened to be here. You see..." Zeke began to relax as he explained how things had been for him and how the town had been organized.

He had come out from Los Angeles to visit some friends and go white-water rafting a few days before the CAT had hit. In a drowsy trance he had assumed it was an earthquake and managed to make his way to the nearest doorway before the small cabin came down around him, but a bookcase fell into the doorway and pinned him against the frame. He was nearly buried alive by splintered wood and plaster as the roof collapsed and the walls buckled, only the thick doorframe had prevented him from being crushed as the house collapsed in on itself.

Once the earth settled Zeke was forced to dislocate his shoulder in order to dislodge it from under the bookcase. Afterward he tried to dig his way out of the rubble with his good arm, but hunger and thirst eventually slowed him down to a still. Three days later the rescue party led by Bess found him nearly comatose...Zeke rubbed his shoulder which now ached with remembered pain.

Jez unconsciously reached for Zeke's injured shoulder as if she could draw the pain from him. Almost instantly she felt the pain course through her fingertips up to her shoulder as her mind's eye saw his memories of being buried alive. Although his pain faded with her comforting grip Zeke remained unaware of Jez's true grasp of his haunting memories. It had taken only two days for Bess to take charge and get the survivors of the area to conduct organized rescue searches instead of the random panicked searches they had instinctively started, but it took her another week to gain enough perceived authority to be able to command an organized clean-up effort as well. Less than a week later an emergency city council was elected to handle the administration of the rescue and clean-up efforts since there was still no sign of government aid being sent – not even the Red Cross had shown up. Predictably, there was no real opposition and Bess's election as the head of the council was a mere formality, but with her authority formally acknowledged she was able to make sure that every able-bodied survivor was assigned to a team and participated in the disaster relief. Even though he had been given a medical release, Zeke had felt compelled to assist the rescuers and convinced Bess to at least assign him to a desk job so she had sent him to work in record keeping.

Zeke explained how meticulous records of the deceased, including fingerprints and photographs, were being kept in hopes that family members might later be notified. They even went to the effort of storing any personal belongings found with the body. Of course, all this required a monumental amount of record keeping, so Zeke's initial frustration with being assigned a "lazy man's post" had quickly been replaced with a great deal of pride, especially after the near round the clock shifts he'd been working over the past several days trying to catch up with the mounds of records that needed to be filed.

They originally had buried each body individually, so the record keeping was manageable. But as the days began to pass into weeks, the number of dead awaiting burial grew and there was still no sign of government assistance – the costs to the living were just too great to continue individual burials. Weaker survivors were steadily growing sicker and dying from diseases fostered in the insects which fed on the piles of decaying bodies, even the shallows of the nearby lake were becoming tainted. Zeke gagged as he described how the stench of death had hovered over the new settlement like a fog until four days ago when the council had finally voted to mass cremate the bodies.

Surprisingly, there were no protests to this drastic action – no complaints were made to government officials, no lawsuits were filed. A few resolute believers in burial had tried to continue individual burials on their own and quickly grown ill from their efforts but they still refused to believe that the number of dead was far greater than the number the survivors would be able to bury. Most agreed that there simply was not enough manpower available to bury all the bodies AND care for the sick and wounded AND provide food and water, so they reluctantly accepted the fact that not only their survival, but apparently the survival of humanity, was threatened by both the health hazard created by the bodies and the damage it did to their spirits. With everyone finally in agreement that survival demanded the swift removal of the dead, the council decided mass cremation was a more dignified choice than mass burial.

Only by the entire town acting as a team and working around the clock in staggered shifts did they manage to dispose of all of the bodies remaining within the settlement's borders before too many more survivors fell ill. With that burden lifted, the townsfolk were anxious and immediately began to shift their efforts toward rebuilding and repairing the few generators, communications devices, and various other pieces of equipment that had been salvaged. Just yesterday the settlement had gained access to fresh well water when the first repaired generator and pump had been successfully tapped into one of the few accessible wells. Zeke glowed with down-home pride as he talked about *his* town. He was confident that within a few days they would have short-wave radio communications restored – if there was anyone left out there to communicate with. And teams were being organized to investigate the condition of the local power plant since they weren't sure of the reasons for the area's loss of power. There were very few left that were willing to wait any longer for the government to begin repairs and Zeke was sure that there must be other survivors out there that would join forces with them in their efforts to restore some basic level of civilization, especially with Bess in charge of coordinating their efforts, as Zeke was sure she would be.

As Jez and Zeke approached the livery, intense feelings of confusion and fear pulsated through her mind's eye and it took her a moment to realize that the emotions were not her own, rather they were those of her equestrian companion Trace. Intuitively she directed thoughts of comfort and safety to him until she noticed the feelings of fear dissipate from her consciousness.

"Hellooo," Zeke waived his hand back and forth in front of her face, "Anybody home?"

"Oh, sorry, I didn't realize..." Jez was still slightly disoriented and unaware of the inseparable psychic bond that had just been forged. She didn't realized that she had stopped dead in her tracks, falling into a deep trance, when she had perceived Trace's panic. "I'm not sure what just happened, but I think that I just experienced some sort of telepathy or something with Trace."

"Are you serious? How can you tell?" realizing that his earlier fear had colored his words with sarcasm Zeke sought to redeem himself, "I mean...if that's what actually happened, that's really cool. You were *gone* for a minute there...you really scared me Jez."

"I'm sorry, I don't mean to scare you, but I am serious," her voice cracked with disbelief of the words coming out of her mouth, "How can this be happening?"

"I don't know, a lot of things have been changing lately, maybe this is just one of them. Either way, I'm sure it's nothing to worry about...just warn me beforehand next time. And besides," Zeke attempted to lighten up the moment, "it's not like you'll be tried as a witch or anything."

"I guess...maybe," Jez was slightly afraid of herself and then suddenly she felt Trace's trust and faith in her as clearly as she could hear Zeke speaking to her – their new connection apparently included even the slightest emotion. "No, you're right. I should be happy that I'm developing my natural abilities and not treat it like some sort of disease," a new confidence filled her fueled by Trace's reassurance. She wondered why she had never experienced such a connection with Puk since she felt as close to him as any human and had raised him since he was a pup. Perhaps it was because Puk had never had a reason to project such intense feelings, he was always by her side and this had all started with Trace's profound feelings of fear at their separation. Puk nudged Jez's hand with his snout as if he knew everything going through her mind even if she couldn't hear what was going on in his...as Zeke had pointed out, things were changing.

Reassured of Jez's safety, Trace suddenly became aware of the scents carried on the breeze. How could he have not noticed her scent before? She was so ripe. Trace paced anxiously in his stall, swishing his tail back and forth and twitching his head. He screamed to be let out, chewing and nudging the small gate. He knew that he was not supposed to go past it, but Jez and the man were gone. Finally, unable to control himself any longer, Trace jolted the gate with his hind legs and as it crashed to the ground he ran toward her scent, he had to find her.

Once again lost in conversation, Jez followed Zeke down the uneven porch stairs, her foot slipping on the air when the step she had anticipated was missing. Almost anticipating her fall, Zeke reached out and she fell gently into his arms. Instantly they dissolved into each other, kissing as if they had never known a time apart from one another...both overwhelmed by some inexplicable passion.

4

But the grieving child is infected with madness,
And casts aside all knowledge and independence,
The silver tongue feeds and darkness enfolds...

The sun eased its way into the horizon, turning the deep purple sky into an icy blue before it slowly melted into a blazing orange. The rays fished down through the clouds on their quest for the earth and the clouds faded in their grasp. Still more determined specks of sunlight penetrated the dense forest canopy as the morning made its way to the camp. The cars and tents were packed into the dense forest wherever sufficient space presented itself, the cars forming a random border between the tents and the narrow trail to the main road. Despite the thick canopy, the dome-shaped tents were aglow and the car windshields sparkled from the sun's rays while the bodies inside and outside of the tents reflexively shielded their faces from the growing light.

In spite of the onslaught of daylight, men and women lay around the camp in various levels of unconsciousness; hands, feet, and faces peering from under sleeping bags and blankets. Inside the largest tent a woman clothed in only a soiled old T-shirt disavowing fur lay beside her naked lover, their legs intertwined, but otherwise they did not touch. Just above her head her small black and white mottled dog lay curled up, close enough so that they could hear each other breathe over the snores and wheezes of the four bodies sharing their tent. The scent of beer and incense permeated every fiber of the campground and perfumed the wind that began to howl as a DJ's voice reverberated out of a retro boom box somewhere and beer bottles and cans littering the campsite clattered against the ground as they tolled the end to a long night of celebration.

Suddenly, a sharp wind began blowing. Tent door flaps whipped and ruffled in the wind and debris flew around the camp. Still, no one stirred. As the wind's intensity soared – threatening to take the tent air borne, the woman's dog began barking in panic. The rumbling in the earth had finally disturbed her sleep and she could now smell the danger. She licked heartily at her companion's face and when the woman failed to respond, the dog barked her full volume into the woman's ear.

"SHIT!!" the woman blared as she was jolted into consciousness, "BAD DOG!!" Her head was pounding and every bark felt like a hot poker burning right through her skull. But the dog refused to be silenced, there was danger coming and they must leave now! "OK, OK. I'm up, I'm up. What the hell do you want?!" the woman screamed irritably. "I need coffee and drag before I can deal with you...Oh fark, that's right, I quit," she threw her warm beer at the dog in an attempt to silence it, "SHUT THE FARK UP!!" Undaunted, the dog continued to bark and pull on the woman's sleeping bag. Others roused as the dog's incessant barking penetrated even the deepest levels of unconsciousness.

"Farkit!" the woman franticly poured cold coffee into her paper cup, then set the cup on the ground beside her and lit a cigarette. Only somewhat calmed and rehabilitated by the infusion of nicotine, the woman fidgeted nervously and reached for her cup but stopped short. She thought she saw large ripples form on the coffee's surface as the ground rumbled, and then she knew that she had when she heard the earth groan just as her cup abruptly toppled over.

"Jesus, what the hell?!" the woman attempted to suppress her growing nausea and fear, breathing in strength from her cigarette, "Jerry, wake up man!" she screeched as she punched his shoulder with her free fist.

"Whaaat?! Can't you see I'm trying to sleep here?" Jerry berated the woman for the uninvited disturbance, "which is hard to do with that damn dog of yours barking its farking head off! Why don't you shut her up?"

"Because she won't shut up, that's why. So are you telling me that you can't feel that?"

"Feel what?" the man chastised her as he buried his head deep under his flimsy pillow, "I'm going back to sleep!"

"THAT!!" the woman screamed as she watched their cars begin to shift from the earth moving beneath them. Suddenly the car parked farthest in the distance appeared to be swallowed up by the earth, "It's a goddamn sink hole! Jerry, we've got to move out of here now. WAKE UP! I said WAKE THE FARK UP!!" The group sharing the tent made various groans of displeasure at the disturbance she was creating. A couple slowly proceeded to begin their day, while the others simply attempted to postpone the start of theirs by covering their heads with a blanket. Renewed with fear and aggravation at the lack of concern around her, the woman made her way around the camp. "IT'S THE FEDS!!" the woman screamed repeatedly, infuriated at the earlier failure of her friends to respond to her pleas. Finally, given the familiar and therefore meaningful motivation, the camp snapped into consciousness and urgently ran to their cars as quickly as paint dries.

Only slightly calmed by her renewed control over the group, the woman apprehensively approached her lover. "Jerry, here's the keys to the VW. I'll follow you in the Jeep," she ordered with a weary sense of crisis. Alarmed and confused by the now apparent urgency of their situation, Jerry welcomed the woman's regular exercise of authority. He was glad she wore the pants in the group, responsibility didn't suit him at all.

"Okay, see you back in town Luv," he gave the woman a hurried peck good-bye on the little mole near her brow even as she shoved him toward the bus, all the while he was pulling up his pants.

The camp began to rock more violently as the hole in the earth grew toward them. This time a one-hundred foot pine disappeared into the earth in the blink of an eye, another and another following right behind, like the earth playing a game of dominos with the landscape. A new panic overtook the camp, which was now sober from fear, and chaos broke out as people in various stages of undress rushed to their cars while cursorily collecting their belongings. The severely hung-over members of the camp would have been left behind by those sober enough to make it to the cars first had it not been for the relentless confusion that plagued the camp. The process of finding the keys to each car and discerning a route away from the campsite in light of the encroaching sinkhole nearly incapacitated the group's collective cognitive ability. The woman herself was delayed when the dog grabbed her keys and ran into the surrounding woods.

"Damn-it dog, come back here!! Here doggy, doggy. Here girl. Come to mama," the woman's voice was full of exasperation and fear. "We need to make it to the car before it gets swallowed up...come on, baby, please come to mama!" the woman cooed through her cigarette.

Torn between her companion's pleas and the need to flee from the approaching danger, the dog hesitantly approached the woman who eagerly snatched her up and grabbed the keys from her mouth before she could run off again. Horror coursed through the woman's veins quicker than heroin as she rushed back to the camp; time was running out quickly and she could feel herself drowning, the sands of time becoming as deadly as quick sand. Falling branches, twigs, and sticks whipped at her flesh as the wind gusted around her faster and faster, and the faster she ran, the more the splinters and thorns stabbed and cut at her bare feet and legs. She could feel the tears blurring her vision and burning the cuts on her face despite her efforts to remain in control of her fear and pain. The camp seemed so far away and she prayed that she would arrive in time.

Suddenly the woman stopped running and simply stood silently still, she had come into view of the former camp. Even as her body continued to lunge forward with the momentum of her sudden stop, she could hear the screams of those trapped inside the cars being swallowed by the earth. She had stoked everyone into action too late, arriving only in time to witness her error. The vision of the bus sinking into the earth faster than Jerry's screams could reach her ears burned into her retinas and the sound of his screams pierced her soul. Why had she been so concerned with saving the cars from the sinkhole? She should have ordered everyone to make a run for it. Why had she not fully understood the danger they were in? She should have realized the risk they were taking! Her mind reeled with repercussions and the world seemed to spin around her faster and faster.

As she stood there paralyzed staring at the sky the sun suddenly appeared to sweep to the east across the horizon. All at once the trees began to rush past her even though the spinning had stopped; someone had grabbed her arm, pulling her along side as he ran, but the woman remained transfixed by her personal terror. She was unaware of taking shelter in a ditch with the surviving members of her camp despite being the center of their tight huddle. Only the eventual grasp of sleep removed her from that endless moment in time.

Other than the early morning melodies of various songbirds, only silence filled the air. The calmness of the earth and the cool breeze nearly caused the woman to forget the events of the previous day as her mind eased into wakefulness. Ever so slowly, visions of the previous morning created a panorama in her mind's eye so hideous to her that she felt they must be the remnants of a nightmare. But as she became aware of the growing discomfort from her multiple cuts and bruises she understood the reality of those caustic memories. A hand gently wiped away the tears welling in her eyes.

"Katie, I'm really sorry, but someone needs to go for help. Mikel broke his leg and maybe...the others... you know... sometimes... they do find survivors..." the man attempted to comfort the woman, "We need to hurry." Katie opened her eyes for the first time since she had watched her lover buried alive and the sunlight felt like acid as her tired, swollen eyes attempted to focus. The man looked into her eyes, not so much to check their dilation as to find some sign that at least a shard of her soul remained. He knew that despite their bickering, Jerry and Katie thrived off each other and he wondered if Katie would be able to carry on with such a large piece of herself so abruptly cut away. "Come on Katie, snap out of it!! We all still need you!!!" he pled as he shook her, hoping for some form of reaction, but Katie just hung limp in his arms like a rag doll, unaware of his pleas, lost somewhere inside herself. Suddenly, she became rigid, an alert unsettled expression creased her exasperated face. Somewhere the rumbling of an engine grew louder and closer. Could someone have returned to the camp and retrieved one of the vehicles?

A young woman poked her head out of the truck's window, "It seems to be running fine, but the damn radio will only pick up static. I can't seem to get in a single station, not even an AM one!!"

Katie shot upright, horror and anger filling every fiber of her being. "STEPHIE, GET OUT OF THE DAMN TRUCK!!!" she blared, her eyes swirling with the intensity of her anger.

"What's wrong Katie?" the woman asked as she proceeded to open the heavy steel door. But Stephie moved too slowly and Katie swiftly grabbed her by the arm and wrenched her from the truck, causing the petite girl to fall smartly to the earth. Due as much to the group's loyalty to her as well as their fear of her current state of mind, no one dared approach Katie, much less attempt to subdue her.

"BITCH, DIDN'T I SAY GET OUT OF THE MOTHERFARKING TRUCK...NOW!!!!!!!!" in a crazed frenzy Katie rummaged through the gear stored in the truck, unsure of what she was so intensely searching for, but as she came across the knife and matches her eyes gleamed with a purposed chaos. Instinctively, she went for the tires first and once she had slashed all four she began to shred the truck's interior, but no one attempted to do more than plea for her to stop. Unaware of the group's petitions and dripping with sweat Katie took a long swig from the bottle of 151 stored under the seat before pouring the rest over the slashed upholstery. With a sense of fulfillment that she had not felt in days, Katie stepped back from the truck and casually lit a cigarette, throwing the match, along with the last of her sanity, into the alcohol soaked truck.

Steam and smoke slowly drifted up from the truck as the last of its interior smoldered into dust, but only the paint around the cabin was cracked and blackened from the heat of the flames since the truck's firewall had done its job and confined the inferno to the passenger compartment, preventing a more serious explosion. Nevertheless, the extreme heat had caused the windows to explode and litter the ground around the truck with jewels of tinted glass before the abundance of oxygen rich air had quickly burnt out the fire. No one dared approach the skeleton of the truck to extinguish the few remaining embers for fear that it might still explode, and no one dared approach Katie as she sat watching the destruction of the contrivance of her lover's death from the edge of the clearing.

Katie surveyed the area as she rose to her feet, noting where each surviving member of the group was silently watching her in the distance. One of the younger men, Brice was his name, had taken her dog and was attempting to keep it out of her sight by hiding the squirming varmint under his sweatshirt. The mere thought of that damn dog made her blood boil. On the other side of the field, Carl and Alex were attempting to stabilize Mikel's broken leg in a splint. She could see tears running down his face which was writhing in pain and knew that he only remained silent in order to avoid disturbing her. That's right, she remembered in a flash of sanity, they needed to go find help for Mikel and the other injured, "Let's get a move on! Everyone grab your gear, we're all hiking out to the main road. Alex, Carl, you're responsible for Mikel," the orders bellowed naturally from her with the authority of a drill sergeant. She picked up her Camelbak and started walking toward the road without hesitating or bothering to look back, she knew the group would be right on her heals.

It had taken them a full day of hiking and climbing around the fallen trees and newly formed hills and valleys to travel the ten miles out to the main road that had originally been only a twenty-minute drive. Now that they had made it back to the highway they were forced to slowly meander their way around and over the mounds of twisted concrete and asphalt. Hunger and fatigue were rapidly mutating the group's perseverance into despair, especially with their discovery that the roadway was nearly completely destroyed, leaving in its wake near insurmountable mounds of debris for the weary group to maneuver around. But Katie, now driven by some unknown compulsion, would not be held back by the upturned landscape and she ordered everyone to form a human chain and follow her as she discerned a safe passage.

Despite her careful trail blazing, the injured continued to lag farther and farther behind. In their effort to limit Mikel's pain and further injury, Alex and Carl had slowed to a pace that left them behind even the slowest of the injured even though very few were able to keep Katie's maddened pace. The group attempted to span this growing distance with idle chatter, endless dirty jokes, and pointless discussions about the weather. But in spite of their earnest attempt at optimism and levity, the group fell silent all too soon. Although the belief that they would soon be rescued by a passing motorist had initially comforted them – after all, sinkholes and earthquakes could only cover so much land – their deserted path through the continued devastation began to cast heavy doubts on their hope. Each step they took caused the voluminous silence to swell as no one risked vocalizing the questions that loomed over them all: Where were they headed and where was help?

The sun's potent midday rays rushed down from the bluest sky to sting skin unaccustomed to direct sunlight. In spite of the fact that the group had enjoyed spending time in the outdoors prior to the sinkhole, the rarity of even slightly sunny days in the prior months had rendered sunscreen an unnecessary precaution and expense. As sweat provoked by the intense heat of the sun's everlasting rays caused their sunburned skin to burn and sting incessantly, the group cursed this newfound burden along with the litany of their other problems. They had lost nearly all of their gear to the earth almost two full days ago and the last of the snacks and water had run out the previous day. Today would be even worse as the group's viscidity threatened to fade in due course. Stephie and some guy had already split that morning, concerned only with their personal survival and frustrated with the group's slow pace.

In yet another instance only moments before, a brawl had nearly been instigated when it was discovered that Eric had been hoarding a pack of gum. The overwhelming tension and despair were palpable by everyone and Katie scoured her impaired consciousness for some means to retain her dwindling control over the group.

"Look...there! We're here, we're here!!" a woman shrieked as she restlessly interrupted her tired assault on the horizon and directed their collective gaze in the direction of her discovery.

"What?! Where, Jessie?" the group chanted in a chaotic chorus.

"Over there! Look! I think I can make out the colors red and blue over by those trees, where all those birds are circling. Doesn't that look like it could be a sign? Like an Exxon or something?" Jessie shouted as she bounced around excitedly. She began to hobble toward the sign, suddenly unaware of her connection with the group as she was overcome with hunger and consumed with her own realization, "Has to be! What else would have a big blue and red sign on the side of road," Jessie chattered on, still not cognizant that she had taken off ahead of the group and was talking to no one. "They all have food stops, don't they?"

A blood-curdling scream rang out through the group's now determined silence as Jessie discovered the reason for the birds circling above the red and blue sign, which turned out to be located at the junction with the highway and a local expressway. Car after car had been tossed and overturned or crushed, trapping the passengers inside. Apparently no one had reported the accident because there were no signs of any emergency personnel – or was there simply no one left to dial or respond to 911 – whatever the reason, all had perished, leaving a trail of death for miles. The stench and carnage were so overwhelming that tears autonomously welled in the eyes of every member of the group with the exception of Katie, who simply had no more tears to cry.

Terrified by the horrific sight, Brice turned around and blindly began to run away, dodging the members of the group in his path and forgetting that the uneven landscape was filled with obstacles.

"BRICE! Where the fark do you think you're going?" Katie blared as she ran after him, "Damn-it, someone help me catch him!"

Panicked, he ran faster as he looked over his shoulder and screamed, "I can't, I can't...You don't under..." Brice violently tripped over a chunk of concrete, hurdling himself headfirst into a ravine before he could comprehend what had happened. The few able bodies immediately rushed to his aid, he was unconscious and bleeding heavily, but he was breathing. His arm lay crookedly out to his side, apparently fractured multiple times as it broke his fall, and his face was a bloody mess. As they worked to stop the bleeding someone in the distance began to wail incoherently and the last of the group's resolution was shattered – now they had two severely injured members, no food or water, and no hope. Obviously the destruction was far greater than they had ever imagined. If there had been no one to rescue the hundreds, maybe thousands, of people injured or trapped on this stretch of highway, how could they expect there to be someone to rescue the handful that comprised their group? Could they be the only survivors in the area? A middle-aged woman sat down where she stood, slowly closed her eyes, and began to weep silently. Jessie and Eric sat down and simply held each other as they shook. Even at their distance from the group, Alex, Carl, and Mikel sensed this final blow to their conviction and sat down. Shortly, the entire group had stopped in its tracks, too tired and hopeless to continue on. Thunderstruck by her sudden sense of failure, Katie sought isolation and continued on into the nearby woods. Finally alone, she dropped to the ground with a thump and laughed hysterically – there was absolutely no hope for Jerry now, he was truly gone forever. She had been so stupid to entertain the fantasy in the first place, but they were all going to die now – there was no help, they were all going to die of starvation, dehydration, exposure, whatever, did it really matter? Katie lay on her side and curled up.

"Okay, FINE! You've farking won!! Where the hell are you Death? Come and get me!! Tell Jerry I'm on my farking way! Fark you Jerry!!" Katie screamed at the top of her lungs to no one in particular as she tensed up every muscle in her wearied body. When she finally allowed her body to relax after screaming herself horse, it was sleep that took her, not death.

S NAP...CRACK...the sounds from breaking twigs and crushed leaves echoed through the silence and animals scurried away from the perceived threat, adding their own scampers to the noise. But despite this growing chaos in the woods beside her and its potential threat, Katie remained lost in sleep, her mind and body exhaustively drained from the ravages of the previous few days and her resignation of her desire to live prevented even her instinctual survival skills from awakening her to the approaching noise.

"Could you possibly make any more noise Josh?!" Ethan whispered emphatically as he glanced around, checking to see if the sound had alerted any predators to their presence.

"Ya watch yer mouth young man! If Sam felt that Ah couldn't do the job he wouldn't have put me in charge! Besides, Ah'm not making anymore noise than the animals," and with his declaration of competence Josh proceeded to trip over a woman's body lying directly in his path.

As yet a further display of his control over the situation, Josh screamed out in pain when his broken arm was jarred in his impact with the ground. Had it not been for the buffer created by the woman's body, his arm might have been broken again. To Josh's further dismay, the combination of his weight pounding down on her and his scream piercing the relative silence forced the woman into consciousness.

"What the hell do you think you're doing?! I thought you assholes didn't want anything to do with me anymore?" Katie screamed before she realized that the man lying on top of her was a stranger. Instinctually she reached for something to use as a weapon against him only to realize that she was helplessly pinned down by the man's bulk.

Ethan noticed her struggles and reached down to help Josh get up as quickly as possible without disturbing his throbbing arm again, "Don't panic Ma'am. We didn't mean to hurt you. My friend Josh here just wasn't looking where he was going. So are you hurt? We can take you to the clinic if you are."

The prospect of help – help that she had given up on ever finding before they were all dead – caused her to rethink her actions, "A clinic...you actually have your hands on a doctor?" the hope and disbelief colored her words.

"Yes, we do have uh doc. Why? Are ya hurt?" Josh intervened.

"Not in any way that you could help with," Katie blurted out caustically before she realized what he was actually asking. Newly embarrassed and somewhat apologetically she finished, "but I have some friends that are hurt pretty bad."

"Well then, let's go retrieve 'em. They shouldn't have ta suffer uh moment longer. The Lord's work is never finished, is it Eth'n?" As hope gleamed in Katie's exhausted soul for the first time since the accident, Josh seamlessly proceeded to assume control over her and her group.

5

Strange bedfellows they make,
The child and the snake,
The circle, the messenger,
Both reel from attack...

A cool breeze danced across her bare skin, sending ripples of goose bumps along its path; reflexively, Jez snuggled closer to the warm body next to her and breathed in the comforting musty scent. God, it felt good to be home...*home...home...* the word echoed through her slowly rousing consciousness, "Home!" with a jerk Jez shot upright in bed, waking her lover in the process.

"Are you ok? Was it another nightmare?" Zeke kissed her shoulder as he embraced her in his arms, attempting to soothe her.

Ruefully, Jez held him close to her, "No...,"she hesitated, "I have to go..." she pulled away as if to get out of bed.

"Are you sure it wasn't a nightmare? We could have an early breakfast so we could talk about it," Zeke continued to reassure her even as an inner panic grew, sending his heart tumbling into his stomach.

"That's exactly why I have to go. The fact that you have to eat before you can talk about a bad dream just because it was one of your mom's quirks..."

"What?"

"It's something you do to remind you of family. My family's still out there Zeke. I have to leave here. I'm getting too comfortable and if I wait much longer I won't be able to leave at all..." Jez trailed off before her voice broke and she choked on her words.

Zeke fought the tears he knew were inevitable, he had known from the very beginning that this day was coming. She had never intended to stay more than a day or two and made her intentions to find her family up north quite clear. From the moment she had fallen into his arms by the stable he had schemed with an innocent malice to induce too much comfort for her to leave. Now he sorrowfully realized that he had only created more pain for her because she regretted having to leave him. He never had a chance of holding on to her while she was searching for her family but he'd been too selfish to admit that before.

Lovingly with a feather soft touch he ran his index finger up along her throat, with his fingers caressing the tip of her chin he gently turned her to face him. The words came out softly, his breath enfolding her as did his hands, "I know you have to go. I've known it all along. Come on, I'll help you get your gear together," and with that he said goodbye to her as only he knew how.

"So you want me to believe that God killed this family over a farking video game? That only people like them who refused to give up their TV's and shit like that were struck down by God? How farking stupid do you think I am? You actually expect me to believe that shit?" Katie retorted skeptically and slightly belligerently. Now that her friends had been cared for and fed the hold that Josh and Sam had over her was waning and they knew it.

Sam laid a gentle hand on her shoulder in a meticulously calculated manner, looking deep into her eyes as he spoke in his eloquent Southern gentleman style, "First of all, at least out of gratitude for the help we've provided, could you please refrain from your incessant use of profanity? I can't take any more of this sailor talk from such a beautiful face," with a rehearsed choreography he innocently caressed her cheek with the palm of his free hand, "Secondly, basically yes, that's what I'm saying. We are the Lord's children to do with as He will. It is only God who decides when life should begin and end. Given that fact and the fact that only those of my congregation that accepted the simpler immaterial life style survived, it is only logical that God did not wish those who were caught up in the materialistic secular lifestyle to survive. Even in your group, those that tried to save the cars – the technology – were the only ones that perished."

"Wait just a god... minute. First of all, I told them that the feds were coming. How else would you expect them to flee the scene? Or maybe they should have just waited around to be arrested? Get ffa...real! Of course they went for the cars, but only to save their asses, not to save the stupid cars. They were just following their instincts. Besides, I am just as hung up on modern conveniences as the rest, so why am I still ffa...alive?!" Katie argued, dismissing his line of reasoning while attempting to maintain her politeness.

"No you're not like the others. You may say that you're materialistic, but if you really were you wouldn't have demolished that truck, would you? But you chose to destroy it even though you knew that one of your friends would have to keep on walking with a broken leg," Sam calmly assured her, his grip on her shoulder slightly increasing.

"I had to, I can't explain it. The damn truck... oops sorry...I just couldn't let them use it," Katie interrupted.

"You may not think you understand why, but think about it. You could have easily gone for help and taken your friend to the hospital in that truck.

The truth is that you knew that Jerry was dead because of the truck. It was modern conveniences, just like that truck, that directly caused your boyfriend's death," Sam persuasively rebutted.

Katie slumped over and buried her head in her hands. Maybe he made some sense. Jerry would still be here if he hadn't been trapped in that farking bus. Why hadn't he just helped her fetch her damn dog? Surely he must have seen her run off into the woods or at least noticed that there was no one in the farking jeep, but he got into the goddamn bus anyway. Obviously he had been more concerned with getting away than helping her. Wasn't he concerned that she might be left behind? Fark! And she had placed the blame for Jerry's death on her dog when it was his disregard for her safety that had killed him. Fark him!

But still, she didn't believe for a minute all that God and Revelations crap. So what did it all mean anyway? If they had just walked away instead of going for their cars they would have all made it through alive! She was sure of that. And she knew for a fact that she hadn't been directed by God to evacuate the camp or chase after her dog. No, it certainly wasn't "God's" doing. Why some people insisted on worshipping a god that could be so hateful, she just didn't understand. It was easier to believe in nothing and she sure wasn't about to start believing in that "God" now just because some farking old man with a charming smile told her to.

The truth was, she'd been so overwhelmed with the loss of Jerry and everything else going on that she hadn't even given the cause or magnitude of the situation much thought. But now, faced with the proposition of it all being some Divine judgment, she searched her memory for possible scientific reasons. She knew the fault lines out west had been more active recently. Hell, California had experienced half a dozen five-point plus quakes over the last several weeks, but that was clear across the country. Katie chuckled to herself, as damaging as the quakes had been, she was actually grateful for their timing because it had given her the argument she needed to block a recent proposal to allow more damn off coast drilling out there.

Really, she couldn't understand why so many people refused to even contemplate the real dangers created by the incessant drilling to the deepest layers of the Earth's crust. How they expected to be able to endlessly rape the Earth of her deposits without ever replenishing any of it and still come back for more without any farking repercussions Katie struggled to comprehend. What if they'd been drilling a new well off the east coast when the big one hit just a few days ago, what havoc would that have led to? Damn it! Katie felt her heart skip a beat as her perception of reality exploded in her consciousness.

Sam politely coughed and mildly squeezed her shoulder and was nearly rewarded with a black eye as Katie reflexively jumped back into reality. She was so tired from trying to work off the debt she felt toward Sam that she hadn't realized she'd gone adrift in her thoughts for some time. She took a moment to compose her response as she stood up and stretched.

"Now Sam, don't think that I believe all your religious mumbo jumbo, but I think I do agree with you on the fact that the modern technologically overloaded world caused all of this mess," Katie thoughtfully asserted, "and if we overload it again then it could happen again," and she was determined to prevent anything like it from happening again because, after losing Jerry, she needed a Cause more than ever.

Knowingly, as he reached out his right hand toward Katie, Sam smiled his Southern gentleman smile, the one with one side of his mouth curled up ever so slightly higher than the other so as to casually emphasize his award winning dimple, "Then we have an agreement. We cannot afford to allow this to happen again."

Katie reached out cautiously and tightly grasped his hand, "To whatever it takes," her voice resounded with a silent strength. She still didn't really trust either him or Josh, but she really didn't have many options right now.

"Ssshhh...someone's coming," the lookout hissed down from his perch in the hunting seat hidden in the uppermost branches of the tree. Although the approaching figures were still too far away to be recognized they were close enough that they should have identified themselves by now. The lookout was new and afraid of wrongfully identifying one of their scouts, so he anxiously studied the movements of the figures hoping to see a signal but there was nothing.

"Is't one uh ours?"

"Ah don't think so," the lookout paused to reconsider his evaluation of the situation, "Naw, they never gave the signal. Okay, ya know the drill." Aware that the seriousness of the situation was growing with every step the stranger took toward them, the lookout ceaselessly monitored the figures through his binoculars, "It's jus uh girl on a horse. Ah think she's got a gun, one of those long ones. She's headed t'ward the site. Wait, there are two horses with no riders following behind her an Ah think there's a dog too," he examined the trail behind her for the two missing riders but spotted nothing, the woman drew closer. "Yeah, it's definitely a dog. An there's alot of gear tagged ta the other two horses...oh, Ah guess they're jus packhorses cause it looks they're leashed ta her horse. That's it, nobody else in the group."

The group's commander, who had been called to the surveillance area after the figures had failed to identify themselves, zealously jumped into action, "Well it's nearly dark so she won't be traveling much farther. Josh, follow her, but don't trip over this one," the commander's eyes gleamed with mischief at the good-natured jab directed toward his trusted friend. "Once she settles down for the night, come back here and we'll send a team to secure her."

Slightly embarrassed and even more determined to execute this assignment flawlessly, Josh rushed off in silence, becoming the woman's shadow.

Newly accustomed to Zeke's gentle touches during the night, Jez awoke abruptly to the feeling of a large callused hand gripping brutally tight over her mouth and the pinch from a cold steel blade against her slender throat.

A gruff voice bellowed in her ear and she could feel the spray of his spittle against her face, "Stay calm. If ya don't struggle an do as yer told, ya'll be on yer merry way tomorrah night. Understand?" Jez's assailant loosened his grip enough to let her silently respond and she carefully nodded her head in agreement, still acutely aware of the cool steel against her jugular vein.

"Good girl," he praised her as he would a small child or dog, "This the deal. Me an my buddy," the man jerked his head in the direction of his accomplice who remained along the edge of the camp, "are goin ta keep ya company till tomorrah night. Don't worry, we're men of God so yer virtue is safe. We don't get our jollies from such ungodliness. But since we don't know ya that well we're goin ta use a little safeguard t'assure yer cooperation." With the knife still dangerously close to her jugular the man proceeded to use his free hand to cuff Jez's hands and feet together, "Like Ah said, we're doin the Lord's work. So if ya try anything ta stop us, you'll pay with yer life. H'ever, if ya continue being a good little girl, we'll let ya go tomorrah night and hopef'ly we'll never cross paths again. Okay?" With Jez securely restrained he finally removed the knife from its position along Jez's throat where its constant presence had left a pink crease in her flesh.

"Okay," Jez's voice quivered with a newly found fear and confusion which overloaded her senses. This was the first time in her life that she had actually been assaulted by someone who she genuinely believed would do her harm. Sure, she had felt a blade or a staff used against her, even faced down the barrel of a gun, but it was always in the controlled situation of a classroom or competition. As such, her self-defense classes had prepared her well for the physical aspects of such an assault, but just now she found that she was caught emotionally unprepared for the real thing. The dark anger emanating from this man of God, combined with the knife against her throat, had caused Jez's intellect to completely, although temporarily, cloud with fear.

With the removal of the knife, the fear began to fade, but not without leaving a permanent scar even when the knife had barely made a mark. Unfortunately, the time for her defensive physical reaction had passed during her emotional expansion and there was nothing that she could do now to help herself except cooperate. Jez's freshly released and strengthened intellect reeled, how could she let this happen? She had thought that she was prepared for anything. Now, as her mind flooded with self-recriminations, Jez was determined to fight back, even if she couldn't seek revenge, her assailants would feel the effects of their violation of her free will! She began to carefully study the men and log their images and mannerisms in her mind, she would remember every detail – these men would not be able to do this to her or anyone else ever again. The man standing watch was really nothing more than a boy of fifteen or sixteen and she committed everything about his tall slender build to memory right down to his hair that was as black as the night in stark contrast to his icy blue eyes. Interesting, Jez took note that he twitched nervously and hesitated before complying with anything the older man proscribed.

As she continued to burn their images into her memory she realized that the older man had wandered off and she fixated on making use of the opportunity, whistling to get the boy's attention. "Hey Boy!" she mumbled loudly, "Come over here!"

Reluctantly, the boy slowly sidestepped to approach her, glancing suspiciously around for his partner, "I'm sorry lady, but there's nothing I can do for you. I don't even have the keys. Please just behave yourself. I...I...don't want to have to hurt you," the boy quivered with fear himself as he attempted to sound menacing.

"There must be something you can do to help me," Jez played on his uncertainty, speeding up her breathing and coaxing out a few tears, "I haven't done anything to you. Please..."

"Please don't cry...it's nothing personal," he paced uneasily and scratched his head, "I know you didn't mean to do it, but you're just in the way of the Mission. I don't think its right, but there's nothing I can do about it!" The boy anxiously edged his way back to his designated post before his lapse was noticed, but it was too late, Josh had noticed her speaking with him. Jez had overlooked the man's obvious distrust of the boy, and worse, she had neglected to monitor him after he had walked away. In a last ditched effort she closed her eyes and went limp, hoping that he hadn't noticed her talking before.

"Boy, Ah thought Ah told ya t'stay on the edge of the camp?" the man screamed as he barbarically knocked Jez unconscious with the butt of her own rifle.

"Whoa!! Easy boy!" Ethan attempted to calm the large stallion tethered to the saddle of his horse before its powerful lunges dislodged him from his perch. His ignorance about how to control such a large animal made his distress noticeable as the stallion snorted and nickered in displeasure. Instinctively, the horse picked up on Ethan's growing insecurity and began to relentlessly buck and violently brandish its head back and forth. "Josh! Help!! I can't control him!" Ethan pled, overwhelmed by the situation.

Josh directed the mare to circle back, "Fine! Hand it over'ta me!" the anger forced his brow into a tight knot as he held his hand out.

Obediently, Ethan dismounted the gelding and freed the stallion's reins from his saddle, keeping a tight grip on the reins as he painstakingly transferred them to Josh's grip. Remarkably, the stallion appeared calm and gentle now that he wasn't being towed by the boy, but Ethan felt compelled to reiterate his concerns regarding the horse's instability despite the its sudden change of attitude, "Careful Josh..."

"He's fine now. Jus leggo of the reins!" Josh summarily dismissed the warning. Diligently waiting for an opportunity, the stallion instantly noticed the lapse in the tension on his bit and seized the occasion to escape. With a grace and speed that left Josh with no time to comprehend or react, Trace jerked forcefully away, dragging Josh to the ground as he disappeared into the wilderness.

Puk sniffed the air, intensely searching for the scent of the two men near the camp, but they were gone. They had leashed him to a tree several yards from the campsite after beating him unconscious during his efforts to protect Jez. Duty bound, he had rubbed the flesh on his neck raw in his initial attempts to break free. Once he realized the rope was too thick to snap he set to chew through it and it had taken him all night.

Finally free of the restraint, Puk raced to find Jez and nearly panicked as he smelled the scent of her blood near their camp, but the sound of her breath quickly reassured him. She was lying still on the ground, slumped on her side with her hands and feet together. He sniffed her over to determine the extent of her injuries and located bruises on her wrists and ankles where the handcuffs had been and found her temple swollen and bloody. His attempts to revive her were futile so Puk provided the only medical care he knew how to give, gingerly licking away the excess blood and dirt around the wound on her head before lying on the ground against her. He knew that she was resting peacefully by the feeling of her steady breath on his muzzle and he monitored her heartbeat by nuzzling his head up to her chest. Now he could only wait.

In due time, Jez awoke to the gentle warmth of Puk sleeping quietly beside her. Her head was throbbing and her joints and muscles ached from their prolonged constraint as she struggled to stand; there was no time to relax. She tried to remember the events of the previous night as she looked around for her attackers. It didn't take her long to realize that the men were gone and so were her horses and gear.

Damn! What the hell was she going to do? Searching for strength while her head throbbed and her mind raced, Jez grabbed control from her determination to stop the men. There was no telling where they were; she didn't even know how long she'd been out, although she was pretty sure that she had been out for at least a day since the sun was hanging low on the horizon and the exposed areas of her skin ached with sunburn. As she reviewed her options she gained support from Puk's physical presence. She could still smell the scent of whatever drugs had obviously been used to knock him out and the various cuts and abrasions along his neck and head still looked fresh, so she figured it couldn't have happened much more than a day or two before. With her panic back in check Jez resumed her survey of the damage.

"Okay, Jez, the horses are obviously gone, so what else did they take?" she talked herself through the motions as she rebuilt her mental inventory. Jez scrupulously scanned the area and noticed her ration bag and canteen sitting next to the burnt out campfire, but the remainder of her belongings were no where in sight. The minor relief of spotting any of her gear quickly evaporated when she found that her ration bag was empty except for a single power bar. Great, her situation kept getting better and better! It was a good thing she'd planned for this moment for so many damn years.

The self-recriminations from the previous night reverberated in her mind even as she forced herself to sample various plants and gather kindling while she looked for her attackers' tracks. Before long Puk began barking wildly and digging by a group of bushes on the other side of camp. Her sense of security permanently disabled, Jez's heart pounded in alarm with each deliberately conservative stride toward Puk who impatiently began dragging a large object from its shallow grave under the bushes. Even from her distance across the camp Jez recognized her mud coated gear bag and in the fraction of a second that it took her to reach Puk her hope was rejuvenated.

"GOOD BOY! OH!! GOOD BOY!!" tears streamed down her face as she rewarded him with a good rub between the ears. She couldn't restrain herself for very long and as she rummaged through her pack she was delighted to find all of her belongings in tact. She even found some packets of peanuts that she knew weren't hers tucked away with a quickly scribbled note: *Sorry, Ethan.* On a hunch, Jez frantically began digging around the hole where her gear bag had been buried and was nearly blinded by her own tears when she uncovered her rifle.

Oh thank you Ethan. I knew you were a good kid, Jez silently thanked her attacker-turned-rescuer. As the relief let fatigue set in, she spread out her bedroll and rekindled her fire before letting herself relax. There wasn't enough daylight left for her to begin her travels again on foot, and she knew that she needed to give herself some time to heal and think.

Her mind rested and her spirit rekindled, Jez packed up her gear and made sure her fire was out as she prepared to start off. She had already decided to continue on her way rather than waste any more time tracking her attackers. Closing the distance between herself and her family took priority over everything else. Anyway, she knew it was ridiculous to go after the two men alone since they had mentioned being part of some group which in all likelihood was probably just as insane – she was confident but she wasn't stupid. Their paths would cross again someday, she was sure of it, and next time she would be ready for them. Karma could be a real bitch sometimes. But for the moment, Jez didn't have any time to waste, especially now that she was traveling on foot – again!

Out of habit, Jez whistled out her call for Trace as she began to grab up her gear, "Now that was stupid. It's been at least two days. Face it, he's gone Jez," she berated her fantasy-like optimism, knowing it was more than the sheer force of habit that had caused her to call for him. She thought that she could sense him nearby and the folly of that caused her to be even more irritated at herself and her situation. Jez increased her pace, all the while Puk increased his stride until he finally raced past her. As he disappeared into the woods it became readily apparent that he was interested in something other than escorting her. A moment later Puk's yelps of recognition followed by an excited whinny told Jez that her optimism had been warranted. Some how, some way, Trace had found his way back to her and she decided to leave it at that. After everything that had happened over the past few weeks, she was beyond trying to figure out why anything happened anymore...it really was a whole new world.

As Jez continued on her way through the northeast wilderness the air was thick with a sense of foreboding that challenged her resolve to keep going. When the smell of burnt nylon filled her senses she finally directed Trace to a halt even though she had only been on the road for a few hours. She followed her nose through the brush and nearly stumbled across the smoldering remains of a burnt-out tent at a recently abandoned campsite. Since she was only a few miles from where she had been attacked, Jez wondered if the destruction at this campsite was related. As with her camp, all the usable gear had been taken, but there were also small blood stains littering the dirt by the campfire. To her it was obvious that someone else had at least been beaten and confined like her. Given the blood stains, she doubted that their captors had looked out for them as Ethan had done for her. It was a good thing she'd thought better of pursuing her attackers alone. She just hoped that whoever had been camping here had found safety by now. Jez pursued the remaining tracks leading away from the camp and was astonished to discover the young couple hiding under some brush not twenty feet from the camp. Obviously terrified that their attackers had returned to finish them off, they were both visibly shaking despite the young man's iron grasp around the woman next to him.

"Are you guys ok?" Jez asked, relieved to find the couple alive and apparently unhurt, but they remained unresponsive and appeared to become more catatonic with every word she uttered. She held out her wrists to display her various bruises and cuts, "See...bruises from handcuffs. I know who you're afraid of, but I'm not one of them," she assured them, but the couple still refused to come out, so she resigned herself to sit and wait – she wasn't going to just leave them to starve to death.

Since she was obviously going to be there a while Jez began to set up camp for the three of them. She quickly brought down a few large birds with Puk's help and as the birds roasted over the fire and their juices evaporated in the flames, the ravenous couple was overcome by hunger and crawled out of their hiding place. They had been huddled there for over a day without anything to eat or drink, and just as Jez predicted, they relaxed once it was clear that she was more than happy to share the meal with them.

With their bellies full for the first time in weeks, Darren and Kit became quite talkative. Before the CAT they had been graduate students studying in the humanities, so when it became apparent what had happened they jumped at the research opportunity. Now they were traveling the coast like Jez, but they regarded themselves as explorers of a new world, visiting and learning about the new social structures that were beginning to arise. They had logged over half a dozen new townships and settlements so far, relaying news about the cleanup and rescue efforts as well as sharing stories about their travels along the way. They had observed very few people traveling as they did and with regular communications still nonexistent, the settlements had started depending on those few as the only means of communication between them, occasionally even entrusting them with mail like the old Pony Express. So many people had taken to referring to them as "Mustangs" that it was becoming customary for them to be introduced as Mustangs to local government officials as part of their initial reception by the settlement. And in the absence of television and radio, the stories about their travels was a major source of public entertainment, so much so that many settlements were trying to schedule and publicize future Mustang visits.

Kit lit up when she recalled a recent visit to a quaint little town comprised of the residents of a former suburb who had survived by taking shelter in the nearby high school. She and Darren had used their engineering and electrical knowledge from their undergraduate studies to devise an electrical grid that linked the output from all the personal generators, basically creating a miniature electric plant. It provided sufficient power to pump potable well-water and provide low wattage lighting throughout the school building which the residents had converted into a permanent shelter. With the success of the power grid, town members were inspired to span out and had begun to make use of the few nearby houses that were still structurally sound. The success fed Darren and Kit's desire to assist other communities, so despite the pleas of the townsfolk, they had left the town as soon as they were certain that the system was running smoothly. The grateful townsfolk had insisted that they accept payment for their services and showered them with much needed camping supplies, including some local vittles and an electric lantern with spare batteries. Darren and Kit's embrace tightened as they shuddered with the memory of how, without warning, their attackers had become violent and torched their camp when one of them had caught sight of the lantern hanging in the tent, "...it hadn't even been turned on!"

"So you're certain that it was the lantern that set them off? How weird."

"Yes, they actually went on a tirade about it... 'How dare we have an electric appliance'...'Didn't we know any better'...They acted like it was some huge hazard, but then they burned down our tent!" Kit shook her head with continued disbelief.

"I'm not sure what to make of it. The kid that attacked me made sure to leave behind all my gear, including my cell phone and that uses a battery," Jez fiddled with Ethan's note which was still in her pocket, "Hmmm, but then again my stuff had been hidden, so I guess maybe he wasn't supposed to be leaving it. The older guy with him was a real ass...we should probably head toward that settlement you mentioned," she regained her focus, "They might have some more information about this anti-technology group since they're so close. And I'm sure you would be able to stay there until you felt safe enough to travel again."

"Okay," Kit and Darren agreed in unison.

"Well, from your description it's a day-long trip to the settlement, so we'll leave first thing in the morning," Jez finished her thought.

They stopped in horror, having reached the crest of the debris mountain shielding the settlement from the main road. The smell of burning wood and flesh filled the air as fumes seeped up from what remained of the former school and settlement. Even more debris and ash fanned out from the school building, clearly declaring where the powerful explosion had originated. With no fire trucks to fight the blaze and no natural fire boundaries, the resulting conflagration had consumed much of the draught stricken town. With an unfounded fanciful hope, the three travelers desperately called out for survivors as they made their way through the debris.

"Oh my God! Darren, the generators—did we do this?" Kit pled in an almost inaudible voice, absolutely horrified that their miscalculation could have wiped out an entire town.

Darren stared into the distance at nothing, stunned at the possibility and afraid to put it into words himself, "No, we calculated and recalculated. Everything was working fine when we left. Besides, the worst that could have happened was a bad fire and the gen room would have contained that...it had three hour walls," he fervently insisted as his mind reeled to find another logical explanation. "No, this looks like the place was bombed," his words floated in the air as the group came into view of their answer. Spray painted in crimson red across the side of the half burnt-out shell of a house was the phrase "REPENT Accept God's Judgment!" Inside the house they found all the appliances vandalized and the electrical wiring ripped out of the walls. It was the same with every other building they inspected as they checked and rechecked for any sign of the townsfolk.

With an eerie foresight, the three reluctantly decided to investigate the school building and carefully made their way into the smoking ruins. The structure was still scalding hot to the touch and the heat penetrated the souls of their shoes, so as Kit directed Jez through the once familiar building, Jez used the tip of her rifle to push open what remained of the fire doors. The farther along they got without seeing any casualties the more their relief turned to concern. When the three finally made their way down the corridor that led to the town's meeting hall and former school auditorium the justification of their concern was almost unbearable. Jez gagged as she attempted to dislodge the chain securing the auditorium doors shut. Even with the fire damage the chains held the doors tight until she and Darren combined their efforts to kick the damaged doors out of their frames, even then a barrier of charred bodies lying one on top of another kept the doors erect. It was clear that those that had not been killed in the initial blast had futilely struggled to escape the inferno that ensued and the horror they must have experienced as they beat at the doors in vain while they burned alive was more than the three could bear to imagine. This was no accident, nor was it judgment, this was a slaughter.

Unable to suppress their disgust another moment, Darren and Kit turned from Jez as they began vomiting uncontrollably.   Although accustomed to death, Jez was still left aghast at the sight of the gore and the ramifications of this discovery made her shudder as an icy chill trickled down her spine. They were not dealing with some random marauders, these were terrorists by any definition. Terrorists that would murder an entire town – men, women, children, and the elderly alike – in God's name. Righteousness was a powerful drug and they had to be stopped!

"Josh, make her shut up," a short stocky man spit out as he brutally shoved a thin middle-aged woman into Josh's arms.

The woman opened eyes bloodshot from tears and swallowed her body convulsing sobs long enough to speak, "No, Ah will not shut up! How can this be the Lord's work? Sam said that tha Lord had spared us because we were his children an had followed his word," the woman nearly choked as she fought to maintain control over her sobs, "so God musta spared those families fer a reason as well. Who are we ta play God an take the lives that God has spared?"

Another moaning sob burst forth and Josh attempted to interject reason into the woman, "Martha, we mustn't challenge the Lord's work. Sam wouldn't lead us contrary ta that, ya know that. Come on, ya have'ta trust him ta lead us. Wasn't his leadership what directed ya in the Lord's direction that spared yer life in the first place? Please, straighten up before Sam sees ya like this."

"Or what? Will tha Lord suddenly find it that mah survival was in error too? Josh, in all Sam's sermons, in all his speeches, we were nev'r told that we would have ta break the Lord's comman'ments in order ta carry out His words. We were never told that we would be spected ta kill!" the pain in Martha's voice nearly cut through Josh's reason but his loyalty to Sam held fast.

"Ya musn't hold yerself responsible for those people's death," Josh held her hands tightly as he spoke, "It was their ties ta the mater'l world that killed 'em. Their own generators caused tha fire that killed 'em…"

"NO! Josh, it was us. We chain'd tha doors. We set tha splosives. There is no way that anyone but God himself is goin'ta be able ta convince me oth'rwise. Ah will not be part of this…do ya hear me? Ah will not be part of this!" Martha declared as the world went dark and she crumpled to the ground.

6

*A connection is made and a pattern revealed,
The messenger and fellows, knowledge they now wield,
As one journey does end, so another begins...*

Surrounded by the sounds of silence Jez laid restlessly by the campfire. Although she had become accustomed to the silence associated with traveling alone and had even enjoyed it at times, the familiar no longer comforted her. It was amazing how her world had changed so dramatically overnight, not once but twice. Long passed were the nights she slept contently in the warmth of a campfire. She now slept in complete darkness with her loaded rifle at her side, her hand resting strategically next to its grip. Every snap of a branch or crackle of a leaf raised the hairs on the back of her neck and aroused her to a state of alert.

She had always believed that this new world would be a better place where everyone would finally come together and realize the error of their ways. She had even envisioned the whole Age of Aquarius/Star Trek type society replacing the everyday rat race. Okay, maybe she had let her imagination run away with her a bit – Jez had never been one to get tied down by the accepted reality – but it had truly seemed that society was naturally moving that way. Or had she simply allowed her fantasy to taint her perception of this reality...Jez drifted off to thoughts of Zeke and Bess and that wonderful hot bath, not to mention Zeke's touch. No, the facts were unmistakable – she couldn't have misinterpreted the impromptu governments of the settlements she had visited or their efforts to deal with all the devastation and damage caused by the CAT. Everyone was pulling together in a level of cooperation that rivaled the camaraderie of World War II America or at least what she had read and watched about that time period. So what had gone wrong? What had turned that group to violence when everyone else was finally feeling comfortable leaving their front doors open again? Maybe a few weeks wasn't long enough to judge if the new system was working, but how did one measure the life span of a new world? Anyway, it felt like it had been an age since the CAT and people had finally started believing that the world would recover from its tragedy, at least until this happened.

Every night since her attack Jez had struggled to understand how this small renegade group could possibly believe that violence was the answer, especially since they claimed to be devout Christians. What ever happened to all that "What would Jesus do" propaganda? Certainly He wouldn't slaughter children and families in the name of religion or God. But what concerned and saddened Jez more was that this state of suspicion and fear that clouded her thoughts was not isolated to her. Once again the world had been infected with fear.

Word about the massacre disseminated with remarkable speed in spite of the continued lack of radio and television broadcasts, leaving in its path a fear that common courtesy was a dangerous weakness. The towns were now suspicious of every stranger and Mustangs that were not already familiar with a settlement put themselves at great risk to carry out the obligations they had previously regarded as elementary. They were suddenly shunned and threatened – over and over again, Jez, Darren, and Kit were greeted with the ring of a warning shot if they had not first been warned of the extremist's boundaries by the body of a Mustang that had not fared as well.

Still, no police came…no FBI arrived. There was no visit from the President or First Lady – not even a press conference was called. Since the majority of the survivors had naturally banded together for mutual support, the general population had been too preoccupied to question the lack of government activity until this point. Communications were still crippled, making it easier to assume that government officials were busy providing aid elsewhere than to address the meaning of its absence and possible destruction. But now with such a horrific act, the public cried out for some official governmental interference and its absence was noted, casting the reality of the Government's disappearance.

To no one's surprise, in the areas where no informal government existed, this realization caused desperation and greed to mix at dangerous levels and widespread looting and vandalism were rampant which in turn spread the fear of anarchy while vigilantes propagated throughout the area and added to the growing mass hysteria. Jez reeled that a religion that had been founded on messages of love and forgiveness had been twisted so far that only extreme depravity was found in its wake.

She hadn't realized how much she had already come to depend on and enjoy the changes to society until now when she felt helpless to preserve it…she hated feeling helpless!

Only the hisses and crackles of water dripping into the fire polluted the early afternoon sounds of the woods, and occasionally the crumpling of paper or the nicker of a horse would interrupt her trance.

"Shit!" the pungent smell of smoke and burning fish alerted Kit that she had drifted off and she hurried to salvage the rest of the meal she had cooking. As she removed the pan from the fire the smoke no longer masked the results of her labor and the sweet peppery aroma of the roasting fish made her mouth water and her stomach churn with hunger. She surveyed the area to see if anyone else was ready to break for the meal and was both relieved and irritated to discover that her earlier mishap had apparently not been noticed. Kit purposefully swished her hand over the pan, directing the delightful aroma to fill the camp, but not only did it fail to elicit any of the usual complements, it also failed to even earn the faintest acknowledgment. Feeling entirely too ignored, Kit decided to extract some recognition through the application of good old fashioned guilt. "Food's done. So who's hungry?" she announced, "the fish I caught earlier are smelling quite delicious, in case you hadn't noticed."

"Hmmm, ok, yes..." Darren mumbled, lost in thought as he scribbled and scratched at the multitude of lines and squiggles on his note pad – another idea that had come to him in his sleep the night before. Although he wasn't quite sure what he was creating, he knew exactly where each line and scribble went and how to complete each calculation. Unconcerned by the illogic of it Darren kept working, he figured that he would know what it was once he was done.

"So I hear Darren's hungry, what about you Jez?"

"Huh? Did you say something Honey?" unaware that he had requested his share of the meal, Darren now jerked out of his trance-like state with the subconscious recognition of his name.

"I thought you said you were hungry," Kit crossed her arms and a frown threatened to swallow her face as she realized that she had been ignored, "Do you want some of the fish or not? It's ready. What about you Jez?" Sensing Kit's increased irritation, Puk immediately leapt up from his station near Jez to present himself for his share of their meal.

Kit directed a stern gaze over to Jez who was rubbing down Trace now that she had neatly removed his saddle and additional burdens, but Jez was lost in thought and failed to notice Kit's stare. The quiet task of grooming her horse usually acted as a stress reliever for Jez since it allowed her time alone with Trace and his calming influence. Now the mindlessness of the task freed her mind to wander to thoughts and memories that she would just as soon forget. For the past several days all she had done was hopscotch between despair and an overwhelming need to focus solely on stopping the terrorists. She had been so confident that her attackers would be stopped, but that was before the bombing, before she truly realized what she was up against...the magnitude of their violence was overwhelming.

"Puk, go get her! She's obviously not listening to a word I say," Kit directed their four legged friend to earn his meal. Obediently and with the same sense of frustration as Kit, Puk prepared to physically drag Jez to the campfire, gently pulling on her shirttail, careful not to rip the fabric. A bit embarrassed at her mental absence, Jez willingly let Puk lead her over to Kit.

"Well I know where Darren's *been*. He's been consumed by another engineering idea again, so I know he'll be of no company until he's figured the whole damn thing out. But where have you been? You didn't even say anything vulgar when I burnt my first attempt at lunch," Kit vented.

"And I thought that you were the ones that needed taking care of. Lately I've been feeling a bit overwhelmed, or maybe 'consumed' is a better word. I'm not sure how to explain it," eager for the catharsis of discussion Jez began to ramble on, "I know I told you two to just forget about the school, it wasn't your fault, yadda yadda yadda. But the truth is, I can't put it aside. The individual attacks were one thing, but to see all those families dead. Burned alive and told to 'repent' by the very people that murdered them. I can't stop thinking about it. I keep trying to figure out a way to stop them, but I come up blank every time. We don't have anyone to go to like the police and we don't even have the ability to warn anyone if we found something since the phones still aren't working," as Jez allowed her wall to come down the tears began to ebb over her lashes and out the corner of her eyes, washing away fine lines of the dust and dirt coating her face. She was grateful for the release the words allowed her and even more so for the comfort offered by the young couple. "I just feel so helpless, like I'm on a plane that's going down and there's nothing I can do to stop it."

Caught off guard by this sudden knowledge of Jez's humanity, Kit sat speechless for a moment. Even though she had known Jez for only a few days, she had gained the clear impression of a steel willed woman that would be one of those people who shaped the world. It had never occurred to Kit that Jez had been as traumatized by the school massacre as she had, "Look Jez, I don't know if this will mean much to you since we haven't known each other that long, but I really feel like I know you so I'm just going to say it any way. You are a very powerful woman and I know in my heart that there is something you will do to help stop all this. But stop thinking that you have to save the world in one day single-handedly. I agree with you about the lack of long range communication being a handicap, but it's also a handicap on the other side as well. So we make do with what we've got and we get the message out there. I'm sure that together we all can figure out something to stop them."

"I don't know about that. I think you're giving me way too much credit," Jez's lingering self-doubt fought to dampen the hope Kit instilled.

"No I'm not, because I know that you're the kind of person that can't sit still for too long and that anything you do will help. Now stop feeling sorry for yourself and have something to eat. We have a long day tomorrow. We have to find a place for Darren and I to drop anchor for a while so that we can cut you free. You've got a lot of work ahead of you missy!" Kit ordered Jez in a mockingly stern voice as she waved her index finger back and forth.

Although she agreed with their decision to part ways, Jez was relieved that it took them another two days to find a settlement willing to harbor Kit and Darren. It had barely been a full day since she had set off on her own again, but Jez found that she was already missing their company. With her walls down, she and Kit had quickly developed a close bond and spent hours in marathon discussions, they had shared their doubts and fears about the future with a cathartic honesty and gained strength from the fact that both had feelings of regret about the disappearance of their old world. Jez came to terms with the sense of loss that she had been unwilling to acknowledge – even to herself – until that very moment, clearing the emotional blinders she had unwittingly adopted. She viewed the change with a whole new clarity that lifted the sole responsibility for saving the world from her shoulders. For the first time since the massacre she was not overwhelmed with guilt as she focused on looking for her family. Jez savored her renewed vigor and even allowed herself to make plans for the future when she was reunited with her mom and sister. She imagined that before her mother could allow herself to enjoy their reunion she would probably scold her for endangering herself. Or perhaps being saddled with her sister for all this time had caused the old woman to mellow out some – Al had that effect on people, her realistic optimism was absolutely infectious. Just thinking about her sister's optimism helped Jez brace herself for the possibility that her family might not be waiting there when she finally arrived. She knew they were alive, she could feel it, so if it turned out that they had left in search of her then she would just have to track them down...and once the communication satellites were restored she could call them. Just another reason for her to do whatever she could to get this world back on its feet...Jez drifted off to sleep as she mentally reviewed the various possibilities.

She carefully smoothed out her well worn highway map on the table next to the massive wall-map pinned on the bulletin board. Beginning at the bottom of the map, she slowly traced her finger along the path she had followed pausing to explain her notations at various points to her counterpart who then applied the appropriate marker to the corresponding spot on the larger map. By the time Jez reached her current location the spattering of various colored flags and push-pins on the larger map was both impressive and disturbing. She took a deep breath and gracefully turned around to greet the group whose arrival had just been announced by the light tapping on the floorboards.

"I'm sorry we're late," an elderly gentleman with the look of a stereotypical eccentric professor apologized as he led the entourage into the room, "it took a while longer than expected to round everyone up."

"That's ok, we've actually just finished with the preliminaries for the meeting," Jez reassured the group. "So if you will all just take a seat we'll begin going over the implications of all this," she pointed toward the colorfully marked map as she leaned against the desk at the front of the classroom.

The Professor shooed the others to take their seats quickly, "Let's get a move on folks, we don't want to keep a Mustang waiting."

"Good afternoon everyone, I'm Jez Kyle," she began as the group situated themselves in the seats located throughout the former classroom. With their full attention on her, she began in earnest, "I realize that you've all heard the rumors about the massacre down south," concerned mumbles circulated the small room, "well I and my friends were the first ones on the scene." Jez quickly continued in order to silence the questions and concerns that threatened to overtake the meeting, "I'll be glad to discuss specifics of that later, but the purpose of this meeting is to pool our knowledge about the rise in crime that has taken place since the CAT," she moved her hand along the map as she spoke, "We've already filled in the map with the episodes that I'm aware of, so I'd like to start off the meeting by adding any other instances that y'all know of." Pausing with a

Vanna-like accuracy over the appropriate markers, she reviewed the color coding system they had developed, "As you can see, we've been color coding the map so that we can figure out if there's any pattern to these criminal events. Blue is for minor, petty theft type things. Yellow is for more serious vandalism and if someone was hurt or killed, then we used red." Jez realized that her hand had been hovering over the red markers for some time and worked to regain her focus as she pointed her index finger at some individual white markers, "You'll also notice that there are white push-pins next to some of the other colors. This means that there was some sort of religious message or insignia found at the scene."

The Professor politely raised his hand as he spoke, "Do you mind if we come and get a close up look? I don't know about the rest of the group, but it's just a blur of color to me."

"Oh, sorry, I should have guessed that," she apologized for the understandable oversight, "Yes, please, come up and get a closer look and while you're up here go ahead and add whatever incidents you're aware of." Over the next couple of hours push-pins and flags were added to and adjusted on the map, slowly developing an even more disturbing pattern in full Technicolor right before their eyes. The blue markers were barely visible in the blur of red and white – never had a sea of red, white, and blue created such an overwhelming sense of dread for the group.

"Does everyone here see the same pattern emerging as I do?" the Professor queried, hoping his analytical skills that had been honed over the years were somehow now failing him.

"I'm afraid we do, Professor. It's clear that the violent attacks are on the rise," someone offered.

"What about all the white markers? Doesn't that seem to imply some sort of cult activity," another interjected. A collective sigh traveled through the room, "You mean like Wako or Jonestown?"

"I think that's a safe assumption. The radical extremist thinking and mind control that goes on in a cult atmosphere would explain the degree of violence and the numbers involved," the Professor deduced as he flipped through the various pages of his hastily scribed notes.

Jez quickly tapped into his line of reasoning, "Okay, assuming that we've established that some sort of religious cult is involved, then why would they be increasing their attacks?"

"Who cares why! How do we stop them? Especially if we're dealing with a bunch of brain washed cult members?" the group's self-appointed spokesman loudly interrupted.

The Professor stood up and identified his heckler, "Now that is quite enough young man," the sternness in his voice communicated his irritation at having his train of thought carelessly interrupted, "'Why?' is the very key to stopping them. We cannot fight an unknown enemy and we cannot know our enemy without knowing what it is that drives him!"

The middle aged culprit swallowed hard and allowed his seat to swallow him, "I apologize, Professor."

"Well, shall we continue then? Professor, I have a theory..." Jez waited for permission to continue their discussion. The Professor waved her on as he took his seat and opened his notepad to a fresh page, "I have reason to believe that for some reason this group or cult is trying to stop our restoration efforts."

"Hmmm," the Professor considered her statement, "What makes you think that?"

Jez made her way to the map to emphasize her point, "Because at the town that was destroyed," she indicated an area of the map tinted pink by the dense population of red and white push-pins, "in the few homes that were left standing they had ripped the wiring right out of the walls and made sure that every generator, vehicle, appliance... everything in the area was destroyed. And every attack that I've heard of or witnessed since then has been the same," she pointed at more markers on the map as she retraced her recent travel route.

"Does anyone here have any similar experiences?" the Professor opened the floor up for discussion when he noticed several people anxious to speak up.

"I heard that one of the cellular towers was bombed right before it was to go back online."

"And I've known a bunch of people that've had their tools stolen or generators vandalized."

"Someone stole my truck but I didn't bother to report it because I figured it would be a waste of time."

"Yeah and last week everyone on my end of town had the gas siphoned from their generators, but we thought it was just some jack-off looting. Do you think it could be related?"

The Professor frantically scribbled in his note pad trying to keep a record of every story being shouted out all at once. When his inability to keep up made it clear that the sheer number of events must indicate a motive or at least a pattern he stood up and reigned in the conversation, "Alright everyone, I think it has become abundantly clear to everyone here that our disaster recovery efforts are a target of this group. 'Why' is another question that we'll deal with, but first of all I think we need to agree to get word out to start guarding potential targets like generators, tools, etcetera. We should probably also start posting guards at every major repair site."

"I agree Professor and I'd be happy to pass this information along to the settlements I pass. I've still got another week or so's worth of travel north," Jez once again offered to go out on a limb, a habit she couldn't seem to break.

"Thank you Jez. We'll most definitely be taking you up on that offer," the Professor surveyed the room, "Does everyone agree that we should start to guard against potential future attacks?" A tidal wave of raised hands made its way to the Professor, "Good. Then with that decided I would like to suggest we table the 'Why' discussion until after our meal break. Let's all meet back here in, say, two hours." Reluctantly the group began to stand and exit the room as the Professor made a shooing motion with his hands. "Please join me Jez," he gave Jez a gentle nudge out the door as well, temporarily sparing her the group's inevitable interrogation.

"Professor, you already know the 'Why' don't you?" Jez asked quietly as they made their way down the dimly lit hallway. He quickly glanced at her through the corner of his eye and she knew instantly that he had the same theories as she did; the two continued on in an understanding silence until they reached the Professor's office.

As the door closed behind them the Professor set his notes down on a small conference table next to the office's only window and poured himself a glass of water, "Just make yourself at home Jez. Someone will be in shortly with our lunch," he indicated that she should take the seat across from him. She quickly scanned the titles populating the bookcase along the wall as she made her way across the room: *Cults: Faith based Healing and Coercion; Road to Apocalypse: Religious Movements and Violence; The Prophecy of Fear: Religion and Mind Control; Cult Mindsets: The Unspoken War in America.*

"So Professor, exactly what are you a professor of?" she made no attempt to conceal her delight at the observation she had just made.

The Professor laughed a slow quiet laugh, "I like you Jez Kyle. You have the keenest sense of observation of anyone I've known. In a former life I was a professor of world theology. I was also qualified by the old federal court system as an expert witness on the cult and group mindset."

Jez caught the growing darkness behind his eyes, "I knew it! So you do think this group is a cult trying to prevent any sort of recovery from taking place?"

"And they will go to any lengths necessary to prevent it," the Professor answered by completing her thought. "What fortune for leaders that men do not think," he sighed.

"Hitler, right?" Jez indicated her understanding of their dire situation when a light knock on the door invaded their conversation.

"Lunch by the window as usual Professor?" the adolescent boy made conversation as he set down the tray and placed their plates in from of them.

"Thanks Joey, you are a great help to me as always," he tipped his imaginary hat to the boy as the young man disappeared behind the closing door.

Jez waved farewell to the guard newly stationed at the outpost as she left the settlement's territory. She was anxious to be on her way again and unknowingly conveyed to Trace her desire for speed – instinctively she tightened her thighs and grabbed the saddle horn to secure herself even as he suddenly launched forward in full gallop. She resisted the urge to pull back on the reigns and was rewarded with the intense sensation of freedom brought with the wind whipping her hair back and the oxygen rich air flooding her lungs. For a short while she allowed herself to be lost in the exhilaration, but once she sensed that Trace had enjoyed a good run she signaled him to slow down to a less taxing pace. The rhythmic sound of his hooves on the well tamped soil barely made an impression on the all too familiar silence as Jez focused in on the sound, seeking companionship for the long ride ahead.

She reached over her shoulder, felt her fingers slip into place around the grip, and whirled her rifle around and into position under her arm in a single invisible motion. Just as seamlessly she slipped the rifle back into its halter along her back, all the while Trace kept a slow steady pace as he navigated the uneven terrain. After a few moments Jez again closed her eyes and repeated the exercise – the long hours of travel had begun to feel quite lonely, but they seemed to go by faster when she kept herself occupied by practicing what weaponry skills she could while on horseback or completing various mental exercises that she had designed to work her growing psychic muscles. In fact, Jez spent nearly every waking moment practicing or perfecting some new skill. As a result, her keen sense of observation began to function as autonomically as breathing and her increased mental and physical proficiencies were readily apparent.

So it was no surprise to her when the low rumble of a growl started growing deep in Puk's throat, she had been waiting nearly two days for the couple she knew was following her to make their move. Jez had been aware of them as soon as their paths had crossed and could identify the moment that they deviated from their route to follow her. She allowed them to believe their presence had remained undetected in order to maintain the advantage of surprise even though her earlier reconnaissance of their camp had assured her that she could easily defend herself against them. The fresh recollection of the couple's complete disdain for outdoor living caused a muffled moan to escape her lips even as the barrel of her rifle slipped into place between the man's shoulder blades.

"Oh shit! Uh, Carl, hold up a minute," the man muttered while he acknowledged the gun to his back by slowly raising his hands above his head as he had been culturally programmed to do.

Carl stopped, spinning around to address the slowdown to their retreat, "Come on Alex, we gotta get outta here. Stop messin around...Oh!" he silenced his complaining and immediately raised his hands as well when Jez choreographed Alex into a turn that revealed her presence. The corners of her mouth curled up menacingly even though she tried to resist smiling at their eagerness to comply with her unspoken commands. She could tell Puk was also amused by the rhythmic change in the pressure on her thigh where he stood against her. Jez wondered if the men were able to notice Puk's wagging tail in light of his curled lips and brazen teeth, especially since she could barely distinguish the playful growl currently punctuating the silence from his normal predatory one.

She finally decided to put an end to the men's suffering when the beads of sweat started to trickle down their faces and she was bombarded with their anxiety. *I really need to work on my shielding*, Jez lowered her rifle into a less threatening stance, "Ok, you can put your hands down now," her irritation at being affected by their anxiety colored her tone so that the men doubted her sincerity and remained frozen in position. "Really guys, you can relax. I'm not going to hurt you," she replaced her rifle in the holster along her back, unconsciously spinning it around her trigger finger in the process, "I just want to know why you've been following me."

With the immediate threat of the gun removed, Alex slowly lowered his hands and wiped the sweat off his brow with the bandana wrapped around his wrist. Carl followed suit, tucking his thumbs in his belt loops and easing forward to stand by Alex's side.

"I'm afraid I don't know what you're talking about," Alex mumbled as he methodically redistributed his weight from the balls of his feet to his heels and back again.

Jez nearly laughed out loud at the blatant deception. Fine, she would play his game, "Well I must have been mistaken then and I'm sure that I'm also wrong about you're not having eaten much of anything for the past couple of days." She took note of Carl's intensified glare at Alex and directed her next statement directly at him, "Since you obviously don't need any help, I'll just let my dog have all the extra food I prepared so it doesn't go to waste." She turned to leave, calling for Puk to follow her, "Good evening gentlemen," she called over her shoulder as she began to walk away.

"Ouch!" Jez heard Alex yelp as Carl slapped him smartly in the back of his head, "There you go, so what do we do now Mr. In-charge? I told you that we should just find our way home and that you were just looking for trouble." He smacked Alex again, "I told you that we should approach her the day we spotted her!"

Alex ducked away from Carl's third attempt to hit him, "What the hell are you doing? This is really not a good time for this…"

"Well when would be a good time? After we've starved to death perhaps?" Carl demanded an answer to his growling stomach. When Alex continued to hesitate Carl threw his arms into the air with desperation, "Fine!" he humphed and then took off running after Jez. "Wait!…Miss, please wait!" he called after her before Alex had a chance to silence him. Anticipating their response, Jez had been waiting just within ear shot, so when she heard Carl closing in she began walking away again, continuing their little charade.

"Miss, please wait! We're starving, please!" his shouts intensified as she came into view, "Please!"

Jez dramatically stopped in mid stride and gracefully swung around on the ball of her foot to face his approach, letting all her irritation at the delay to her travels show, "Look, I really don't have time for these games. So either you come clean or I'm leaving and you're on your pathetic own again."

Carl stood hunched over with his hands on his knees as he panted and tried to regain his breath. He could hear Alex coming up the trail behind him and forced himself to stand erect, "Look Alex, I know you're afraid that if word gets back and they find us, but if we don't get help we're just as dead," Carl pled with his mate and then turned back to Jez. "We have no food or supplies, We'll tell you whatever you want to know, but you have to promise to help us...Please?" he let his desperation flow out. Defeated, Alex collapsed at Carl's feet and buried his head in his knees.

At the sight of the two companions breaking down in front of her, Jez's initial amusement at their ineptitude was quickly replaced with compassion, "Come on guys, I'm sure the food's still warm. Follow me," the questions burning on the tip of her tongue could wait until after the men had been fed and rested.

Carl helped Alex to his feet and tenderly wiped away his tears before they made their way with Jez to her camp. They were genuinely surprised and grateful when they saw that there was indeed enough food for three waiting – a couple of roasted rabbits and warm rolls filled a pan resting next to the campfire. Jez offered them a blanket to sit on near the fire and Puk sat next to them, his tail stirring up the dirt and leaves as he eagerly awaited any scraps that might be left over.

Jez served them a generously filled plate of food before she got herself situated, "Puk, I don't think they're going to be leaving you even the smallest crumb. Now stop you're begging." Puk reluctantly stood up with his tail between his legs and walked to her side where he slumped to the ground, resting his head on his front haunches and looking up at her. "I will not let you manipulate me like this," she again scowled at Puk and turned away from his forlorn gaze. As she redirected her attention to the men, Jez noticed that Alex was sobbing again with his head resting on Carl's shoulder, "Is everything ok?" genuinely concerned she directed the question to Carl.

"Oh, he'll be fine. This is all just a little overwhelming," he indicated the whole of the camp with his free hand, "We are very grateful, by the way." Alex leaned up to say something softly in Carl's ear and then smiled at Jez. "We'd like to go ahead and start. We've got a lot we'd like to get off our chest," Carl sighed as Alex quenched his sobs by taking a drink, the gravity of the impending discussion clearly upsetting him anew.

"I was planning on waiting till you were both fed and rested, but if you want to start now, I'd love to hear your side of things," Jez spoke as she cut up her food to give Puk his share. With Puk enjoying his meal and Trace off grazing, she made herself comfortable and gave them her full attention. Given Alex's current state of mind, she had decided against the formality of taking written notes even though she was reticent to trust her newly developed photographic memory, she would just write everything down in her journal later.

Surprisingly, Alex took a deep breath and began speaking, "Jez," his voice barely more than a whisper as he began. "I want to make sure that you understand that we didn't know what we were getting ourselves into. By the time we did, it was way too late," his voice trailed off as he searched for the strength to unload his burden.

"Okay Alex, you have my word," she looked his square in the eye as she reassured him.

Carl intertwined his arm with Alex's capturing Alex's hand in his own, "We'll do this together Alex."

Alex smiled and increased his grip on Carl's hand, "Okay."

Carl could feel Alex's hand tremble as he spoke, "I guess we should start at the beginning of our trip...before all the earthquakes and all hell broke loose," Carl's voice seemed to pick up as he spoke of the recent historical past. Jez couldn't deny her amazement as she gasped when they described how their campsite and all their supplies had been suddenly swallowed up by a giant sinkhole. As they spoke of witnessing the deaths of their friends Jez thought of her father and was grateful that at least she had not had to watch him die. She tried to imagine how much worse her mental state would have been if she had been caught off guard like Alex and Carl had.

"Jez, it was just so awful," Alex took over before Carl had a chance to break down too, "We were as gentle as possible, but Mikel was in so much pain every step made him cry out. So we were having a really hard time keeping up with everyone else, but we could still hear their sobs. I don't think I ever understood the term 'wailing' until people started noticing that Katie had disappeared." Alex sighed and increased his grip on Carl's hand, "She was the one who had kept us together and convinced that we would find help, so when she just up and disappeared we all just froze...like a deer in headlights – we were doomed and we knew it."

"But you're here now, so you obviously found help," Jez questioned his look of absolute desperation.

"Actually help found us. Turns out that Katie had decided she could find help faster if she forged ahead alone. Took her almost a full day, but she showed up late that night with a group of people that helped us back to the clinic they had set up! Mikel and a few others with broken bones were actually able to have their breaks set and real casts put on!!" he paused to wipe his brow and clear his throat, the continuing turmoil weighing down his eyes, "I just don't know how to describe the emotional roller coaster we were on Jez. Maybe the elation we felt at Katie's finding help only felt so great because we had just felt so low. Or maybe, in retrospect, it's the other way around. Either way, we couldn't have been more grateful. I still wonder if we haven't jumped to conclusions about them."

"We didn't Alex," Carl chimed in, his composure restored by his conviction, "At the beginning everything was great. We had food, shelter, medical care. Like Alex said, we were overwhelmed with gratitude. I honestly can't remember anything negative from those first couple of weeks and I certainly can't remember anything that might have warned us what this group was really about. Thinking back, I wonder if we weren't blinded by their generosity. Anyway, I guess the reason isn't important because it doesn't change anything that happened."

Jez raised her hand as she interrupted, "May I say something Carl?"

"Oh please do."

"I think the reason you can't recall anything bad is actually very important. You do still have friends with this group don't you?" Jez continued at his acknowledgement, "Personally, it's my opinion that you and your friends were absorbed into a cult and if we are to separate your friends from this group's influence, then we need to know what is being used to control them."

"Really?" Alex blurted out almost enthusiastically.

The crease in Carl's brow deepened as he considered her comment, "I guess so...maybe. What makes you think that?"

Jez carefully reviewed her knowledge of the two men before continuing, "I'm just speculating right now...from what you've told me and what I've observed so far, I know that this group has you fearing for your lives, has a very extremist view point about something, and that you worked with this group to do something that you greatly regret.

Am I right?" Alex and Carl nodded their agreement and she continued, "Add that to the fact that the disaster – the CAT – placed you in a life/death situation from which this group rescued you. You were clearly influenced by that in a way that made you reliant on them and therefore compliant."

Carl sighed, "Okay, so where do we go from here? Do you even need to know the rest of what happened?"

"Oh yes Carl, please continue," Jez urged him, "I think what you have to say is invaluable. You're the first people from the inside of this group that I've been able to have an honest conversation with."

"Okay Jez, but first I want to know how you know so much about us before we've barely told you anything."

Jez answered by sharing her recent discussion with the Professor about mind control techniques and cult mindsets, along with her mapping of all the recent activities. As she relayed her discovery of the massacre while indicating its relative location on the map Carl's breath got stuck in his chest as he seemed to forget how to breathe. He gasped, taking in the much needed oxygen, "Alex! No!" but Alex just shook his head "yes" as the tears welled up in his eyes, "Jez...please don't say any more. I don't think I can handle any more."

She caught his gaze and held him there eye to eye, "You were there, weren't you? You helped do this...You're NoTechs?"

"Yes," Carl answered simply, held captive by the truth, "we were there."

Alex found a spot on the ground and steadily monitored it as he wept, "Jez, we didn't know about the bomb!" She could sense how this new revelation would be more than he could stomach if he dared to look in her direction. "We thought they wanted the people locked inside so they couldn't stop us from going through their houses. Sam only told us that they were a danger to us and had to be stopped...Jez I swear that we didn't know anything about a bomb! Those people were alive when we left and we never heard an explosion!!"

A solo tear began to find it's way down the creases in his face, Carl's increasing anger having stemmed his earlier sobs, "Alex, remember that woman who flew into a rage when we got back?" he continued without waiting for Alex to retrieve the memory, "Remember how she raved about something not being 'God's work' or something like that? She didn't shut up about it until Josh knocked her out...she knew!! This is obviously what she was talking about!"

"Slow down guys, you're losing me," Jez reminded the men of her presence, "so if you didn't know all of those people had been murdered, why are you running for your lives? And who is this woman and the other two men...Sam and...Josh?"

Stunned by the interruption to their epiphany, they sat there silent for a moment before Carl continued, "Um, I'm sorry. Sam is their preacher. But after what you've told us I don't think that he deserves the respect that comes with that title. Besides, he always acted like more of a tyrant anyway...It was pretty clear from the beginning that he got off on ordering everyone around."

"Man of God, my ass," Alex burst in, "You know he has the hots for Katie! And she knows it too!"

"I know, but she'll never admit to playing him. She's too obsessed with being able to control people. Ever since he died she's determined that she has to save everyone from themselves!" Carl paused as he reviewed his 20/20 hindsight, "You know Alex, we should have known Katie would do something crazy like this."

"How? Katie was always so mellow. She and Jerry wouldn't even let the dog chase squirrels, remember?"

"That's just it, Alex. There's no more Jerry. Remember what she did to the truck? And how she almost beat the crap out of Stephie?"

It was Alex's turn to loose his breath as he made the connection to their ultimate responsibility for the mass murders, "That Bitch! We've been manipulated since the moment we were *rescued*!" Alex caught his breath as Carl grabbed his hand and cupped it in his own, quietly conveying his support and understanding, "Oh Carl! You were so right, but what can we possibly do to make this right?"

Carl just shrugged as he embraced his now sobbing partner, "It's okay Alex...It's okay..."

Seizing on the unscheduled break, Jez retrieved her journal and began to organize her notes. By the time she had finished Alex and Carl had managed a good purging cry and were eagerly awaiting to return to their previous discussion.

"Jez," they spoke in unison before Carl took the lead, "We've been talking and we think we've figured out how to make up for our part in all this."

"You guys know that I will do whatever I can for you."

"Thanks, but we were thinking of something the other way around. Even though we apparently were in the dark about the obvious, I think we remember enough between the two of us to be a real help to you."

"You did say that's what you wanted, didn't you?" Alex anxiously added.

"Well, yes, I was hoping that you would be willing to do that," Jez accepted their offer, "You don't mind if I start taking notes now?"

"Oh no, not at all," Carl made a welcoming gesture with his free hand urging Jez to move closer before he began reviewing the details, "Actually, why don't you sit closer and we can start off by drawing you a map of the camp."

Jez's eyes beamed with genuine hope, "Do you think if I showed you a map and where we are on it that you might be able to retrace your steps to the camp?" not waiting for an answer she smoothed out her fading map in front of the two men, tracing her finger along the map searching for the indication she had noted earlier.

"Um, maybe...with your coaching we might be able to," Carl and Alex searched their memory for potential clues.

"Ok, this is about where we are now," she took the lead, making sure the men were following her on the map, "and this is where I first noticed you guys. That was a couple of days ago."

Alex coughed nervously.

"Wait, you mean you noticed us before we even decided to follow you?!" Carl stuttered as he gave Alex an *I-told-you-so* look.

"Yes, I'd be dead a dozen times over by now if I didn't keep my eye out as far as I do," Jez said matter-of-factly, "Now, I figure from what you've told me and by how slow I've noticed you travel, that the camp must be somewhere in this area," she laid out the perimeter in string on the map. "So do you remember anything distinguishing near the camp? A mountain...a road sign...a lake... anything?"

Now it was their turn to light up, "Yes! There was a river or stream nearby! That's where everyone bathed and did laundry," Alex shouted the good news.

Jez reviewed the map's details with a forensic scrutiny, "Okay, well there are a couple of those in our search area. Was it a large or small river?"

"Small, I guess, I don't think you could fit a real boat on it, but you could probably go white water rafting in it," Carl offered.

Jez's finger zeroed in on a search area, "Okay then, according to the map's legend, this is the only one in our area that is small enough. That means the camp has to be somewhere in here," she circled her finger around an area about the size of a quarter, its enormity bringing a scowl to her face.

"I'm sorry, I wish we could be more helpful," Jez's visible disappointment spurred Alex to attempt making amends.

"Oh no, it's not your fault. It's just very frustrating knowing that we have the technology to locate these people in a matter of hours, only none of it is operational. So instead it's going to take us weeks to find them if we're lucky!" she made note of the area on the map before folding it up, "This all has my mood spiraling downward. What do you say to us taking a break and finishing our meal? We can pick up with this afterwards."

Carl eyed their plates of now cold food and realized that his stomach had been grumbling for quite some time, "I think that's a great idea. Now that you bring it up, I am starving."

"I know, I didn't even realize that we'd stopped eating," Alex mumbled as he chewed on a fresh bite of cold rabbit.

Puk moaned and looked up at Jez with his ears laying back flat against his head and his tail between his legs, thoroughly conveying his unhappiness at the situation.

"I'm sorry Puk, but they can't come with us. We've already been through this," Jez denied his plea to bring Alex and Carl with them.

Puk let out a final whimper before sniffing the air ahead of them and trotting off to scout their trail. When he reached the main road he stopped, turned to smell the air from each direction, and looked over his shoulder at Jez.

She took a deep breath, closed her eyes, and blurted, "North," she had been laboring over this decision for the past couple of days and finally resigned herself to follow her gut. As much as she was personally obsessed with the compulsion to stop the terrorist cult, she knew that it was not the time and she had obligated herself to spreading the information north. Her Mustang duties were more important now than ever before considering the menace the cult was quickly becoming. Traveling was dangerous enough these days and she knew that even with her new skills she would not be safe going to their encampment alone – her cause would die with her. To do it right, the search would take time, time she didn't have right now. A sudden jolt in her loins as Trace increased his pace in response to her subconscious desires snapped her back into reality just in time to respond to her friends' trailing shouts of reassurances.

"...nder control. Don't worry, we'll find the camp!" Alex's promises reached her ears and she waved good-bye over her shoulder before grabbing hold of the saddle horn and situating herself into a more comfortable position in the saddle. With her feet securely positioned in the stirrups, her thighs gripping hold of Trace's sides, and a firm hold on the horn, Jez commanded her friend, "Okay Trace, the sooner we get there, the sooner we can return to help. Let's defy time! Geeit!" she clicked as Trace burst forward in full gallop.

Puk stopped and let out a howl of recognition. "Good boy Puk. You're right, we're home," Jez leaned down from her perch atop Trace to give Puk an affectionate rub behind his ears.

Someone had restored the old street sign – *Revolution Drive* – although they had scratched off the "R". Despite the anticipation that coursed through her with this evidence of survivors in the area, Jez cautiously moved down the street with her rifle drawn and her eyes dancing from side to side, searching for any signs of trouble. Assured that the area was safe, she increased her pace and finally caught sight of the remains of her childhood home about halfway down the block.

Parts of the roof had collapsed and were sliding off into the yard and the nearby street was still littered with debris. Even though the house was almost roofless and was leaning to one side, it was still standing – confirming that her family must have survived the initial shifting and tremors. A single tear that went unfelt began to stream down her face as Jez confronted the possibility that she had somehow never allowed herself to consider. What would she find inside her childhood home nearly a month after the CAT? Nearly a month after she had ventured roughly seven-hundred miles on foot and horseback and helped to dispose of countless other bodies – far too many of whom she knew had survived the CAT only to die of disease and hunger in the aftermath.

A few houses down a man quietly cleared the debris from his lawn. He looked up at her, seemed to make a mental note of her presence, then returned to his work. Jez distracted her thoughts and postponed the inevitable by turning her attention his way. The laundry drying on the line by the side of the house swayed in the breeze, otherwise, there was no movement aside from the man's. It had surprised her that she had been able to just ride into town totally unmonitored and unsupervised when she made no effort to conceal herself or her weapon. And now this man had seen an armed stranger appear and he simply acknowledged her presence, then went back to whatever he was doing. Before Jez could continue on with her thoughtless analysis of the neighbor, Trace halted and she realized that she had arrived at her parents' house.

With no where further for Trace to go, Jez simply sat there in a daze, afraid to go inside. Her fear of the worst weighed her down like the infamous albatross she remembered from her high school reading. Who was is that wrote that? Jez searched her mind for the trivial information that was suddenly vitally important in her attempts to once again distract her thoughts. Although she had become nearly desensitized to death, Jez didn't know if she could dispose of a body that she had known as a living person. Her gaze returned to the man next door, she could certainly enlist his help if her worst case scenario turned out to be true. The implicit duty to provide aid to a fellow survivor assured her that she would not be alone in this task, but that still didn't ease the pain of having to confront a family member's death.

Reluctantly, Jez forced her body to dismount Trace and enter the house.

"Mom...Al...is anybody here?" the silence that followed sliced through Jez causing her heart to sink into her boots, tearing through her guts in the process. She could feel her skin turn to ice from the tips of her toes to the lump caught in her throat as she slowly, almost catatonically, made her way into the crumbling house. Grasping for hope, she checked for the survival packs first, tears flooded her eyes and spilled down her face, blurring her view of the empty storage cabinet. Foil wrappers from ration bars sparkled like fine diamonds as they littered the area, Jez picked up the shinny wrappers, smelling and holding each one as she did so. She neatly folded one and slipped it in her breast pocket as relief coursed through her every fiber and she convulsed with joy, her gut was right – her mom had obviously survived both the CAT and the aftermath! Filled with a new energy and purpose, she made a chaotic search for a note or any clue to her mom's whereabouts but found nothing. The house began to moan and screech as the earth continued to settle, sending chunks of plaster and paint raining from the ceiling and adding more dust to the grime, tears, and sweat already coating Jez. There was no time for a closer inspection – for now she would have to be satisfied with the fact that her mother was alive somewhere. She placed her hand protectively over the pocket containing the wrapper, feeling the beating of her heart through the plastic foil as she said good-bye to the world of her childhood and carefully made her way out of the would-be tomb.

Jez placed a chunk of concrete on the man's rock pile, "Hi. Jezzelle Kyle," she politely extended her right hand out to the man in greeting. He looked her over, appearing to size her up and causing Puk to bare his teeth protectively.

"Hey boy, I promise I'm harmless," the man reassured Puk as he quickly took Jez's proffered hand in greeting, "Jez, the name's Fitch. How can I help you?"

"Actually, I think we can probably help each other, I don't mean to sound rude, but you're either very brave or very foolish to be working on your house alone. Haven't you heard about all the recent attacks?"

Fitch chuckled politely as he took advantage of the unplanned break by grabbing a fresh drink from his cooler, "Actually I'm neither. We've got a good surveillance system set up."

"Really, I didn't notice anyone on watch when I came in," Jez questioned his confidence.

"That just means they're doing their job right."

"Oh," she blushed, "I get it."

"Besides, there really hasn't been that much terrorist activity around here and rats don't come out in the sunlight. All the same, I do appreciate the warning and I'd like to know any insight you have on the group, what do you call them?"

"NoTechs."

"NoTechs, that's right. Yes, I've heard that name before. From what I've heard about the group, they haven't made it up here. We mostly have problems with looting and there've been some pretty intense brawls because everyone's looking for someone to blame for all this, whether it's God or the government," Fitch commented as he wiped away the sweat streaming along his brow and neck.

Jez mentally reviewed at length the data she had gathered on the NoTechs, "Now that you mention it, I haven't seen any evidence of NoTech activity for three or four days now. So you guys must be getting things pretty much back to normal since you don't have to worry about them."

"Yeah, that's true, but we are no where near being back to 'normal', whatever that is. There's just way too much to be done and not enough people to do it. We do have some radio communications with the nearby settlements and I hear they're working on getting either cell phones or some other long range radios working, I'm not really sure of the specifics."

"So can you get a message to the President or Governor to have them send the National Guard or whatever, someone's got to stop those people," Jez blurted, excited by the news of actual radio communications taking place, "You have heard from Them, haven't you?"

The lack of response from Fitch foretold his answer, "I'm sorry, we've tried, but there's no one responding."

"No one..." Jez's voice trailed off as the significance of the news took hold.

"No one, and I've heard rumors from some Mustangs coming from the northeast. They claim that the ocean is much closer to us than it used to be."

Jez sighed as she processed this confirmation of her suspicions, "Well, I can't say that I'm surprised, I've sorta always known that was going to happen one day...but it doesn't make it any easier to accept the reality of it."

"Oh, you're one of those," Fitch rolled his eyes playfully at her.

"Yes, I'm a 'those'. It's why I'm here today and not a corpse rotting off the highway. So do you know what happened to the couple that lived there?" Jez indicated her parents' house with a lingering glance over her shoulder, "they're my parents."

Fitch breathed out a sorrowful sigh, "I'm sorry, but I'm really not sure what happened to them. I was held up inside for probably a couple of days and after I got out I still wasn't really all there. I do recall seeing some people mulling around outside the house, but it's like they were there and the next moment they were gone. Wish I could be more help."

Although Jez hadn't expected to find out much from Fitch she struggled not to choke on her disappointment, but no amount of self-control could keep it from showing on her face, "It's amazing how much that still hurts even though I knew that's what you were going to say, guess I'm just a foolish optimist, thanks anyway for your help," she struggled to bear the weight of the incredible burden she faced, "I've got a long trip ahead of me, so I guess I'd better be going. Can you point me in the direction of your town hall?"

"Hey, if you want I'll help you plan out a route back home while you get a good traveling meal in your belly. I happen to have enough food to feed a very small army and I have been keeping up with the Mustangs in the area," Fitch opened his industrial size lunch box and proceeded to split the meal between them. "The soda's warm, but at least it's not flat. I hope you don't mind drinking from the same can because I didn't pack a cup," he handed her the can to do the honors of popping the lid.

"Oh my god, a *real* sandwich and soda! You are being way too generous. How can I ever pay you back?" Fitch's generosity finally put her over the edge and allowed Jez to release the tears she desperately had been holding back.

"Jez, it's okay," he put an arm around her and she temporarily hid from the world in his shoulder, "You can pay me back by sharing whatever info you have on these NoTechs and I'll help you plan a route back that includes the towns with radios so you can find your folks. We're square, alright?" she shook her head in affirmation into his shoulder, "Now eat up."

Jez managed to regain control, easing her sobs and wiping away her tears with her shirt, "Thank you Fitch...for everything."

"Not a problem. Now do you have a map or something I can write on?" unconsciously he scribbled in the air as he spoke.

She stood up as Trace appeared by her side and removed her map from a saddle bag, "Yes, right here. You can just indicate the radio towers with a symbol like this," she made a quick note on the map's legend, "and I'll explain what all the other markers mean after you're done."

He let out a long low whistle as he got a good look at the map for the first time, "Whew, no wonder you were looking at me like I was a mad man. Have there really been these many attacks?"

"Yes, I'm afraid so."

"Well Jez, I think that I owe you alot more than half my lunch...we've got a whole lot to talk about. So were you going to discuss this at the town hall?"

"Yes, I can't go after my family until I've passed this information along," she unconsciously glanced to the sky to check the position of the sun, obviously anxious to be on her way.

Fitch stood up and retrieved his knapsack, "Well then, let me help you move things along," he pulled a flare out of his sack and released it, "the people you need to talk to should be here inside a half hour."

Jez coughed to cover up her surprise, "I thought you had radios working again?"

Fitch laughed and sat back down next to the map, "We do, but the flare was much more dramatic don't you think?"

"I'll give you that. You definitely snapped me out of my mood," she smirked.

A beep suddenly erupted from Fitch's bag, "Speak of the devil. Fitch here," he answered into his Nextel.

A distant voice crackled from the handset, "I thought that flare came from you. It better be something really big to justify wasting that flare!"

"Definitely Boss, I've got someone here that you need to talk to yesterday. A Mustang from the deep south," he spoke without pause to prevent the voice from interrupting. Jez could see Fitch was exceptionally pleased with himself. "...and it's worse than you thought."

"Really? Worse?" the voice sounded caught off guard.

"Alot."

"ETA fifteen minutes," the voice crackled.

7

A bread crumb, a gift, the messenger finds,
Her children she blesses with abilities new,
But their path they must uncover and no harm must they do....

A faint electronic beep pierced the silence, causing Jez's heart to skip a beat before she eased Trace out of his gallop. It had been so long since she had used the stopwatch that she was startled by the foreignness of the once familiar sound and fumbled awkwardly for the proper button combination to silence the irritation. "Farkit!" she cursed her lack of grace, *If this was a hot spot I'd be in a lot of trouble now!* She glanced at the display before purging the readout with the sound, based on her elapsed time and the directions Fitch had given her – Jez manipulated the numbers and sequences floating in her head – the township was about five or so miles away. Still she should be able to navigate by sight once she found the antenna tower among the tree tops. Although the trees were less dense here and had not begun to take on fall color, the blinding angle of the sun made it difficult for her eyes to focus on the distance even with her scope. She attempted to compensate by adjusting the polarity, but that reduced the contrast as well, and she finally decided that a methodical visual and mental search of the panorama was her best option despite the helpless position it put her in. She alerted Puk to be on watch, providing her with some protection while she focused entirely on the search, and proceeded to get comfortable in the saddle, wiggling her hips and cracking her neck, before switching her concentration to probing the area. As she slowed her breathing and concentrated her mind on the visualization of the tower, Jez began to take on a petrified appearance, with the only signs of movement coming from her eyes. Starting to her left she began visually dissecting the horizon, making a mental note of every tree, branch, or anything else that pierced the blue skyline. At the same time she used her developing sixth sense to sweep for signs of anything man made. It didn't take long for her to sense the energies being cast out by the tower and direct her eyes to the area at her two o'clock where a flickering light caught her attention.

"Needle in a haystack, that's what he should have told me I was looking for," Jez mumbled to herself as she retrieved her scope and directed it at the point of light. "Well, that explains it! They're covering it with cam!" she directed her discovery to no one in particular.

Sensing Jez's change in demeanor and the route evolving before them, Trace began to trot in the direction of the tower before she had a chance to finish her thought.

Jez deepened her breathing allowing the musky scent to penetrate her as she massaged the oil into the saddle leather. She could feel her hands as well as the leather soften with each circular stroke. Slowly, the leather began to take on a sheen that gave the well worn saddle a feeling of newness and Jez a feeling of accomplishment. She reveled in the simplicity of the task, allowing her mind to wander. She had been disappointed at first when she learned that the radio would not be operational for another day or so, but now she was grateful that the Universe had intervened and forced her to take some much needed rest. Jez was bordering on exhaustion and although it was only slight, she could sense that her developing sixth sense had dulled a bit. She subscribed to the practice of mind over matter, but she had to accept that her brain was still human and subject to some natural physical limitations.

With an admiring glance at her rejuvenated saddle, Jez habitually surveyed the area while she decided whether she could afford a nap before the festival began that afternoon. There were people in the distance apparently busy setting up tents and booths, but her immediate area was clear, save for one figure. A red headed woman had settled herself just outside of the perimeter of what might be considered stalking distance. Jez knew she was being watched, but didn't feel threatened by it enough to postpone her nap. She yawned and stretched, giving a final wave to the red head as she sprawled out in a beach chair that had been left behind by some other camper.

She was aware of every cell in her skin as the sun's rays tingled across her face. Jez meditated on the sensations as she felt the process of her skin tanning and the sweat forming deep in her skin and rising to the surface. Relaxed in the warmth of the sun, she closed her eyes and gave into the effects of the satisfying hot meal by reclining the beach chair and inhaling deeply. The late afternoon breezes stirred across the field, carrying the scents of the ongoing feasting while diffusing the heat of the day. Her belly was too full to sample any more of the local delicacies and Jez now appeased her desire for them by savoring the aromas of the roasting meats and vegetables and various distilled beverages, as well as the fragrances of burning sage and hemp. Occasionally the aroma would intensify, confirming her perception that someone was passing by. She rather enjoyed the scent of the burning herbs and as she breathed in their essence she envisioned the wisps of their smoke swirling around her and lifting away all her stresses of the day.

"It's ok, I'm awake," she addressed the figure she knew had sat down next to her before opening her eyes and shaking the proffered hand, "Jez."

"McDowd," the seasoned man replied, "I noticed that you've been over here alone for quite some time, so I thought I'd introduce myself."

Jez smiled, "Well thank you. It's nice to meet you McDowd."

"Would you care for a smoke," the man generously held his pipe out to her.

"No thanks, I don't have time to get that relaxed, but if you have some, I'd love a smudge."

"As a matter of fact, I do," he reached into his fanny pack and retrieved a small bundle of white sage and a lighter, "So you're one of those Mustangs I hear. Is it true what I hear about DC? Did it really fall into the ocean?" He handed Jez the burning sage bundle.

She allowed the sweet smelling smoke to wash over her before speaking, "Most likely, I haven't seen it with my own eyes, but I have heard stories from reliable sources. And I think the silence of Washington is making itself fairly apparent," she eyed his pipe and smiled.

"You're most right about that. If you ask me, aside from these NoTechs, things have been running smoother than ever without it," he paused as he took a puff off his pipe, "Politics has a way of making everything dirty and right now we can't afford to waste time and effort on bureaucracy," he tapped his pipe as if it emphasized his point,

"Don't get me wrong, I understand the need for government, it's just the resulting politics that I think need to be done away with."

"Do you mind doing my back?" Jez held out the still smoldering sage, "Oh...and I most definitely agree with you. It just worries me," feeling the heat of the smudge leave her back she let her hair fall back down, "without the organization and implicit domination of the federal government, how are we ever going to get these NoTechs under control?"

"Touché," McDowd waved the smudge around his head before snuffing it out and returning it to his pack, "I'm sorry, I've totally imposed on you. I know you're supposed to be taking some R&R. I heard you haven't taken a break for weeks, right?"

"My, word travels fast. Yes, that's true," Jez rubbed her temples, "Guess I need a mental vacation every so often and if I don't take one the Universe will force one on me," she smirked as she spoke.

McDowd stood up and walked behind her, resting his fingers lightly on her temples, "Well then I insist on repaying you for the imposition. You just relax and let yourself drift off."

"Only because you insist," Jez acquiesced, letting her eyes close and her body go limp. The tension released with each stroke of his skilled touch and immediately washed her away from the realities of the world.

She sat at the desk cross-legged in a soft Italian leather office chair with her chin comfortably resting on her fist. Jez would have appeared quite serene had it not been for her eyes darting from gage to gage on the various control panels occupying the make-shift command center. The mounting hush had reached a disturbing level and was only broken by the crackle of white noise punctuated by the crinkle of paper from Jez unconsciously crumpling her notes. Everyone in the room was on edge, making the natural tension of the situation almost suffocating.

The weight of the group sat squarely on the radio operator's shoulders and his thirst for air was audible as he sighed before delicately tapping the tuning dial once more. The resulting moment of utter silence was quietly acknowledged by the group mind.

"Bravo..." the fatigued voice crisply escaped the small speakers on the desk and was immediately engulfed by the hooting and hollering that filled the room, "Tango...Niner... This is Alpha...Bravo...Tango...Niner... Is anyone out there?"

The operator waved his hands and silenced the celebration before depressing the button at the base of the microphone, "Alpha...Bravo...Tango...Niner, we copy you. This is Charlie...Tango...Niner... Delta...Do you copy?"

"We copy! We copy...Charlie...Tango...Niner...Delta! Thank God, we copy!" the elation on the foreign voice rang through the room, "So what's your twenty? By the way, I'm Becka," the voice abandoned formal protocols before signing off.

"Well Becka, good to meet you. We're in Rocky Mount. What's your location? Oh, and I'm Jack. I've got a room full of really happy people here," Jack motioned for the others to shout a hello before ending transmission.

"Hello Jack and friends," a collective voice responded before Becka took over the com, "Same here Jack. We're actually just south of you by maybe fifty miles. I'd heard on the grape vine that Rocky Mount was getting back to normal, but I'm glad to hear it first hand. So shall we set up a regular time for our daily debriefings?" Becka was obviously anxious to get to the business at hand of official gossip.

"Same bat time, same bat channel?" Jack suggested as he jotted down the current frequency readings in his log.

"That sounds great Jack. Most likely you'll be chatting with me, but just in case I'm not available, it will either be Derek or Mojo. Guys say hello," Becka prompted her colleagues to speak up.

"Hello Jack," Derek and Mojo chimed in.

Jack added the names to the log before summoning Jez to the mike with a beckoning wave as he opened up the channel, "Good to meet you gentlemen. Before we get down to our normal debriefing, I'd like to let our Mustang friend Jez here speak with you, if you don't mind," he slid the mike in front of Jez.

"No problem Jack. We've always got time for a Mustang," Becka's genuine enthusiasm echoed from the speakers, "Nice to meet you Jez. So how can I help?"

Jez shifted her weight in the chair and smoothed out the creases in her notes as she cleared her throat. She could see her hand shaking as she pressed the transmit button, "Hi Becka. What I need is actually on a personal level," her voice quivered with her anxiety and anticipation.

"Oh, do you want me to have the guys leave the room?"

Thrown off guard by Becka's assumption, Jez laughed nervously as she tried to will the blood from where it had rushed to in her face and cheeks, "Oh, Becka, I'm sorry," she attempted to stem her growing embarrassment, "I didn't mean *that* kind of *personal*." Jez fanned herself with her notes as she spoke, "I just meant it wasn't official business."

"Wow! I'm sorry Jez," Becka apologized for the confusion, "Well then, I'll just have the guys stop snickering and let you ask your question," the whomp of a rolled-up magazine making contact with Mojo's head escaped the speakers before the transmission ended.

Jez paused a moment to allow herself to finish laughing before opening the mike, "Thanks for that Becka," more giggles powdered her words. "Seriously, what I'm trying to find out is if you could check to see if Sylvia or Alzatia Kyle might have passed through your area," she breathed deeply and swallowed before continuing, "Sylvia's my mom…Al's my sister…I've been tracking them for weeks now," her final words were a mere whisper directed at herself before she let up the com button, her fingers lingering on the mike.

"Jez, I sent one of the guys to check our guest books. If they stayed in town we'll have a record of it. Why don't you give me a description and I'll circulate that as well," Becka's voice commanded confidence, "don't worry Jez, you'll find them. I know you're concerned, we got the reports on that NoTech cult, but we haven't really noticed anything like that around here."

The air rushed briskly over her lips as she emptied her lungs of the breath she had been unknowingly holding. Jez fought to keep the tears from her words, although her eyes remained stone dry with her resolve to shed only tears of joy at their reunion it was so much harder to keep her growing disappointment out of her voice, "Thank you Becka," she articulated, fighting the spasms in her gut. "I know you're right, especially now that communications are getting back up," another deep breath, "Anyway, my mom is about five foot four, a hundred thirty-five pounds, blonde shoulder length hair, and very fair skin. Oh, and her eyes are green. Did you get all that?"

"Got it...green eyes, blonde, fair complexion. So what does your sister look like? Does she look a lot like your mom?"

Jez's brow furrowed as she considered Becka's question, "Well, you can probably see a family resemblance, but I wouldn't say they really look alike. Last time I saw my sister she had died her hair a deep brunette and she keeps up a good tan. At first glance you might not even think they were related, but they do have the same nose. Al is quite a bit taller, she's five nine and slender and she's got my dad's brown eyes. Jez out," the room went silent and Jez felt each pause of her watch's second hand while she waited for Becka's response.

"Copy that Jez. Brunette, tan, tall," Becka reiterated, "We'll keep you posted through the message boards. It was good meeting you Jez, good luck," the sound of papers being shuffled filled the void while Becka switched gears, "Well I guess we should get back to business now while we wait for the guys to get back. Is Jack there?"

"Thank you so much Becka, I really mean it. I know air-time is precious as gold these days, so here's Jack," she slid the mike back to the operator as she rose from her seat.

"Jack here," he seamlessly continued the transmission, "Why don't you cover your business first Becka? Jack out."

"Thanks Jack. I'll begin with the personal messages..." Becka's voice faded into the distance as Jez quietly stepped out of the room.

Jez's skin glowed orange and red as the light from the bonfire reflected off the beads of sweat streaming down her face and body. The rhythm of the drums and the beat of the rattles enveloped her chanting, creating a palpable electric mist in the air and she reveled in the chilling tingles running down her body despite the heat of the fire. Her chest pounded faster, her voice grew louder, and she tightened her grasp on those next to her as her entire being was swept up in the rhythm of the beating drums during their spiral around the fire. She became oblivious to the heat of the flames and the loudness of the music while the energy of the dance filled her and she released herself to the rapture of her ability to physically feel the music.

In unison, the drums went silent and the group circling around the fire stopped the dance and dropped their hands to the ground. With her connection to the physical world restored, Jez became aware of the red headed woman staring at her from across the circle and took advantage of their current connection to study her more closely. If it wasn't for the woman's height, Jez might have assumed she was just a girl since her demeanor and frail frame betrayed her otherwise unapparent maturity and the brown sundress she was wearing was styled like something a child's doll baby might wear. But the contrast of her fair complexion with her copper locks made her quite stunning, she was definitely no girl. Jez wondered if the redhead was interested in her or perhaps she reminded the woman of someone she'd lost in the CAT.

Her curiosity piqued, Jez impulsively focused her full awareness on the woman. Suddenly the world faded away and she was engulfed by a cool silvery mist that seemed to pass right through her. The murmur of a crowd was coming from every direction although she was aware of nothing beyond the sweetness of the mist.

"Where the hell am I?" Jez screamed for an explanation.

Where the hell am I? her own voice answered through the mist.

What are you doing in here? another louder voice demanded and Jez became aware of the redhead's growing anxiety.

"Oh my god, I'm in her head!" Jez instinctively withdrew behind her own psyche's shield, but the sensation of the other woman's intense anxiety lingered despite terminating the connection. With the foreign anxiety buzzing in her ear, Jez was unable to avoid confronting the redhead any longer and decided to confront her directly this time, so she caught the woman's gaze and forced eye contact. A moment later the woman stood up and moved toward Jez as if she understood her thoughts, then without exchanging a single word she followed Jez to her campsite on the far edge of the bonfire. Relieved by the relative privacy offered by the distance from the festivities they sat down in silence next to the smaller fire. Jez sensed something familiar about the redhead, so when the woman grabbed her hand unannounced, rather than pull away or strike out, she relaxed and waited.

Your last name is Kyle? the voice seemed to originate from inside Jez's head as the question challenged her consciousness.

She wasn't sure if she had heard the question spoken out loud or not and paused a moment, "Yes, my last name's Kyle. Why?" the shadow of a thought flashed through her mind and desperation filled her voice, "Have you seen my mother or sister?"

They passed through here a couple of weeks ago...they're searching for you, the silent voice answered.

"My mom was here?" Jez's voice was barely a whisper as surprise robbed her of her breath. It wasn't until she processed the good news that her mind was clear enough to realize that the voice did indeed sound only in her mind and the potential of this new reality set her mind off spinning again, "I'm sorry but could you please tell me that out loud. Hearing someone else's voice inside my head is just too much strangeness for me to handle right now."

"Oh, I'm sorry...It's just that...since you were in...my head...earlier, I thought...You just seemed like the kind of person that would be okay with it...I'm sorry, I'm still getting used to it myself. I figure the more I do it the faster I'll get over the strangeness of it. Anyway, I'm Kara," the young woman apologized, her physical voice eerily similar to her voice in Jez's head, "Your mom and sister were here a couple of weeks ago I think, but I'm very bad about keeping track of time. They stayed here for a bit but they didn't socialize much, which is probably why no one else has put two and two together."

"So how did you know who I was?" Jez began the interrogation, "I know you've been watching me ever since I got here. Did my mom talk to you?"

"I recognized you from the pictures your mom showed me. She's a really open person, which I guess is why Al kept a tight reign on her. Anyway, she told me all about you and how you saved her life before she'd even been here a half day," Kara laughed as the comment caused Jez to roll her eyes.

"Yeah, that sounds like Mom. So what else did she tell you?"

Kara sighed, "Quite a lot. I'm sorry, but she told me your father is still missing," she paused to allow Jez time to react and bombard her with questions.

Jez turned away and blinked, "I know...I've had this *feeling*," she rested her chin on her fist, "Please go on."

"Okay, well your sister said that he had been on his way to work so after everything settled down they retraced his route as far as they could, but most of the roads were impossible even on foot. I guess you're well aware of all that," Jez nodded in affirmation, "Anyway, Al said that once everyone got over the shock there was so much looting going on and fighting for food that she just didn't feel safe being a 'sitting duck'. Your mom wanted to stay behind and wait for FEMA and your dad, but Al wouldn't hear of it and convinced her to move on so they might find you along the way."

"Oh, Al...thank you," Jez mumbled to herself.

"She said you always knew what to do," Kara squeezed Jez's hand as if she might be passing along a hug from her sister.

"Thank you," she feigned a smile but she knew Kara sensed her disappointment.

Kara scratched something in the dirt with a stick, "I'm sorry they didn't leave me a real message for you, but I don't think it ever occurred to any of us that you might actually show up here." She pointed at an area on the ground with her stick, "They did have a map though. I can't remember the road names but I do know this is what they had highlighted as their planned route," Kara made an "X" to mark the spot, "and I think this is where we are now. Does this help any?"

Jez beamed, her smile almost completely absorbing her face, "You bet it does! If I can match the shapes of the roads you've drawn with my map, there's a pretty good chance I can pick up their exact trail!" She jumped up and gave Kara a bear hug before running to collect her map.

Jez anxiously ran her finger along the path she had translated from Kara's stick drawings in the dirt. She could barely contain her desire to be back on her family's trail, but her duties as a Mustang came first these days and that required her to stick around one more day to attend meetings at what was quickly developing into an impromptu regional conference. Once word had spread about the nature of the information she was carrying several nearby settlements had sent representatives to attend the meetings. Jez reveled at how fast information could travel even when it was just by word-of-mouth.

As if she had been broadcasting her need of a distraction until the meetings, she felt a gentle mental nudge before Kara's voice echoed in her mind, *Jez? Sorry to intrude, but I never had the chance to really talk to you about this earlier. Do you mind helping me out now?* the pleading nature of her voice came through as a sensation rather than an inflection. Jez scanned the horizon for Kara, and sensing her behind a tent, directed her response simultaneously out loud and silently, "Kara, you don't have to hide from me. Of course I'll help you. Besides, this is something I'd hoped you'd teach me...*If that's even possible,*" Jez kept the last thought to herself.

Kara shot from behind the tent, symbolically covering her ears, "Okay, you don't have to shout!" she screamed aloud to emphasize her point, "and it is possible."

"Sorry, wow, you even got that last remark?" Kara smirked her acknowledgement, "I wasn't even directing that at you. Told you I needed the workout more than you." Jez whispered playfully, "So how did you figure out how to use telepathy anyhow?"

"We can only speak..." Kara looked sternly at Jez as she switched seamlessly to her mental voice, *telepathically. You're supposed to be helping me practice, remember?*

Jez giggled and focused on a more relaxed tone, *Okay, is this better?*

Much, Kara settled down next to her, *Anyway, to answer your question, I'm not sure how or even if I learned it. I just one day realized I was reading people's minds...it's been about two months now, I think,* she looked up as if she was searching the corner of her brain for the memories that might help her answer, *like I said earlier, I'm really bad at keeping track of time. Anyway, I'm positive that it was after the CAT. Does that help?*

Quite a bit, Jez's mental tone fluctuated as she found her voice, *I have a question. Before, when I accidentally went into your mind, I heard...a lot of...murmuring...Do you hear that as well?* she focused on maintaining a level tone but could tell by Kara's occasional winces that much more practice was in order. She paused to take a deep calming breath to avert her growing frustrations, *I'm just curious because for me, ever since the CAT, it's almost like something in me has been uncapped, like some latent gene I had was activated.*

Oh that. It used to be a whole lot worse. When I said before that I was reading peoples' minds, I meant that I was reading ALL of them ALL the time, fatigue stained her face, *it's taken everything I have to be able to focus in on just one voice at a time, so I just decided to get used to the murmuring.*

Jez leapt at the chance to repay her kindness, *Well then, I've got something to teach you as well. I bet no one ever taught you how to shield,* she furrowed her brow when her mental voice squealed like a boy going through puberty, *You taught me how to open up to the mental voices, so it's only fair I show you how to lock them out.*

Kara cradled Jez's chin with her hand, forcing Jez to look her squarely in the eyes, *Relax Jez.*

You're trying too hard. Just look me in the eyes and speak.

Jez blushed, embarrassed at hearing the same advice she so often administered, *Okay, let's start over,* she closed her eyes and calmed her breathing. *Hi, I'm Jez and I'm a recovering control freak,* she focused on Kara's eyes as she spoke.

By George, I think she's got it! Kara managed to add a proper English accent to the thought.

The rain in Spain falls mainly on the plain, Jez kept a straight face and pointed her nose haughtily in the air.

Quite right Eliza! Kara giggled, sending Jez over the edge and soon their laughter filled both their ears and their minds.

The cloud filled sky glowed shades of peach, gold, and pink as the sun eased its way into the sky. Ribbons of golden light seemed to beam straight from heaven where the clouds had broken, leaving the impression that the sunlight had forced its way through in its desire to experience the waking earth. Below, a light mist covered the ground and drifted up from the field with the breeze giving the whole area an otherworldly appearance.

It strangely resembles the inside of Kara's mind, Jez thought privately to herself and smiled, expelling the sweet medley of her personal amusement as she quietly giggled through her nose. It wasn't cold enough for Kara to see the giggles escaping, but the press of the icy aluminum against her thighs eventually caused her to shudder – there was a modest chill in the morning air lately although the days remained almost repressively hot. Jez resituated herself closer to Kara to take advantage of the blanket she had wrapped herself in.

I told you the bleachers would make you get cold, Kara shot Jez an "I-told-you-so" as she scooted over to make more room under the blanket for her friend.

I know, I know, Jez looked down, feigning regret, *I apologize for my transgressions Oh Knower-of-Everything.*

Kara pulled the blanket tighter around them and nestled her head against Jez's shoulder, relaxing in the increased warmth. *Oh Jez, I wish you didn't have to leave already,* she sighed as she spoke.

Jez reached over and cradled Kara's head with her free hand, *I know K, but I promise I'll come back for a visit as soon as it's safe for me to take some time off. Besides, it's not like we won't be able to talk,* she tapped her friend's head for emphasis.

You don't have to sell me. I know the spiel Jez, Kara smirked, gauging Jez's reaction through the corner of her eye so she wouldn't have to abandon her choice position, *too dangerous for me to come...more people can learn to path if we split up...blah...blah...blah...*

"Ouch," Kara squealed out loud as she shot erect in reaction to a thunk on the back of her head, "What was that for?"

You were beginning to wallow, Jez bluntly answered Kara's mock indignation.

Oh...yeah, you're right, she quickly snatched her blanket from Jez and nearly toppled her down the bleachers in the process.

Jez laughed at the turnabout, "Come on, let's go grab some grub before there's nothing left. I don't want to hit the road on an empty stomach," without waiting for a response, she swiftly began descending toward the amalgamation of picnic tables and patio furniture that populated the former football field.

"Hey, wait for me!" Kara shouted as their quiet of the bleachers interchanged with the clatter and clank between dishes and utensils and the hum of conversation.

Kara's fading calls inspired Jez to make this a true race and she forged ahead at full sprint. Assured of her victory, she turned to witness her friend's struggle to catch up and a giggle escaped her lips only to be silenced with the thud of a sudden impact. Jez grasped her shoulder as she recoiled, "Shit!" the pain radiated down her arm, "Ffaaark..." she moaned as she regained her clarity.

"God, are you alright?" Jack bellowed in unison with Kara.

"Oh, I'll be fine," Jez shook her arm as she would a soiled carpet and channeled the pain out her finger tips, "nothing's damaged...except my ego."

Kara grabbed Jez by the shoulders, "Oh Jez! I felt that, are you sure you're okay?" she gently squeezed Jez's arm from the wrist to the shoulder, tenderly inspecting it for any signs of injury.

Jez indulged the girl's poking and prodding, "I'm fine Kara," she wrapped her arm behind her head and grabbed her opposite shoulder, "See, the pain's already gone."

"Okay you two, you can rehearse for the circus later. I need to get back to the office," Jack good naturedly mocked Jez's genetic flexibility.

"Oh, we're sorry," Jez and Kara chimed.

"Perfectly alright. I'll even forgive you for not checking to see if I was okay," Jack winked at Kara from atop his six foot eight frame, "Jez, I just wanted to let you know that Becka had some news for you."

His words immediately swallowed their laughter as it knocked the breath from Jez, "Oh," the air spoke as she searched for her breath, "Jack, please, what...what is it?"

A formidable smile emerged on the goliath's face, "they came across your mom and sister's names in their guest logs," Jack braced himself for the inevitable assault but still nearly toppled over as Jez sprung her full weight against him, instantly wrapping her arms tightly around his thick neck and her legs about his waist.

"Oh thank you Jack! Thank you! Thank you! Thank you!" she squealed with delight and kissed him hard on the cheek before allowing him to pry her off, "Oh Jack, so what did Becka say?" Jez tugged at her short cuffs and wiped the tears from her eyes as she waited for him to finish his sentence.

He scratched his head and stared at his feet, "Hmmm, now what was it? I knew I should have written it down," he attempted to sound serious and masked his laughter with coughing, "Gee, I must be coming down with something...Now where was I?"

"You were mentally abusing me because I just assaulted you," Jez focused her big eyes on him with all the longing of a lost puppy, "Please Jack, don't make me beg," she fluttered her eyelashes in afterthought, escalating the degree of absurdity to an unbearable level.

Jack was the first to break, his loud bellowing laughter reverberated on the wind even as he pounded his fists against his thighs to stop the spastic laughter that now controlled his body. With tears streaming down her face, Jez cradled her gut, nearly unable to stand upright while her initially delicate laughter grew to rival Jacks. Kara fought against the disability as well but soon infected their laughter with a snort and the bizarre laugh volleyed between them until the pain from their aching abs freed the group from the infectious laughter.

His eyes swollen and red, Jack applied pressure to his diaphragm as he attempted to speak, "Thanks for that Jez," he cleared his throat but his voice remained horse, "Becka said," he paused to verify that she was listening, "your mom and sister stopped overnight there ten days ago. The logbook indicates they only stayed the one night. That's all the news they have at the moment."

Jez leaned against Kara who reassuringly stroked her hair with her fingers, "Thanks Jack. At the very least it saves me a stop," she reached out, burying her hands in Jack's, "Besides, it's been so long since I was able to get any word on them at all that any news is good news to me."

"You are something special Jez," he pulled her into a hug before partially releasing her. "You two were headed to breakfast, right?" he intuitively draped his free arm around Kara, "Come on, I'll walk you guys there." With a beautiful woman on each arm Jack oozed charm, "Of course you don't mind if I join you."

Jez inhaled deeply the still crisp morning air before she took a running leap and mounted Trace, unable to wait a moment longer to resume her travels despite Kara's good natured pleas for her to stay. The events of the last few days had re-energized her hope while her telepathy drills with Kara had exponentially increased her other extra sensory skills – now her mood was literally contagious and readily infected Trace and Puk with an equally irrepressible anticipation.

Trace nipped at his bit begging to gallop as Puk jetted back from scouting the trail ahead, gave a howl encouraging Jez and Trace to join him, then ran back up ahead. When they failed to catch up Puk ran back and howled again, this time prancing with his head cocked backwards so that he could monitor their progress. Obviously outnumbered, Jez resigned to her impatience, waving farewell to her friend as she spurred Trace into a light gallop.

8

As the serpent and company do plot and scheme,
From inside weakness builds along the seam,
The circle they do wish to break,
Yet the mother reveals herself to the snake....

Sam lithely hooked one foot on the bench next to Katie's thigh, leaning his torso ever so slightly against her back, his knee brushed her bosom as he looked over her shoulder at the map. She was lost in thought and merely cleared her notes away to acknowledge his presence so he instinctively fed off her lack of concern at his imposition, gently brushing a stray lock of hair away from her face under the pretext of clearing his line of sight, his tender hand drifting softly across her cheek up to her ear.

"Yes, God is certainly looking out for us. We couldn't have prayed for a better set-up," he breathed into her ear. With a mastered subtlety Sam had manipulated his stance so that his face was aligned so closely with hers that he could hear her breathing and feel the heat rising from her skin, which he quietly savored.

"The hospital is reported to be here," apparently still oblivious to Sam's strategic maneuvers, Katie ran a callused finger along the map to the areas she had highlighted with lip liner, "which will be about a four hour hike from where we'll set up camp and," she traced the ruby red path with the fingers of her other hand as she turned to address Sam's remarks and unwittingly brushed her cheek against his face, "about a day from the site of the power plant." She ignored his proximity and focused on business, "We need to cause as much havoc as possible – we only get one chance at this. We should strike the hospital as soon as it's full dark. The blaze will probably be visible for miles so all the neighboring townships," Katie marked each known settlement with an "X", "are sure to send all available manpower to help."

"And while they're busy battling the blaze and organizing rescue efforts, we'll be a full day's hike away," he squeezed her shoulders in his growing excitement, "By the time the sun comes up and they realize what happened, the Lord's work will be done." Sam's eyes gleamed with a wicked pleasure at the genius of their Divine plan as Katie felt something rub against her back.

Startled, she edged forward on the bench and continued their discussion, "Exactly, plus we'll be long gone and they'll be too busy to chase after us.

Now we just need to work out the details," she pushed the map down the table and grabbed her notepad, "Damn, you know this is getting to be a ffa...uh...nightmare to organize?"

Sam frowned at her verbal slippage, "Katie, please. Yes, I understand your stress but I have full faith in your abilities," he gave her a reassuring squeeze on the shoulder as he stood up, "Anyway, you've already gotten things off to a great start!"

Katie stepped up from the bench and tossed her notepad at Sam, "Do me a favor Sam," she waited for the smirk on his face to fade before continuing, "At least make an effort to not sound so damn patronizing. You can work on this alone for a while," she shot a derogatory glance at his waist line, "I need a **farking** break!" She stormed out of the tent, compensating for the lack of a door to slam by stomping her feet as she left.

Mortified, Sam monitored her exit with a blank stare and placed his fist in his mouth to muffle the frustrated laughter he expelled once she was out of ear shot, "Lord help me to understand why you have sent me such temptation and torment." He prayed quietly once he regained his composure, "I would say that vixen bewitched me, Lord, but I know you selected me because of my strength to resist such things. You preserve me to complete your Mission, but why must you test me so?" Sam reviewed his behavior since Josh had brought Katie and her group into his fold, but could find no reason for the woman to have gotten under his skin so deeply. She was abrasive and crude, not to mention his ideological opposite. Yet there was something strangely familiar about her.

"This is nonsense and I will waste no more time on nonsense until the Lord's Mission is complete," Sam mumbled to himself as he sat back down at the table to review Katie's notes. He laughed nervously to himself, stunned and impressed by the neatness and organization that had gone into the documents. There were tables delineating the personnel assigned to the new camp and their scheduled dates of departure, lists of equipment needed, and inventories of the equipment in stock. He traced his finger along a meticulously detailed timeline and found himself enamored with her penmanship.

"Lord, this woman lacks faith in you, yet she is so dedicated and committed to your Mission... Why?" he mused as he followed a cross-reference to a notation on the map.

"Knock, Knock," Sam emulated the familiar request for entry that tent living precluded.

The wearied voice barely pierced the fabric door panel, "Who is it?"

"Katie, its Sam. I brought your dinner," he sounded almost apologetic, tapping the plate as if to verify his story. When there was no immediate response he continued, "Martha fixed your favorite tonight...and the biscuits are still warm." He fanned the rising steam toward the tent's entry in hopes the aroma would speak more eloquently.

"Come in Sam," she verbally unlocked the door from her perch in the hammock chair dangling from the military surplus tent's epicenter. Torn between the promise of Martha's famous biscuits and the comfort of the hammock, Katie moaned as she stood up while Sam made his way to the small table at the far side of the tent.

"You seemed really distraught earlier today," Sam increased the wicks on the two hurricane lamps illuminating the room, "So I thought you might prefer to eat in the privacy of your quarters." He pushed Katie's seat beneath her as she sat then reached for the room's spare chair, "Do you mind?"

She hesitated a moment, but ultimately relented, gesturing for him to pull up the chair. She was still curious about their earlier meeting and he did seem genuinely concerned about her, "No, go ahead," she forced herself to sound more pleasant, "I know we've still got a lot to get ready for tomorrow." Katie swirled the thin pasta noodles around her fork as she spoke, "But you have to come clean before we get into that."

Sam nearly choked, "Alright," he had known this was a possibility and had come prepared – Katie would not be a threat to his Mission. He turned to face her directly, lightly brushing the barrel of the gun hidden under his shirt as he adjusted his chair accordingly. Sam flashed the smile that Katie was all too familiar with, it was the look a cat often gave a mouse he had finally cornered, "but you must also promise to keep your composure and watch your language," he placed both his hands on the table, "What is it that I need to come clean about Katie?"

She pried open one of the steaming garlic and cheese biscuits and popped a delightfully warm piece into her mouth. "I need to know if I'm just spinning my wheels or not," when Sam raised his brow in confusion she moved on, "Okay, what I mean is that I don't want to be wasting my time. This mission is really important to me. I can't let something like those earthquakes happen again, but I'm not going to pour my heart and soul into this if you're just going to second guess or ignore all my efforts just because I'm a woman."

"Oh..." he hummed thoughtfully as he quickly composed an answer, "but what have I done to make you think I wasn't utilizing your efforts? You practically run this camp," Sam swept his arms out to emphasize the camp's size even as he forged a subtle lock on their eye contact.

"Well," she spoke as she quickly swallowed the bit of bread she had been chewing so that she could focus on her words, "first of all, it's your attitude in general," she unconsciously glanced at his lap, "You're always going on in your sermons..."

"Wait," he playfully interrupted, "you listen to my sermons? I thought you didn't believe in any of that gobbledygook?"

"I still feel that way. But with no radio or TV or anyone," her voice trailed off for a moment, "Well...you're a good speaker and I enjoy listening to your voice," Katie confessed after her unwitting admission.

Sam leaned back in his chair and took on a more casual demeanor despite his intense gaze. "Oh really? Well that's good to know," he strategically paused...*I knew she would come around,* "So what were you saying about my sermons?" Sam attempted to sound coy.

"Well, before you interrupted I was saying that you're always going off on how inferior women are to men and how they should know their place," she rolled her eyes and took a sip of her tea as she organized her thoughts, "That's obviously not me, so how am I supposed to believe that I am an equal in the project? I just feel like you're humoring me. That all you're interested in is using me," she intentionally glanced at his lap, still unsure if that was a topic she wanted to approach, "and my friends."

Sam sensed the Lord's plan evolving – he would make Katie understand the opportunities before her. "Katie...Katie," he shook his head as he spoke, "You have clearly misunderstood my message," he lightly squeezed her hand, "I do value you and your efforts tremendously. Now, let me see if I can find a way to explain what I meant in your terms." He began to rub his chin the way he often did when he was composing a sermon, Sam knew the power of words better than anyone and now that he had confirmation of his influence over Katie he wanted to choose them very delicately, "Do you agree that a marriage takes teamwork?"

"Of course, but what does that have to do with your point? Is this a proposal?" Katie suppressed a sneer as she tried to remain objective.

Sam waved his hand to hush her and broke out in a warm smile as he watched the lump travel down her throat from an unspoken thought, "Just let me finish before you jump to conclusions. You'll see what I mean in a minute. So we agree that a marriage is like a team," he waited for her to nod before continuing, "Okay, let's look at some other team relationships. Say, basketball for example." Sam ignored her groans and went on, "Someone has to lead the team, right? Otherwise the game will be chaos with everyone going in different directions. So how many coaches does a team usually have?"

"Two or three, I think," Katie struggled to maneuver his argument to her favor.

He could see her foundation slipping but only nodded his comprehension of her point, "Yes, but how many of those are *head* coaches?"

Katie shrugged and looked at her food as she spoke, oblivious to her inevitable defeat, "One..."

"Exactly, and the others are assistant coaches, so it is the nature of their position that they assist the head coach. Isn't that right?" Sam continued without pausing for her answer, "And as part of that they may even express an opinion that is different from the head coach's, right?" He once again drew Katie's gaze as he continued to chip away, "isn't it their duty to the team to defer to the head coach's judgment when there's a difference of opinion?"

Katie eyes fluttered as she processed his argument over the grumble growing in her belly, "Well, yes," she was eager to display her understanding of such basic coaching concepts, "because they can't exercise a play if everyone is following different directions. That's obvious."

Sam could barely believe that he had manipulated her opinion so well, but here she had just stated his point and he savored her comprehension, "Precisely! So you see, my point is not that women are inferior or incapable. It is that the man is the head coach." He took Katie's free hand and held it firmly while he gazed into her, "Katie, you are going to help me lead this team to victory!" he casually released her hand a moment after he sensed her comfort level had been breached, "Now, are you ready to start going over the plans for tomorrow?"

Katie's eyes were focused on her formerly captive hand as she rubbed it to restore some perceived loss, of what she wasn't sure, "Uh, what?" she fought to regain clarity, "Oh yeah, sure...where did you want to begin?"

Sam smiled inwardly, "Why don't you bring me up to speed on the local activities and then I'll review what I learned in the field."

Suddenly aware of the barely touched tray of food in front of her and the increasing complaints from her stomach, Katie wistfully buttered the remains of a cold biscuit, "Oh, da...rn," she ignored Sam's smile, "I can't believe you got me so distracted that I forgot about Martha's hot cheese garlic biscuits sitting right under my nose!"

"I'm going to go grab a tray for myself," Sam authoritatively informed her as he stood up and grabbed the cold biscuits, "and I'll get you some biscuits that are still hot." He playfully juggled the cold biscuits as he made his way out of the tent.

He lightly ran his fingers along the delicate brown skin, memorizing each bump and divot. The moist skin felt cool in his rough hands and he held it for a moment longer before beginning. With a surgical precision the razor-like blade sliced through the thin skin as it quickly followed along the natural curve, sending a thin coil of skin twisting in gravity to the top of the growing pile.

"You owe me a steak!" the young man growled lightly through the frown permanently engraved in his flesh, "I told you I could do it! Another perfect peel! And in record time too!" he proudly retrieved the spiral of potato skin and tossed it at the stout man sitting across from him.

"Fine, Larry, next time they serve steak you get my share," the man wiped the potato from his face while retrieving a fistful of peels with the other hand. Without warning he forcefully directed the mass at Larry's eyes, "But don't you touch me again!"

Stung more by the sudden malice than the potato acid, Larry backed his stool away, "Jeez! Man! I didn't mean anything by it!" realizing that he had been shouting, he quickly hushed his words, "I was jus trying to pass time. I'll leave you alone from now on…Swear!"

"Okay, boys," responding to the commotion Martha made her way over, "if ya'll can't control yer tempers it'll git a whole lot worse than peel'n taters."

"Sorry Ma'am," Larry apologized against the glare of the other man, "We didn't mean nothin by it."

Martha grabbed his bucket of potatoes, "Come on Larry, ya kin help me mash'em now," she ignored the angry stare as she directed Larry to follow her to the far side of the kitchen area. "Ya'll need ta chop'em up an boil'em first," she instructed as she set the pail on the work table.

"Thanks for that Ma'am."

"Oh that? That was nothin. Ah've had ta deal with uh bunch worse lately…bahlieve me," Martha cryptically dismissed the need for his gratitude, "So why don't ya update me on what happen'd at the meetin? Sometimes Ah feel like Ah'm chained ta this here k'chen."

Larry seated himself in front of the bucket and grabbed a potato, "Do you want to hear about everything or just the transfers?"

"Why don't ya start with mah request and than go on ta the other stuff," she placed a large pot of water on the camp stove and sighed, "We've gotta whole lot of taters taggit done."

"I figured as much. Yer being sent to the new camp on account of your organizational experience," he tossed a handful of chopped potato into an empty pot, oblivious to the momentary gleam in Martha's eyes.

"Well, Ah spose that's for the best," Martha spoke matter-of-factly as she stirred the pot, "Ah could use uh change a scen'ry anyways. So what else happen'd?"

"Not much really. They announced the next group leaves with Pastor Sam in three days."

"Thray days?" Martha burst, ignoring the steam and smoke rising around her as water lapped over the edges of the pot under her intensified mixing that was triggered by her excitement rather than the panic she portrayed, "How am Ah sposed ta train uh raplacem't in thray days?"

"Do ya want ta hear the rest or not?" Larry playfully threatened as he grew comfortable under Martha's supervision. Once she stopped stirring and nodded he carried on, "Okay, sorry, but ya got three days. So don't shoot the messenger," he flashed a wink at Martha that made her blush. "Anyways, Pastor Sam also announced who's being sent ta check out the rumors of a hospital, a *real* hospital," he made a quick look around before leaning across the table to Martha and speaking under his breath, "I hear they've got electricity and runnin water. Not ta mention all those gadgets that get used in a hospital."

Martha covered her mouth as she gasped melodramatically, "Naw! So what's this mean?"

Larry continued in a whisper, "I dunno," he quickly looked around again, "but Ethan an Jack will find out. An once they get back I'm sure the Pastor will be able to figure out how ta protect us."

"Eth'n? But he's only uh boy! Surely somebody like Josh's better suited," Martha fished as she deposited more chopped potatoes into the boiling water.

"Yeah, Josh was pretty upset he wasn't goin. He made a real big stink bout the horses he brought back an how Eth'n was too young ta be trust'd. I'm surprised the Pastor didn't knock him down a peg," Larry absently assaulted his last potato like he was chopping wood, ending his sentence with the loud thunk of the knife impacting the table.

"Naw Larry, ya really shouldn't speak bout Josh like that. He's like uh son ta Sam," she scolded him with the party line as she refilled the bucket of peeled potatoes, "Ah'm sure Josh will be much more h'lp now that he's assigned ta…what was it?"

"The plant, I think. An maybe the new camp," he spat out a wad of raw potato, "hey, do ya have anything I can snack on? I'm starv'n here."

"Ah actually have some pie left from yesterday," she watched his eyes anxiously follow her as she fetched the pie from the dry storage bin, "Why don't ya take uh break an have some." Martha set the pie tin in front of him and handed him a fork.

"Ma'am, that's awfully considerate of ya," Larry buried a large chunk of pie in his mouth, "I don't b'lieve nuthin they says bout ya. Yer not crazy the least bit."

Martha buried a laugh in her smile, "Well Larry, Ah do appreciate yer kind words. An ya've been very helpf'l," she winked and tilted her head to indicate the pie and the locked storage area,

"There's more where that come from for helpful folk such as yerself. Ah treat mah friends right."

Larry smiled as he swallowed, a drip of cherry glaze dripping off his chin, "You're my bestest friend Ms. Martha."

Martha's face shimmered with streaks of tears and her eyes gleamed. She cupped her hands over her mouth to conceal her gasps as she tried to speak through her sobs, "Oh! Sam...Sam...," he led her by the shoulders as he twirled her around to fully take in the view of the stocked cafeteria kitchen, "Really?! It's okay fer me ta use all this?" Martha's surprise was genuine as she lustfully ran her hand down the stainless steel countertops.

"Well, the refrigerators obviously won't work, but you can still use them for storage," he pulled open a door to reveal the fresh vegetables and other foods that had been sequestered, "And I don't see any reason why you can't use the gas stoves until we run out of propane. The simpler life of the Lord doesn't require us to live like animals, only to extricate modern distractions," he flashed a beguiling wink at her, "I wouldn't classify eating as a distraction. In fact, I'm pretty sure your biscuits qualify as sustenance."

She forcibly wrapped herself around the tall man, "Oh thank ya Sam!" she dripped with enthusiasm.

"Don't thank me Martha. It's all part of the Lord's plan," Sam couldn't help but smile, her gratitude infusing his divinely inspired ego, "you're going to have a lot more mouths to feed down here and He has provided you with the facility to do that," he squeezed her shoulder affectionately as he spoke.

"More people?" Martha promptly released her grip on Sam as she gasped and nearly fell over backward, "but Sam, Ah was barely able ta keep'em fed before! How many more? How long're they gonna be here? When they gettin here?" she stealthily seized the opportunity and quickly rattled off her questions in mock horror. "Ah need ta know! This's goin ta take plan'n an creative cookin, else these extra people yer referring ta are gonna starve! Oh, Ah'm gonna need some full-time help for preppin an laundry an..."

Sam looped a finger under her chin and reestablished eye contact, "Martha," he interjected, putting a finger across her lips when she kept on, "Martha! Everything will be okay...calm down."

Under his intense gaze she immediately complied, retrieving a tissue from the stash in her ample bosom and wiping her brow. Martha took a deep breath, "Ah'm so sorry Sam," she fanned herself nervously with the tissue, "Ya can't jus spring someth'n like that on an ol'woman. Ya rightly sent me inta panic!" she masked her nervousness. Wondering if her gamble would pay off, Martha fought the urge to begin pacing and instead accelerated her fanning, flopping the tissue wildly in front of her face.

Sam shook his head and laughed while he flipped through his notepad, "All right, 'Ol'woman,'" he playfully winked at her again, "I'll see what I can do about getting you some more help, it shouldn't really be a problem since we'll have more volunteers to draw from." Martha watched him flip back three more pages, "As far as how many and when, you've got a week or so to get things organized. Plan on feeding, say," he tapped his finger along the page, "maybe twice as many."

Martha feigned a swoon and grabbed the countertop for support, "Oh Sam, ya give me far too much credit," she whined. "Ah'll do ma darndest. Ah best get started right off," she familiarized herself with the facilities as she spoke, opening and closing cabinets, "D'ya have anyone that kin help me now? Maybe tha older kids?"

Sam reviewed his list again, "Why don't you get Ethan to help you right now. He's a smart kid and he's not assigned to anything for the next couple of days. Tell him I said to organize the other free kids into an extra kitchen and laundry detail."

"Eth'n?" Martha scratched her head inquisitively, "Oh...yeah, Ah think Ah know'em," she pronounced with uncertainty as she continued to conceal her ability to comprehend much beyond her duties of cooking and cleaning.

"Young, tall lad with dark hair," Sam politely offered, "You'll find him down the hall in room two seventeen. It's on the adolescents' hall," he quickly sketched her a map of the facility - the last thing he needed was for her to be wondering around lost. "Right here," he directed her on the map, "and you're here."

She sighed and blotted her eyes with a fresh tissue, "Oh Sam, Ah jus wanna thank ya for all ya've done fer me," she allowed herself to choke on her words as she carefully tested the waters, "Is jus ever since tha school, ya know, well the change in scenery's doin me good. Ah'm so glad ta see we've moved on from that sorta thang."

Sam possessively wrapped his arm around her shoulders as she turned to leave the room, "Martha, I hope you trust that I will always lead you in the direction of our Lord," he smiled when he felt her shudder under his words, "and I promise you we are moving exactly as He has directed." Sam took in the whole of the campus with a sweep of his hand, "Why else would he have led us here?" his conviction echoed along the empty hallway.

Martha felt the growth of his consuming ego and, despite the revulsion she felt, forced herself to relax into his embrace as if content at his reassurances. With her head resting gently against his chest she quietly listened to the pounding of his silent excitement while she let out a restful sigh, "Yes Sam, Ah'm listening. Ya know Ah'll always falla His Word."

"Good," he tenderly stroked her head. "Well, here we are and Ethan's right where I thought he would be," he pointed to an older boy engaged in a game of blocks with several pre-school aged children, "Ethan, come over here and help Ms. Martha." Once the boy acknowledged him Sam confidently peeled away from Martha and continued down the hall without a word.

The wicker chair harmonized as Josh leaned over to grab the wooden mallet that had just landed at his feet. As he tossed the mallet in his grip to assess its weight he watched his would be assailant's face flush with embarrassment and decided against throwing it back. "Really Joey, if ya don't care fer the way Ah assigned yer duties, ya should've just spoken with me in private," he handed the mallet back to the boy with a feigned cautiousness.

The featherweight boy flushed an additional two shades of red and his already fluctuating voice quivered as he spoke, "I...I...uh...it jus slipped...uh...Sir," he held the mallet tightly with both hands, "I'm so sorry Mr. Josh."

Stunned at the boy's apparent fear of him, Josh knelt down beside him and gently squeezed his shoulder, "Now, really boy, it's okay. Ah was jus mess'n. Ah know ya didn't mean nothin by it." He looked the boy in the eye, "We square?"

"Yes...yes, Sir," Joey's tone was now much lighter as he demonstrated his new technique for swinging the mallet by holding its handle with both hands, "See?"

"Good," Josh moaned as he rose to his feet and limped back to his seat by Sam. He pretended not to hear the wicker groan under his weight as he sat back down, "So Sam, do ya really think it's necessity that ya leave so soon? It should only be uh day or so til we have it all set up proper," Josh attempted to conceal the fact that he found himself completely overwhelmed at the prospect of managing an entire camp without Sam present, "then there'd be someone free ta ride back up with ya."

Sam brushed the comment off with a polite laugh, "Josh, I really must get moving. There is simply too much to be done."

"Really Sam, are ya sure it can't wait jus another day," he spoke with the confidence that he knew Sam wanted to hear but he didn't really feel, "Ah'm worried about ya riding alone with uh hurt hand."

Sam unconsciously rubbed the edge of the bandage covering the renewed wound on his palm, "Josh, it's just a minor burn. People burn themselves cooking all the time."

The boy winced as ointment was spread along his palm. He focused on the quarter-sized circular pattern of reddened flesh to avoid glimpsing the nurse's pointy white cap and yet another reminder of his mother. The memories of her were still more painful than any of the burns and his father made sure that he had plenty of opportunities to realize that.

"Samuel Brown, you really are the most accident prone boy I know," the nurse lacked any of the compassion of his mother as she scolded him, "Make sure you come by tomorrow so we can put a fresh bandage on. That really is a nasty burn." She

lifted him off the table, "I'll let your father know he needs to keep a better eye on you." The nurse shooed him out of the door with a light tap on his bottom.

Sam winced at the pain that radiated up his arm like acid as he absent mindedly rubbed his palm, "I'm perfectly capable of traveling by myself," he scowled as he masked the pain with anger, the intensity of his voice erecting the hairs on the back of his neck and causing the veins in his forehead to visibly throb.

Blindsided by the sudden verbal lashing, Josh almost got physically sick as his heart plummeted into the pit of his stomach and a cold sweat broke out down his back. He could feel Sam's eyes burning through him. Sam had never spoken with such anger before, especially toward Josh, and now Josh's already overtaxed mind threatened to simply shut down. Fixating on the ground as he chewed at his fingers, he reminded Sam of a remorseful child, "Ah'm sorry," Josh wailed, "that's not what Ah meant Sam!" He peered up from the corner of his eye still fearful of another backlash, "Please don't leave here thinkin that. Ah was jus feelin like Ah was in over my head and thought Ah could stall ya till Ah got myself t'gether...honest," he desperately sought forgiveness from the only father he could remember.

Sam reached over and slowly pulled Josh's hands from his face, "Joshua, I shouldn't have snapped at you like that. I'm the one that should be apologizing," he felt Josh tighten his grip on his good hand but Josh still wouldn't look at him, "And I should have consulted with you before I decided to put you in charge here. But for what it's worth, Josh, I didn't ask because I knew it was something you were meant to do." Sam spoke in the gentle authoritative voice he reserved for his sermons, "The Lord placed you with me because he knew this day would come. Joshua, you are one of the most faithful men I know."

"Really?" Josh looked up only to be caught in Sam's gaze. His pounding heart slowed and the knot in his stomach faded as his earlier panic began to dissolve into gratitude and he fought to resist the tears welling in his eyes, "Am Ah really that important?"

Sam smiled as he continued to direct Josh's confidence to the required levels, "Of course you are, Josh. I can't do this without you and there is no one that I trust like you. Really, you are the only reason I feel confident enough to continue the Lord's work." Sensing Josh's revival Sam momentarily tightened his grip before finally releasing him and reclining back in his chair.

"Thank ya Sam," Josh swallowed as he digested the pride Sam's confidence instilled in him, "Ah guess the Lord was jus try'n ta teach me some sorta less'n. But if ya think Ah can do it, then Ah can do it!" he proclaimed as Sam's influence took seed. Josh rocked from side to side and settled deeper into his seat, the panic was gone and he savored the feeling of confidence that now filled him. It wasn't long, maybe a handful of breaths, before he had completely forgotten his former state of dread.

Sam easily recognized the emptiness glazing Josh's eyes and waited for it to pass before ending the silence. "So do you still need me to stay on a few more days?" he needlessly inquired to solidify Josh's commitment.

"Thank ya for the offer Sam, but things will run jus fine here without ya," he replied as if his earlier lapse in confidence had never occurred, "There is far too much work ta be done for ya ta waste yer time play'n house here."

"Good," Sam clapped his friend on the shoulder before closing his eyes and reclining in his chair once more. He basked in the glory of success, everything was falling into place so easily he could almost feel the Lord's hands embracing him.

Josh shook Sam gently by the shoulder as he stood up, "Sam, Ah've got ta go check on some things. When will ya be leave'n?" He rocked impatiently on the balls of his feet while he waited for Sam to answer.

"Oh, yes, just after breakfast, Josh," Sam reeled back into reality. "There are several potentially sympathetic parishes nearby and I plan to pay them a visit on my way back home," he attempted to stand but Josh politely held him down.

"Ah can take care of thangs on my own. Ya've gotta bunch of travelin ahead of ya so stay here an Ah'll send someone ta fetch ya once breakfast's ready," Josh's eyes gleamed with impiety now that he had accepted his authority over the camp.

Sam relented to the burgeoning ego and relaxed back in his chair, "All right. I can see I've made a monster," he laughed and closed his eyes.

"Beautys'n the eye uh the beholder," Josh chuckled as he walked away.

Although fading, the sunlight seemed to gather strength as it glistened off the surface of a lone forgotten tear. Slowly, as if afraid of discovery, the tear meandered its way down the trail of wrinkles in the old man's face until finally the tear escaped with a drip of sweat off the man's chin.

Sam was not one to show weakness and he would have denied the tear if he had known it was there. But for all the control Sam had over his growing congregation, there were still some things beyond the grasp of his will. And now, without Sam's knowledge or permission, his journey to the church of his childhood had finally severed the chains of an unnamed beast that had begun to stir only recently. He wasn't even aware that the beast had been seeded deep in the recesses of his mind ever since his mother had abandoned him, rather he had unknowingly nourished it with denial to the point that it now threatened to consume him.

The boy began to rub the sleep from his eyes. He and his mom were knelt beside a wrinkled old woman lying on a cot in a crowded hallway.

"Ok, you first want to hold down the skin next to the bandage with a finger, then grab the edge of the bandage with your other hand and gently peal it away from the skin..." she explained to her son as she kept her eyes locked on the old woman, monitoring for any signs of pain during the simple procedure. This wasn't the first time he had watched his mom change a bandage since he often accompanied her to work when he got out of school. Once he could tell she was done he emptied the tin bowl into the red garbage bin and looked up in time to see her smile with pride. That's why he did it, just for that smile. They made their way to one of the areas hidden behind the pretty blue curtains where an older boy was sitting on the examination table.

"Hello, I'm Nurse Brown," she introduced herself as she reviewed his chart, "This is my son Samuel. You don't mind if he watches, do you? He's training to be a doctor some day," she turned her head and subtly winked at him. Samuel struggled to contain his embarrassment at her praise, but a nervous giggle still managed to escape his reddened face.

"Well, I guess not. Can we just get this over with?" the boy watched his kicking feet as he spoke, appearing more embarrassed than Samuel felt.

His mom firmly placed a hand on the boy's knee, "You'll want to keep still," Samuel noticed how his mom exercised as much care with the impatient boy as she did the old woman, "See Pumpkin, how nicely this is healing," she urged him to come forward and take a closer look at the stitches on either side of the boy's arm, "Dr. White did a really pretty job, don't you think?"

"Yes Ma'am," he answered proudly as he stepped back into the background again.

She returned her attention to the boy, "Luckily for you young man," she clipped and removed the stitches before swabbing ointment onto the healing wound, "the bullet was small and went straight through your arm without breaking the bone or hitting a major artery. I hope you've learned your lesson from this...you could have easily lost your arm." She spoke as if he was her son while she fixed the clean bandage in place, "Ok, you're free to go."

"Thanks, Ma'am," the boy leapt off the table and was gone.

"Now honey, would you like to practice on mommy? Here, the dressing on my arm needs to be changed and I think it would be good practice for you," she sat him on the table so that he could easily reach her arm. Slowly he began to peel away the tape as she had shown him. He tried to watch her face as he pulled the edge of the bandage like he had seen her do with the old woman, but it only caused him to slip and pull too hard. Still his mom never even winced.

"Sorry," he apologized as he fought back the tears.

"Honey, it's okay. You're doing just fine," she encouraged him in her gentle way.

"Ma, how come it's only me that changes your bandages? Why don't..."

"Doesn't..." she lovingly corrected despite her obvious pain.

"...doesn't Dr. White fix you too? He fixes everybody else. No one even asks if you are hurting," the boy asked as he continued on at his mom's encouragement.

"Honey, it's not because they don't want to. It's just easier for mommy to have you help me," she barely grimaced as he poured antiseptic on the circular burns along her forearm, "That way I don't have to waste time with all the paperwork you've seen the patients fill out. You know mommy is very busy between working here and keeping the house the way your father likes it. I know I should ask for help, but I just don't have time to fill out all the papers," she smiled at him as she spoke. She always smiled when she spoke to him, even when there were tears coming from her eyes – it was a smile that would haunt his memories forever.

"Okay Mommy," his hands were dwarfed by the bandage as he gently rubbed the tape into place, "Did I do a good job Mommy?"

"Yes, you did. You were very gentle," she caressed his face in her hands as she leaned her forehead against his, "You promise Mommy you will always be that gentle even when you grow up big and strong like your daddy?" Her face was so close to his that he could only focus on the mole next to the bridge of her nose and never saw the tears welling up in her eyes.

Sam wiped away a tear, but the memory would not fade. His mom's disappearance still haunted him despite the depth of years he wrapped it in. He couldn't remember where she had gone or why she had left without even saying good-bye, but he knew that for all the light she had brought into his life, his father and her disappearance had filled it with darkness. Sam ignored the pain radiating from his palm as he put his hands together in prayer.

"Boonng...Boonng...Boonng" the deep baritone of the church bells eerily flowed across the silent landscape like a mist, "Boonng..."

Drawn by the distantly familiar tones, Sam looked up to search for the source. In the fading light he nearly looked past the dark stone bell tower, but the Lord signaled him with the last of the sun, gleaming it off the freshly polished bell as it swung back and forth. Sam listened to the Lord's message as he approached what was left of the ancient church. Every toll of the bell spoke of the enduring strength of the bell tower which now stood high above the ruins of an obviously modern addition to the building, the surrounding landscape was merely punctuation. He smiled his understanding – here, at the very birthplace of his devotion to the church, the old clinic that had immortalized his mother's disappearance existed only as the burnt out skeleton of a building.

The elderly round man struggled to embrace Sam despite the fact that his bald head barely reached Sam's shoulders. There were only a handful of hairs brave enough to hold on to the man's shiny scalp and he had more than his fair share of chins, all of which jiggled with his delight, "Oh thank ye Lord! Sam! Sam! Ah can't tell ya the number uh times Ah pray'd for yer saf'ty!" Pastor Frank panted. "Have uh sit," he directed Sam to the chairs arranged around a weathered card table set up under a shade tarp, "Care fer some sun brew'd tah? It's naught prop'r ice tah on account of no ice, but we all mus make sacrifices in times such as these are," he looked longingly at the glass as he eased himself into the aluminum beach chair which squealed with it's own agitation.

"Yes, we must," Sam answered softly as he passed the pitcher of warm tea back to Frank.

"Honey, this here is Sam, mah boy," Frank gripped Sam's shoulder affectionately, "Sam, this is mah new wife Honey."

Honey nodded, "Yes, Ah remember. Ya raised him after his father was called up in the service, right?" She stood up and extended her hand to Sam, "It's good ta finally meet the man Frank is always talking about. He's so proud of ya!"

"A pleasure to meet you, Miss Honey," Sam oozed Southern charm and politely kissed her hand, "Frank, you have certainly been blessed by the Lord to have such a beautiful wife."

Honey giggled nervously at the complement, "Why Sam, ya are uh charmer."

"Yes, ya certainly are, but with an air uh truth. The Lord has most definitely watched out fer me," Frank emptied the pitcher of tea, "Honey, go fetch some vittles fer Sam an mahself."

Sam waved his hands 'no' over the table as he swallowed, but the Pastor's wife was gone before he had an opportunity to speak, "Really Frank, please don't go to any trouble."

"Nonsense," Frank cut in, "Ah made uh promise ta yer Pa that Ah would look out fer ya an Ah don't tend ta fergit such thangs!"

Sam absently ran his thumb along his bandage, "Yes, I remember."

Hidden under the covers, with only the illumination from a small flashlight, the boy slowly peeled the bandage away from his palm. The air stung the freshly exposed skin and would have caused him to cry out in pain if he had not steadied himself against it by biting down on his lip. As the shock passed and the pain faded into a simple ache he started to relax and focus on his damaged palm. The blistered skin glistened with ointment and the creases of his palm were blood red. The boy wondered if the scar would be as perfectly circular as the original blister and held the flashlight closer to study the progress of his healing skin. The warmth of the small light on his skin was comforting and he closed his eyes and imagined it was from his mom's touch.

Suddenly the silence was broken with a loud clatter and the boy's heart froze. He quickly switched off the light and held his breath, afraid to make even the slightest sound.

"Yoo hoo!" the Pastor's wife cheerily interrupted, "Lunch's ready. Ah hope everyone is plenty hungry," she set a large platter of finger sandwiches on the table between the men just as a young boy appeared with a salad bowl filled with cantaloupe and melon chunks. "Oh good, jus sit that down an be on yer way," she directed the boy as she set a place setting in front of each of the men, "Okay boys, enjoy! Frank, Ah'll be at the laundry iffen ya need me." She was gone before anyone could remark on the presentation, the tune she was humming lingering in the air along with the clatter from her multitude of bangles.

Frank lowered his head and reached out for Sam, "Sam, would ya be so kind as ta lead us in pray'r?"

Sam gratiously cleared his throat as he accepted Frank's hand, "I'd be honored," he began in a deep baritone, "Dear Lord, we thank you for this bounty before us and humbly accept your extraordinary gifts of fruit and meats in such trying times. Lord, we also want to express our sincerest gratitude in the compassion you have shown by keeping our loved ones safe," he purposefully squeezed the Pastor's thick hand, "when disaster surrounded us. Your Word sustains us and gives us hope. We see signs of your message everywhere Dear Lord." Sam ignored the ache in his hand as he tightly clenched his fist in the throws of his own enthusiasm, "the beauty of the stone and mortar bell tower presides over the ruins of man's modern world. The music of prayers and hymns that are no longer drowned out by the chatter of a television or radio…"

"Yes Lord, thank ya," Frank mumbled blindly.

"The conversation between family and friends now that there are no malls or video games to lure them away," Sam seamlessly continued pausing only long enough to catch his breath, "Lord, we thank you for the growth in our characters that simple chores have nourished now that machines are not available to make such tasks mindless. You have shown us the path to a simpler way of life that is more truthful to your image," the vision of himself on the pulpit flashed through his mind's eye and the smile on his lips filled his words, "through simplicity we are able to truly practice our devotion to you and honor you. Lord, we honor you for this opportunity you have given us for our salvation. In Jesus' name we do pray." Sam narrowly opened his eyes and fixed his gaze on Frank, "Amen."

"Amen," the Pastor paused as he wiped the tears from his eyes, "Sam, mah son, Ah don't know where that come from, but it was one of the most beaut'ful prayers Ah've heard! Ya've given this ol' man much ta ponder," he finished his sentence with a bite off his egg salad sandwich.

"Thank you Frank," Sam toasted his friend with a swig of lukewarm tea, "but I should be thanking you. I got the inspiration for it from you," he easily maneuvered his way into Frank's current need for a sense of purpose.

Frank swallowed, "Really? Ah'm honor'd but how so?" He subdued his growing embarrassment with more warm tea and another bite of his sandwich without taking his focus off Sam.

"Well ever since I heard those bells as I was riding up, I've been thinking about what I would say to you and all the things that never got said because we were too distracted by the world," Sam took a deep breath and locked eyes with Frank while grasping the man's thick forearm. He could sense Frank coming into alignment and crafted his words accordingly, filling them with the deep affection of a son for his father, "I owe you so much Frank. I'm just glad that the good Lord saw fit to give me the opportunity to say it."

Frank coughed, attempting to regain his composure yet again, and decided that another sandwich would do the job better. The mouthful at least provided an alibi for his silence as he struggled to sequester his rampant emotions.

"Uh hmmm," a delicate cough politely interrupted the sudden quiet, "Ah'm sorry. Ah didn't mean ta overhear, but yer prayer mesmerized me Sam." Honey blushed as the two men looked up at her in bewilderment, "Ah jus brought more napkins for ya," she waved the napkins erratically as she spoke, "but ya were already deep'n prayer."

Sam reached up and caught the napkins mid-flight, "Thank you," he smiled deeply at Honey, "I'm glad you enjoyed the prayer."

Honey blushed again, "It was jus'so beautiful Sam...what ya said about how thangs are now," she hugged her clasped hands to her breast and sighed melodramatically, "Ah jus can't imagine why anyone'd want ta go back ta the way thangs were before!"

"Sam," Frank's chair squealed as he maneuvered closer to his friend, "Ah must agree." Frank latched on to the change in topic and unwittingly aligned himself with Sam's cause, "The Lord's most definitely given ya the gift uh words!" he lovingly wrapped an arm around his wife as she stood by his side, "An Ah must admit Ah do enjoy the quietness now an the night sky is ever more beat'ful than it was." Frank could feel Honey's heart pounding and his sense of indebtedness to the Lord grew with each beat, "Ah am so truly grateful an Ah appreciate everything the good Lord has given me," he raised his tea glass, "Ya may be the one with the gift Sam, but Ah'd like ta go ahead'n make uh toast anyway." He waived his glass around until Sam raised his, "Ta Sam. Thank ya for takin the time ta wake this ol' man up an remind him uh the beauty that is everywhere now," he clinked his glass and winked at Sam.

"Here! Here!" Honey concluded with an overenthusiastic giggle.

Sam closed his eyes and smiled as he drained the remainder of his glass.

Honey fussed over the many knots that fastened the satchel to the bulky saddle, disguising her distress with aggravation, "Now Sam, ya sure that's gonna hold? Ah jus hate fer all mah hard work ta be wasted on varmints if that comes loose," she tugged on the satchel, nervously testing its attachment.

"It will be just fine," with a premeditated precision Sam pulled her hand away from the satchel and wrapped a hug around her, giving her a soft peck on the cheek before pulling back far enough to look her in the eyes. "We'll all be just fine," he carefully spoon fed her the reassurances she demanded, his words laced with confidence that ensured she wouldn't undermine him once he was gone.

"So ya have mah letter, right?" Frank inadvertently interrupted, "Pastor Carl and Reverend Peter are sure ta come onboard once they know yer mah boy," his voice boomed with pure adoration for his adoptive son.

Sam leisurely moved toward his horse, savoring the allegiance of his former mentor. "I've got it right here," he tapped his breast pocket, "and you have the map? They'll be expecting you five days from now," he locked eyes with Frank as he verified his commitment.

Frank tightly clinched the papers in his fist, "Right here! We'll be there!" he choked as he struggled to suppress his pain at Sam's departure. Frank had given Sam up for dead after the massive quakes, so his appearance on the coattails of a message from the Lord had truly felt like a resurrection for him and he could barely comprehend his protégé leaving yet again.

As if on cue, Sam patted Frank on the back and embraced him so tightly that he nearly lifted the hearty man off his feet, "Thank you for the hospitality Frank. It felt good to be home for at least a little while," he carefully released Frank to his own accord and then swiftly pulled himself into the saddle.

Filling the emptiness created by Sam's choreographed release, Frank wrapped an arm around Honey who had started to sob at the sight of Sam poised to go in the saddle. "An thank ya Sam fer gracing us with yer presence. It's been uh glorious few days!" He shouted over Honey's increased sobbing, "God bless ya. Travel safe!"

As Sam breathed in the final breaths of home he resisted the images developing in his mind's eye, focusing instead on the image of the bell tower. His inner struggle thoroughly concealed behind his smile, he waved farewell and directed the horse forward, "God bless and good-bye!" Sam spurred his horse into a gallop in a futile attempt to escape the waking memories.

Barely a moment later Honey's sobs transformed into wails and Frank struggled to console the wiry woman within his embrace, "We'll see'em soon enough Honey," he began to walk toward their tent with her head still buried in his shoulder, "Come on, we need taggit pact. There's no time fer waste'n like this." Frank drew strength from Honey's weakness as he transformed into one of Sam's apostles – there was much work yet to be done.

9

Deception is a double edged sword,
The serpent refuses to see,
When the clock is ticking and the lies are told,
Its use must eventually, the innocent set free...

Blood dripped down her chin from where she had bit through her lip in an effort to ignore the pain of her disguise. Slowly, it pooled in the spatter stain on her blouse which was also being fed by the blood from the fine cut on her forehead that ran into her eyes and down her cheek before she was allowed to wrap her head with a bandage made from an old T-shirt. Again Susan took a deep breath and held it as she steadied herself for the next assault. She gasped and bit into a rag as Josh slit a three-inch gash into her forearm, carefully missing any major arteries. Once more the wound was allowed to bleed a bit before Ethan was permitted to wrap it. He was so covered in blood, his own and hers, that his hands were slippery and caused him to lose his grip on the bandage several times before successfully tying it tight enough to stop the bleeding. The gash in his chest throbbed and burned as the raw flesh was rubbed between the bandage and his ribs, but he was blinded to his own pain by his concern for the obvious agony that Susan was going through. She had held on to him for support and was unaware that the pain had tightened her grip to the point where she had left him with bloody bruises from her nails cutting through the flesh on his arm. Ethan was nearly besieged with the bloody mess that they had created – only the silent fear of his growing doubts being discovered kept him from being sick or passing out.

In contrast, rather than appearing sickened or disgusted with his duties, Josh was covered in smugness as thickly as he was blood. Sam's earlier infusion of confidence had done more than boost his pride and unconscious desire for leadership, it had an unplanned side affect: a darkness that had been feeding off Josh's hidden fear and guilt since childhood had been released.

The hospital reconnaissance mission was his final opportunity to exercise his newly discovered leadership skills and Josh planned to thoroughly impress Sam. He had no doubt that he had done his job well: those heretics would, without hesitation, lower their defenses to this family who was bloodied and bruised from top to bottom. The deep knife wounds were a touch of genius, they would never suspect anything like that was self inflicted. Josh gave himself a mental pat on the back as he wiped the blood off his brow with a damp rag before helping Ethan carry Susan's limp body back to her room.

"Well, Eth', Ah believe we do real good work tagether," Josh commented as the two laid Susan on her cot.

"I guess so sir," Ethan whispered.

"Good then. Well, Ah've gotta run, There's some newbies that Ah gotta meet with."

Once Ethan heard Josh's footsteps fade away he waited a few moments more to make sure that he wasn't coming back and then began to gently wash the blood from Susan's face and eyes. Before he left Ethan checked that her head was propped up and he loosely wrapped a blanket around her. Satisfied that she was resting as comfortably as possible, he struggled to stay on his feet as he staggered to his own room. He was in too much pain to eat, but he would at least get some rest before they left the following afternoon.

A lthough windows ran down the entire length of the wall she was sitting by, the woman was having difficulty finding enough light to work by. She put on her reading glasses and squinted while holding the vial at various angles in an attempt to read the label, but the fading light eventually forced her to accept that it was time to go spend supper with her family. The woman placed the vial back into the small refrigerator, checked the adjacent generator's fuel level, and satisfied with the level, she removed her gloves and washed the powder lining off her hands. Once she was safely out of the lab she removed the thong that had been holding her hair in a low ponytail, shaking her head from side to side to ease the tension in her scalp – if only it was that easy to assuage her frustrations from working in such archaic conditions. She fought the grimace she felt creeping over her face and slowly changed her focus to the all too short visit with her family.

The doctor semi-leisurely made her way down the hall and was greeted with waves and smiles from the patients that littered the corridors. She smiled and waved back, solidifying her decision to release her frustrations and avoid spending her precious free time reliving unpleasantness. As she turned the corner she quickly popped her head into an open doorway, "Hey Tyler! Did you finish all your vegetables?"

"Doc Evie!" the boy looked up from his half eaten dinner tray, "Almost...you heading home for dinner?"

"You know it. You'd better be done by the time I get back," Evie tussled his hair before jetting out of the room, "I'll be checking in on you!"

"I promise," he called out after her.

"You'd better," her voice echoed down the hall as she approached the exit. She could see her walking buddies waiting patiently by the door and hastened her pace to meet them, skillfully dodging the obstacle course of patients and equipment.

"Hey guys, thanks for waiting," she half-panted half-giggled as she popped up from behind the group.

"No problemo chica. I'd wait a lifetime for you," the young orderly acknowledged her tardiness with an overzealous flirtatiousness, "like we would leave youz to walk alone with those crazies out there," he rolled his eyes melodramatically.

Evie threw her arm over his shoulder and they began walking in step across the parking lot, "Lions and tigers and bears...Oh my!" she laughed.

"Good Gawd! If I have to put up with this for the whole two miles back to the residences I'll go stark raving mad!" another nurse chimed in.

Evie laughed again and it soon spread across the group, fed largely by their collective exhaustion. With the current staffing level barely a third of what was really needed, the group spent nearly every conceivable hour at the hospital. Now, as they walked punch drunk back to their families and homes, the five colleagues reveled in their fleeting moments away from any responsibility.

"Hold on. I think I heard something," the orderly held his hand up as a signal for them to stop and remain silent. He nervously thumped the baseball bat in the palm of his free hand as he looked for the source of the suspicious sound.

Instinctively the group closed in and began to visually comb the area for would be assailants. The growing dusk made it too easy for someone to be hiding unobserved in the shadows of the nearby woods, at least with animals you could see their eyes gleam, but they were searching for human predators.

Adding to the air of danger, the breeze picked up, swaying the tall grasses and rustling the leaves to further camouflage what lay beyond the shadows. Still, time continued to pass without incident and as the seconds faded into minutes they began to wonder if what they had heard wasn't just a byproduct of the wind.

The nurse held his finger to his lips as he broke from the group and walked like a ghost to the edge of their path. As he peered down into the tall grass he struggled to focus his tired eyes beyond the whishing grasses, relying instead on his keen sense of hearing to direct him. A moment later he resisted the urge to forge ahead while he anxiously waved the rest of the group over.

"Oh my god!" Evie quickly checked their vitals, "help me clear away the grass. Be careful not to move them," her concern overrode her cautious silence. The noise had not come from the wind or some terrorist sneaking through the woods, but rather it was a last call for help from more innocent victims of those damn NoTechs. She quickly established that the three were only unconscious so she proceeded to carefully examine each one before disentangling their arms and rolling them onto their sides in a stable recovery position. She had to bite her lip to keep her composure as she realized that this wasn't just three strangers, rather it was a family – a middle aged couple and their adolescent son – and they had nearly been exterminated by some faceless group of terrorists!

"We've got to get them back to the hospital," Evie combated her rage by jumping head on into procedure, "Zandre and Leslie, you run back to the hospital and get some stretchers and help...Go!"

As he rolled on to his side Ethan was roused by the pain coursing through his chest and instinctively reached for the source of the pain. He startled awake as he felt the fresh bandage that covered the gash on his chest and soon realized that his entire body, as well as his wounds, had been cleaned and he was clad in only a fresh pair of boxers. He was sure that he must be dreaming or dead since he was convinced that he was lying in a real bed that had a real mattress and a real pillow. It even appeared that he was inside of a real hospital room with a window next to his bed.

"Cool, you're finally awake! I've been up for hours," a young boy in the bed next to him stirred Ethan from his daze, "I'm Tyler, the Doc said that I should keep an eye on you and let her know when you woke." He took a deep breath, "DOC! DOC!! HE'S AWAKE!" Tyler giggled, "Sorry if I scared you, we don't have no call buttons here," he winked with mischief at Ethan.

"Jeez, you could have told me that before!" Ethan laughed, "If they don't have call buttons, I sure hope they have one of you in every room. So what do you guys do for door bells around here?"

Tyler giggled again with innocence, "You're funny. What's your name? You look like a 'Gilbert' to me."

"'Gilbert'? I do not look like a 'Gilbert' that's a geeky name," Ethan threw his pillow at the boy and puffed out his chest like a proud rooster, "My name's Ethan."

"So Ethan, I see that you are feeling better today," the doctor proscribed from the doorway.

Ethan's jaw dropped and he could feel the blood drain from his face with the shiver that ran down his spine. He coughed out the lump in his throat, "Yes...yes Ma'am. I'm feeling much better... I'm sorry for the horse play."

Tyler giggled, "Hi Doc Evie!" the boy's smile gleamed as he spoke, "Can Ethan be my brother?"

"I don't know, you'll have to ask him about that. So Ethan," Evie handed Ethan his pillow and smiled warmly at him until she noticed him relax, "do you mind if I take a look under those bandages? By the way, your parents are fine. They're both still sleeping, but as soon as they wake up I'll let you see them."

Ethan had been enjoying himself so much that he had forgotten about his "family" until that moment, "Thank you Doctor Evie. I'll try and be patient," he masked his remorse with disappointment.

"Now please don't be all gloomy and formal with me, Ethan. You call me Evie just like everyone else. I should apologize to you because I see how upset you are about being separated from your parents, especially under the circumstances. So we'll just pay them a visit right now so you can see with your own eyes that they are all right." Evie gently replaced the bandage and combed the hair back from his face with her fingers, "I'm sure your mom is very proud of you. Now let's get you out of this bed," she handed him a robe and left the room.

Without thinking, Ethan slid to the edge of the bed and jumped to his feet, immediately regretting his haste. Even before his feet hit the ground he felt a chill go across his forehead and down his spine as darkness enveloped him.

"HELP! EVIE! HELP!" Tyler's frantic screams cut through the darkness and Ethan became aware that his knees were going soft. In a panic he grabbed for the bed rail to steady himself and was relieved to find the doc's supportive grip instead. Without a harsh word she guided him to the awaiting wheelchair that she had gone to fetch.

"Guess I should have ordered you to take it easy. You're not invincible young man," Evie shook her finger as she lightheartedly lectured him.

"Thanks, Evie. You're right," Ethan belatedly answered after he regained clarity. As Evie wheeled him down the hall, he was bewildered by all the smiles and friendly greetings as they passed. There were beds squeezed into every available room and corridor, but no one seemed to mind the lack of privacy. Instead he observed patients not only caring for other patients, but also engaged in lively conversations and games with each other. Unlike the quiet oppressive corridors he remembered from when his baby sister was born, this hospital was buzzing with laughter and cheerful voices. Ethan was completely overwhelmed with all there was to take in and even thought he saw a clown giving someone stitches. He contemplated asking Evie if the clown was really a doctor, but was afraid it would make him appear nosey and decided not to ask any questions. As they pulled into his parents' room the jovial sounds faded into silence, reminding him of his real reason for being there and his turmoil was visible.

"Ethan, I know you're concerned because they're still unconscious," Evie's concern was both maternal and professional, "We just gave them a sedative so they wouldn't wake up while we were working on them. They are going to be just fine." She knelt down to eye level and squeezed his hand, "Please don't worry about them because they're getting the best care possible right now. You will all be going home in a couple of days."

With the grief for his real family surfacing, Ethan began to sob and impulsively put his arms around the doctor, "Oh Ma..."

Those damn NoTechs! Evie's heart bled and she pushed aside her anger with compassion as she comforted the secretly grieving boy.

"Hey Doc Evie, Guess what," Tyler greeted the doctor as she pushed the wheelchair into the room, "Ethan said he always wanted a baby sister or brother..."

"Did he now? So I take it that you're going to give him his wish," Tyler giggled again and nodded a very big "yes". Evie parked the wheelchair next to Ethan's bed, "Ok, get in. I've got someone I think you'll want to see."

Ethan's eyes lit up with excitement and he quickly hopped off the bed and into the chair, this time without incident. It had been nearly two days since his visit with his parents and he had almost managed to erase their reality from his memory. His breakdown at their earlier visit had convinced the Doc that seeing them unconscious was too painful for him, so she had stopped offering him information about them and he never asked. Rather, Ethan had seized the opportunity presented by their lack of consciousness and blossomed outside of Sam's watchful eyes and the fear they instilled in him. He joyfully immersed himself in life at the hospital, interacting with kids his own age for the first time since the quakes.

He started to forge relationships with some of the other kids and even had a crush on a girl he met at the daily wheelchair races. She had broken her leg jumping from her bedroom window when someone had set fire to their house. When he asked she had blamed some gang called the Nauteks, at least that's what he interpreted through her unfamiliar accent. He thought that might be the same gang Evie had mentioned when asking about his attack, but had been too shy to ask the girl to repeat herself and instead tried to pry the information from Tyler. So he was positive the girl was that someone the Doc was taking him to see now, Evie probably wanted him to console her since she thought they were attacked by the same group.

"Don't I get a clue?" Ethan clasped his hands as he begged.

"No you don't," Evie was mockingly cruel, "Now buckle up, it's going to be a bumpy ride!" She began to push him down the hall at what felt like a very unsafe speed, so he begged her to go faster. Before long they rounded the corner and Evie slowed his chariot to a reasonable speed before they entered the cafeteria, but he was laughing so hard it took him a moment to realize that they had come to a stop. He caught his breath and looked up to see who it was that Evie wanted him to meet so badly and his heart sank draining the blood from his face. He forced his smile back and hoped they wouldn't realize the true reason for the tears in his eyes.

"I thought you might like to have dinner with your parents!" Evie announced, delighted that her surprise had the reaction she'd hoped for, "They've been asking about you ever since they woke late last night. You are one lucky family!" Evie put her hands to her heart as she addressed the family, "It's so good to see such a happy ending. I just wanted you to know what an inspiration your family's story is to the hospital staff..." she glanced at her watch, "Sorry, but I've got to run. I'm going to spend some quality time with my kids." Evie quickly kissed Ethan on the forehead, "You two have raised a really wonderful boy," she turned to leave but paused. "Oh," she spun back around on the balls of her feet, "and I want you to know that you don't have to worry about those NoTechs. I've alerted the local guard unit and they're on the lookout for them...Well, have a great dinner," she waved a final good-bye as she briskly exited the cafeteria.

"Well, Sam was right about ya boy. We certainly can expect great things from ya. So did they give ya a tour?" Jack spoke quietly as he scooped a spoonful of mashed potatoes into his mouth.

"Yes sir. I don't really feel like talking about it right now," Ethan darted his eyes nervously and glanced over his shoulder several times as he spoke, "Can we talk about it when we get *home*?"

"Oh, yeah...Son," Jack mumbled as he too glanced around the thickly populated cafeteria, "The Doc said we'll only have ta stay here uh day or so more, so we can catch up on tha ride home. Til then, what say ya run off an explore with yer new little friends?" he punctuated the comment with a wink.

Ethan let out a deep breath and settled down into his chair, "Yes sir, that's a good idea," he concealed the joy he felt at the temporary reprieve from their watchful eyes, "I'll go right after supper."

"See what uh fine polite boy we've raised," Jack clapped Susan on the back. She coughed in pain, but otherwise made no perceivable change to her slow silent consumption of her meal. It had been nearly a week since Susan had spoken or displayed any hint of emotion, but other than

Ethan, no one who knew her seemed to notice. "See Eth'n, yer ma agrees," Jack callously remarked as he again failed to notice the tip of his nose, "Naw why don't ya run off."

In the warmth of the small pale blue room, the stainless steel felt cool against his exposed skin causing him to reflexively jerk away.

"Oh, does it still hurt that badly? I hope you're not getting an infection," the Doc grew concerned.

"Oh, no, your stethoscope was just cold," Ethan laughed, "that cut is actually not bothering me at all. The nurse said it's not even swollen any more."

"Good to hear it. Then let's try this again. Take a deep breath for me," this time Evie rubbed on the stethoscope to warm it up first, "Well young man, if I didn't know better, I'd say you're in perfect health. We'll probably release you and your parents in the morning. Until then, I suggest you take it easy and get some rest. You don't need to stay confined to the wheelchair anymore, so try going for a walk or maybe you could push Tyler around, just to get your sea legs back before you leave," Evie encouraged him as she helped him to his feet.

"Thanks, Doc. I'll go do that right now. Hey, can I ask you something?"

"Shoot."

"Where are Tyler's parents?" he scratched his head as he nervously twisted in the doorway, "I know I've only been here a few of days, but I still thought theyd've visited by now."

Evie's laughter disappeared and she took on a somber look, "I'll tell you, but don't let Tyler find out that you know. He's a remarkable kid, you know, and he doesn't want people to feel sorry for him. Understood?"

"Understood," he allowed the door to close as he stepped back into the room.

"A month or so ago some Mustangs from the north brought him in. He was in pretty dire shape...multiple fractures, you name it. As I understand it, his family operated one of the outposts that provides shelter and supplies to Mustangs. Anyway, some group had attacked the camp during the night and burned the whole place to the ground. The Mustangs found Tyler unconscious at the foot of a tree house. My guess is that he must have been in his tree house and seen the whole thing happen and at some point he obviously lost his footing and fell to the ground. We have no way of knowing if he has family alive somewhere else," Evie's voice faded with her frustration, "everyone else at the camp was dead."

"Even his parents?" Ethan mouthed, unable to speak.

Evie closed her eyes and nodded in affirmation.

"So the only reason Tyler is alive is because they probably thought he was dead?" Ethan found his voice in anger as he digested what had happened, "Do you know who did it? Was it the NoTechs?" He could feel his face flush and he knew the vein across his forehead was visibly throbbing.

"We're not sure," Evie sighed, "but probably. Who else would do such a thing?"

Ethan could barely control his growing despair at her confirmation of his suspicions and started to pace before the adrenaline pumping through his system clouded his thinking too much. It seemed the more he learned about the "evil doers" of Sam's sermons, the more it became apparent that the only acts of evil being committed were by himself and the others under Sam's, Katie's, and now Josh's leadership. If Sam would do this to strangers he felt had wronged, what would he do to someone in his congregation accused of doing the same? Ethan was terrified for himself and for Tyler and the others. "Doc, why doesn't someone stop them?" the tears began their long delayed journey down his cheeks, subduing his burning rage along the way.

"There's a lot of reasons I guess," Evie's eyes appeared to roll into the back of her head as she searched her mind's library for a simple answer that didn't exist, "Personally, I think people just don't want to accept that there's a war going on, especially after all that's happened in the world."

"War?" Ethan's adolescent mind struggled to process this new possibility, "You really think there's a war going on?"

"Yes I do Ethan," Evie hated giving bad news, but she could sense that this was something he needed to know.

"But how can we be at war?" Ethan didn't like the prospects that a war suggested and fought to discredit her presumption, "No one's invaded. There's no military involved."

"Ethan, you don't have to be invaded for there to be a war. Haven't you covered the Civil War in school yet?"

He shrugged, "I think so, but school seems so long ago."

Evie shook her head in frustration and mumbled to herself, "How can we be expected to learn from our past if it's not being taught well enough to be remembered." She looked back to Ethan and took a deep breath before continuing, "I'm not going to re-teach you American History, but suffice it to say that it's kind of the same here – American against American, brother against brother. Only this time they're not settling for seceding from the Union. This time they're using force to impose their will on the entire country."

"But what if they're right? What if this is what God wants?" his fear visibly pained his face.

"Ethan, don't you think if God wanted to end the world or get rid of one group of people he could do it without the help of a bunch of zealots?" her voice cracked as she struggled to remain objective.

"But what about the military? Why haven't they been called in?" he begged the Doc for reassurances.

"Ethan..." Evie sensed his dropping blood pressure and wrapped her arm around his waist for support, "the reason the military hasn't gotten involved is that there's not a military anymore."

"No military? How? Why would the President do that?" his breathing became erratic as the truth of his situation finally revealed itself and he collapsed into the doc's grip.

Evie guided him back into the wheelchair. "I'm sorry Ethan, I didn't realize that you hadn't even suspected that," she apologized before continuing, "Ethan, there is no more Washington...it's gone. Those earthquakes several weeks ago, they weren't just local. It happened all over the world. Billions of people probably died."

He blinked with disbelief, unable to focus on the onslaught of information as he felt his skin grow cold and was engulfed in blackness.

"Ethan...Ethan...stay with me," Evie ran the smelling salts under his nose until his body tensed with consciousness, "Are you okay?"

He blinked as he gathered all the thoughts that flooded in, "Oh jeez, Doc, I'm sorry. Please don't tell my parents about any of this," he pled in self-preservation.

"Promise. Now let me get you back to your room," she moved to release the brake but Ethan grabbed her hand.

"Wait Doc," he quivered and continued to hold her hand for comfort, "I'm not ready to go back just yet. I'm scared and I don't want Tyler to see me until I've got a handle on it."

She knelt down beside him and cradled his hands in hers, "Oh Ethan. I didn't tell you to make you afraid. I'm so sorry, maybe I should have kept quiet."

"No, I'm glad you told me. I'm too old for people to keep *protecting* me from the world," he took a deep breath as he reigned in his emotions, "Trust me…this is something I *needed* to know."

Evie smiled at him reassuringly, "Okay…good…" She blew a lock of hair from her face, "Well, just so you know, I get scared sometimes too. But Ethan, I promise you that as long as you're here you're safe," her face was stern with her conviction. "Besides, I don't believe for one moment that even the NoTechs are so bad that they would attack a hospital. Even religious fanatics respect the sanctity of a place of healing and dying. And I'm sure they'd just as soon attack a church as they would a hospital."

Her words forced Ethan's stomach into his feet and he swallowed in protest, "I just don't know doc. I don't think they should be trusted even that little bit."

"Maybe so. Guess it's just the healer in me that won't allow me to see anyone as hopeless," she winked at him and let out a small giggle, "Anywho, there are others who think like you, so we're prepared, just in case you should be right."

Ethan visibly relaxed and the color slowly returned to his face, "Thanks Doc, that makes me feel a lot better. You know…'Live for the best, prepare for the worst,' my parents used to say that a lot," he laughed sadly as he reminisced about his Mom and Dad. "Doc, don't you think that these NoTechs need to be punished? I know you said you're ready in case they attack, but what about all the people they've already hurt? What about justice?" his voice cracked as he tried to mask the true despair he felt.

"Ethan, the right thing to do isn't always the obvious or easy thing to do. And you're right, there needs to be justice," Evie rubbed her face in frustration, "but the fact is we barely have enough people to function now. At the hospital there's not even a half dozen doctors total! And we've all spent nearly every moment since the quakes working to keep people alive. If we started sending people off to fight there'd be no one left!"

"But the NoTechs are evil. Somebody needs to punish them!" Ethan's guilt now filled his words.

"You're right, they should be punished, but I don't think anyone is evil..."

"How can you say that? How can you not think they're evil?" he vehemently interrupted as he finally lost his hold on all the emotions he had been suppressing since his parents' death.

Evie wheeled her stool closer and embraced the sobbing boy in an effort to console him. "Ethan, it will be okay," she cooed softly into his ear, "Everything will work its way out. It always does, you just need to have a little faith." She continued to rock with Ethan until she felt him relax and his sobs quieted.

"Doc...thank you," he mumbled as he wiped his nose on his sleeve, "I didn't realize how much everything has upset me."

"Are you going to be okay?" Evie's concern was evident as she habitually checked his vitals.

He let out a cathartic laugh, "Yes, I actually think I'm feeling better than I have in a long time."

"That's good to hear," she offered him a wet towel to wipe his face with, "You do seem different somehow."

As Ethan handed the towel back to Evie she realized that she almost didn't recognize the boy in him anymore. She couldn't put her finger on it, but she sensed a significant change in him.

Ethan carefully studied the earth under his feet and kicked another pine cone out of his path as he walked. He watched it skim across the leaves littering the ground and then bounce off of a tree root before it found its final resting place on the edge of the path. With the end of the momentary distraction, he returned his gaze to the path directly below his feet. A cool breeze off the water came through the trees allowing him to feel the contrasting warmth of his breath against his chest. Ethan breathed deeper and sighed.

"Eth'n, could ya lift yer end uh little more? Yer startin ta drag," Martha called from behind, but her voice sounded faint and far away.

Without removing his gaze from his own footsteps, Ethan tightened his grip on the basket's handle and straightened his posture until the resistance from the dragging subsided.

"Are ya okay, Eth'n? Ya've been awfully quiet since ya got back," Martha pried now that they were within the privacy of the woods. She had recognized the change in him the moment he had returned to camp, but she had ignored it – she knew better than to do anything that might cause anyone else to take notice.

Ethan sighed and increased their pace, eager for the camouflage of the swift moving river. He was fairly certain that Josh was having him followed, so the natural sound barrier created by the moving waters was the only way he could keep his secrets from prying ears without raising any other suspicions. As they set their burden down near the bank of the river he scanned the area, darting his eyes to alert Martha of their observers' location before grabbing a handful of laundry and a bar of soap and settling on the riverbank. A moment later, Martha did the same and sat down next to him.

Making sure to always face the water, Ethan spoke quietly while scrubbing someone's ragged old T-shirt, "Martha," he sighed, "I can't go through with it...the people there were so nice. They're good people and they don't deserve this...ya know what they're planning, right?"

From a distance Martha appeared to be singing hymns like she always did while she worked. Her body rocked and her arms swayed with the music as she sang quietly, "Than Eth'n...ya need ta stop'em...Go back'n warn'em whilst there's still time...Sam 'eez still out thare..."

Ethan scrubbed at a difficult stain and moaned, "But they're always watching..."

Martha built up a good lather, stretched, and reached for a high note, "They'll leave or tire evenchally...Sam left yester morn...so nothin's keep'n em in line..." she took a deep breath and continued her serenade as wads of soap suds flew off her hands, "Than ya'll leave...than ya'll leave...folla tha rivahhhh..." Martha wound herself up for the big finally, "AMEN!" she hooted loud enough for the sound to carry over the rushing waters.

The sound of slopping wet clothes and water dripping on tile heralded the severity of the situation as Martha stormed into the meeting room. Her tears were lost in the rivulets dripping from her hair, but her sobs and gasps memorialized their presence. Gasping for breath, Martha collapsed to the ground as she nearly blacked out. She had rushed back to camp faster than she had ever dreamed she could run, but now it appeared that her speed had robbed her of the voice she urgently needed.

"Oh Dear, someone help her!" Martha could hear someone yell and realized that she was suddenly being surrounded by people.

"Okay, let me through. Martha, what's wrong?" she recognized Josh's bellowing voice as she rested like a limp rag doll in someone's embrace.

"Eth'n...hurreh..." she struggled dramatically for the breath to speak. "Rivah..." Martha managed to give way to the darkness before the word had fully left her lips.

10

Empowered with knowledge of frailty and fault,
The fellows prepare, the snake they will halt...

The growing rumble in his stomach was so loud that Ethan was surprised he could hear himself think. It had been two days since his last meal and the hunger pains were now so intense that he found it impossible to sleep or even just relax. He had been avoiding the well traveled paths, afraid of discovery by the thugs he was sure Josh had sent after him, but it was too dark to find his way through the deep woods. So after wasting what felt like hours lying awake in misery, Ethan decided to take his chances along the main road. Being two days away from camp, he figured his chances of finding help were marginally greater than getting caught and he could always claim he was lost and trying to find his way back since

Martha assured him that she would make them believe his fall into the river was nothing more than a tragic accident. Besides, if he didn't find help soon then the risks he had taken by escaping would have been for nothing because he was sure that he would be dead. Desperate, Ethan gathered the last of his strength and started to make his way to wherever the trail led.

As the minutes and then hours passed painfully like the stones beneath his feet, Ethan failed to notice his stride evolve into a stagger when his hip went numb from the stress of his uneven gait. But as painful as his physical traumas were they were paled by the mental ordeal of his growing delirium. The near drowning during his tumble down river was barely a memory as his mind raced between thoughts of food – burgers sizzling on a grill...a super sized order of fries – to visions of Tyler's and Evie's lifeless bodies and landscapes blanketed in blood, each vision intensifying his anger while simultaneously loosening his grip on reality. He pushed blindly along the forest trail driven by a growing anger that threatened to overwhelm him...Oh, how he hated Sam and his hypocrisy! Sam had gone on and on about living simply and not taking any shortcuts, but he had not hesitated one moment about using the horses they had stolen. Ethan fed his starved and broken body with his anger for Sam, making it an even greater struggle to hold on to reality. He was barely aware of anything beyond his next foot step, yet the familiar sound of hooves clapping on the hardened trail behind him managed to grab the last threads of his consciousness.

SAM!!...Ethan screamed the name in his thoughts. Sam had found him first! He had failed! He knew there was no avoiding capture as he heard the clatter of hooves accelerate and grow louder. He was helpless to save himself, much less Tyler and the others. Once again, everyone he cared about was going to die and it was all his fault! Martha had warned him that Sam was out here and he had still chosen to risk the main road. He should have just waited till daylight!

Suddenly, the hoof steps came to a stop directly behind him and Ethan decided to make one last attempt at freedom. He breathed as deeply as he could through his sobs and pushed his body into a sprint toward the cover of the woods. But it was more than his starved body could handle and his footing slipped, sending him rushing head first toward the hardened ground. Ethan's clouded mind didn't even register whether everything went black before or after his head hit the rocks.

With the waxing moon's surrender to the full moon almost complete, the night-time landscape was illuminated with a haunting glow. The pearlescent light caused the world to take on a dark emerald hue and the deep indigo sky sparkled with the shards of a mirror reflecting a bygone world. Still more moonlight reflected off the rocks and shells embedded in the now well traveled dirt road, making it appear that a luminescent trail was unfolding before her eyes with each step. Jez allowed her eyes to wander and take in the beauty even as she maintained her extra sensory observation of the path before her. It was a quiet night aside from the rhythmic tapping of Trace's hooves on the shells and the barely audible roar of the nearby river. Occasionally the light breeze would pick up enough to rustle the leaves, allowing the moonlight to dance all around her. Jez took a deep breath and savored the fleeting relief from the day's heat and the incessant threat of the NoTechs.

With the summer entering its peak, the darkness seemed to provide less and less relief from the heat even with the daily rain showers. But then, comfort had little to do with Jez's decision to travel only at night. That had been a purely tactical decision since the darkness and shadows provided her with a distinct advantage now that she had developed her extra sensory abilities to the point where she could perceive the reality of one location while simultaneously experiencing her own immediate physical reality. The tricky part was being able to distinguish between the two, so she had enlisted Puk as her Watcher. Whenever she felt disoriented she would whistle an "SOS" and Puk would pull her back into her own reality. With each episode the rapport between Jez and Puk had grown, so that now he would appear often as the first note left her lips. Having such a strong bond had given Jez the confidence to venture farther and farther away each time and she finally had established the range to use the perception to not only scout the area ahead of her, but more importantly, to hone in on her family's trail. Once she visualized her mother and her sister traveling, her mind made an intuitive leap to their side and she knew which way to go. Having picked up their trail earlier in the day, Jez was now focused only on detecting any NoTechs or other dangers that might cross her path.

She instinctively tightened her grip on the hilt of the rifle resting in her lap, slowly and steadily raising the muzzle and causing its cool steel to grow warm in her grasp. In unison, Trace slowed his gait and Jez quickly leapt back to review her own immediate surroundings more closely after detecting the presence of someone along the road a few hundred yards ahead of them. She had been so shocked by the level of anger radiating from him that she had withdrawn before discerning anything else. Being able to project her consciousness ahead of them was great for detecting potential hazards, but she needed to have her full wits about her in order to do anything about it. As if in agreement with her, Puk decreased the distance between them and kept his teeth bared in challenge to anyone that might consider approaching the group.

The trio paced the remaining distance to the stranger in a cautious silence, their bond allowing them to interact as a single being and assuring them a degree of invisibility. Now, as they moved along the shadows Jez studied the man in the moonlight. In her earlier vision she only had time to note that he was a tall male, but now she was able to make out his features. Despite the relative darkness, his unkempt state was as clear as his tattered clothing and his erratic stride. There was something eerily familiar about this dark haired man, but Jez was distracted before she could make any connections as his intense anger suddenly evaporated into an equally intense fear. Her curiosity aroused by the change, Jez urged Trace forward to approach him.

"O happy day...O joyful hour! When freed from earth my soul shall tower...Beyond the reach of Satan's power...To be forever blest..." Sam's taxed voice still carried across the dark forest as he fervently sang his favorite hymnals in a desperate attempt to drive away the memories that had relentlessly pursued him since his visit home. As if he might outrun them, he had pushed himself to ride nonstop, losing track of how many days had elapsed, or even how much distance he had covered.

The oppressive heat wore on him and he struggled for relief. He stood for a while in the stirrups and adjusted himself in hopes that he might assuage his growing discomfort at least a bit. His hand ached where he had chafed the old wound raw again and he involuntarily stroked the sweat dampened bandage. His mother would have been so disappointed in the state he kept the aggravating bandage. A scowl edged its way across his face, sealing his lips against the songs he had used as a shield. With no other means of escape, the tune in his subconscious sought release with each breath and before long Sam was humming a melody that had only haunted his dreams until that moment.

"I feel so lonely baby...I feel so lonely, I could die..." the deep voice from the radio blended with his mom's soulful voice as she sang to pass the time while she went through her nightly routine in the kitchen, washing, rinsing, drying. She had a beautiful voice and he wondered why she only sang at night when she thought she was alone. The boy knew he was supposed to be asleep, but he loved to listen to his mom sing and this was the only way he ever got to hear her since his father had declared that he was too old for lullabies.

So he sat quietly in the dark by his bedroom door which was cracked just barely enough for him to rest his ear along the opening and listen. Samuel fought the urge to hum along because he knew that she would not just be upset that he had disobeyed her and stayed up, but she would stop singing. So he sat there still and quiet listening in the dark and with each chorus the boy found it harder and harder to stay awake. Maybe he wasn't too old for lullabies after all.

"BITCH!" Samuel shot up at the sound of his father bursting into the house. He could feel the walls shake as the front door slammed shut and

the floors echoed with each forceful step of his father bounding toward the kitchen. Still half asleep, Samuel continued to sit quietly in the dark, confused by both his father's untimely return home from work and the angry screams rushing down the hall.

"I'm sorry...I'm sorry," he could hear his mom plead over the crashing of pots and pans.

"BITCH! You told that damn doctor of yours," the anger in his father's voice and the breaking glass sent chills down the boy's spine, "He came to see me at work today!"

"Honey...please...you'll wake Samuel," his mom's quivering voice was barely audible over the running water and the clatter of her sweeping up broken dishes. The boy wrapped his arms about himself to keep from shaking as he slowly walked barefoot down the hall. "Just let me clean up in here and we can talk about it outside...Please," the despair in her voice terrified Samuel and he froze now that he could see into the kitchen. His mom was frantically trying to finish the last few pots and pans left in the sink even as his father continued to throw what was left of the dishes at her. He could see the tears streaking her face and nearly cried out when he noticed her cheek was all purple and bruised. "Please...honey..." she begged in a whisper.

For a moment there was complete quiet aside from the radio and running water and Samuel edged closer to the kitchen. His father was pacing, the anger visibly radiating off him like the steam that rises after a storm on a hot summer day. He was intent on punishing her so deeply she would never consider disobeying him again. And in the next instant his father had his answer as his mom contemplated the risks involved in shutting the radio off, her eyes briefly darting to the object of her thoughts before returning back to the dirty dishes.

The following moment his father struck out at his mom's very soul, "You WHORE!" he cursed her as he aimed all his anger at the radio, sending it flying.

Busy scrubbing a greasy pie tin, his mom only looked up when something flashed in her peripheral vision, but it was too late.

"No..." the single syllable managed to escape her lips before the radio sank beneath the suds and the circuit was complete.

Samuel stood wide eyed in the kitchen doorway, unable to move, lost in time. Finally, his father nudged his mom with his boot as he turned to leave the kitchen.

"This never happened," his father casually walked past without a second glance.

The boy watched over his shoulder until his father disappeared into the living room and the noises of a million different voices began to trickle out. Slowly, as if walking on broken glass, he tiptoed across the room to his mother. Sam grabbed his mother's wrist to take her pulse and was confused when her rigid body resisted.

"Ma..." he wailed and shook her by the shoulders to wake her, "Maaaa..."

"SAM! Stop! You're hurting me," a distant voice pled.

Sam's abdomen ached and he transferred his own convulsions to her as he continued to shake his mother, "Maaa...wake up...come on Ma...I know you're still here!" the boy screamed as loud as he could, he didn't care if his father heard him.

"Please...Sam..." the voice grew fainter.

"Mama...I can hear you...that's it. Wake up Mama," Sam encouraged his mother, "I'll never let you go again!" he embraced her with everything his little nine year old frame had.

"Can't...breathe...Sam..."

"Hey, take a look at this," Becka handed the binoculars to the man lying next to her while she simultaneously dipped another chip into the bowl of salsa resting in the fold of her lap.

"Not unless it's an emergency. It's your watch," the man grumbled and pushed her offering away, rolling over so that his back was to her.

"Ok, then. It's an emergency!" she squealed, but a sense of mischief was in her voice, "Now look!" She quickly popped the salsa laden chip into her mouth so that her chewing would disguise her laughter. The call had come in over an hour ago and she had only been able to contain her excitement from him because he was asleep. Now she fought to conceal her news until the last possible moment because she wanted to see his reaction.

The man finally announced his surrender to her prodding with a loud groan as he sat up, rubbing his face and stretching in the process. Becka again handed him the binoculars and indicated the area that he needed his attention. Slowly both his eyes and the viewfinder came into focus and he nearly lost his breath, "You've got to be kidding me! Is that really who I think it is?" he sought confirmation from the mischievously smiling woman.

"It surely is!" Becka burst as she wiped salsa from the corner of her mouth, "So does this qualify as an emergency?"

"I can't believe this! I really thought I'd never see her again. Did you know about this? Can you take charge here? Let Bess know what's going on?" the man rattled on nervously as he pled for his release.

"Go! Zeke," Becka reached out for the binoculars he tossed at her as she spoke and he was gone before she had even tightened her grip.

With the skill of a seasoned fire fighter, Zeke hooked each foot along the side rails of the ladder and quickly slid down, leaping to his feet before ever touching the ground. In his excitement he had forgotten to grab his flashlight, so as he ran through the moonlit courtyard he awkwardly fumbled for the spare he kept tucked in his belt. Zeke refused to stop for even a second, afraid that some unknown danger would tear her away before he reached her. Almost from the moment that she had disappeared into the trees, he had regretted their separation. He couldn't even remember what on earth had compelled him to stay behind. What an idiot he was, any other man would have followed a woman like that to the ends of the earth. But now Zeke felt blessed beyond words, his Jez was back!

Jez had felt his familiar presence long before the settlement was visible. He was sleeping. She could even feel the softness of the down pillow his head rested on and smell his light musk scent, which made the back of her neck tingle. Jez smiled and ran her fingers along the erect follicles down her neck line, even before she had developed her present abilities she had always known when he was near. They had a bond that only the greatest poets had ever dared describe with mere words. She had nearly abandoned the search for her family because of the intensity of her feelings for him and even though she had managed to leave him to continue on her journey, that bond and her feelings for Zeke had never faltered. It was only by suppressing a part of herself behind a very thick wall of denial that she had been able to ignore the pain of their separation and stay focused. Now that she was finally close enough to "feel" him again, Jez could sense her carefully built wall coming down, then a light in the darkness appeared and the wall was gone. Only the weight of the unconscious man in her lap restrained Trace from bursting into a full gallop from Jez's deluge of anticipation.

With the shaft freed from his belt loop, Zeke effortlessly switched on his Maglite as he ran and nearly doubled his pace. He could hardly tolerate the anxiety as he grew close enough to see her distinctive silhouette approaching and he effortlessly increased his speed again to meet hers, filling his ears with his heaving breath and the rushing wind. Zeke strained his eyes to see clearer in the passing darkness, but Jez seemed to be cloaked by the shadows. He wondered if she had taken to wearing camouflage but restrained his desire to see her face, keeping the beam low on the ground to avoid blinding her and Trace as they grew closer. Instead, he focused his body on eliminating the distance between them and time seemed to vaporize. He was sure that not more than a heartbeat had passed from the moment he first recognized her silhouette to when he was finally able to make out her features by the moonlight. Zeke could feel the smile engulfing his face and was glad that he had refrained from shining the flashlight on her. He had forgotten how she seemed to actually glow under the moonlight and for a moment he lost track of the world and nearly called out to her between breaths, unaware of and unconcerned for the sleeping settlement. With their eyes locked he was paralyzed in her gaze, suddenly they were together – he could feel her inside of his mind as if they stood there with their bodies in a tight embrace.

Hey, I've missed you, Zeke heard with both his mind and his ears.

"Cool trick. Now get down here," he acknowledged her mental greeting as he held the limp body steady so she could slide off the saddle, "So who are we rescuing now?"

As Jez slid across Zeke during her dismount she gently caressed his cheek while quickly kissing him hello, "I don't know. I was on my way here and he passed out on the trail right in front of me. He hit his head pretty hard and I think he's dehydrated. Anyway, help me get him down, we've got company coming," she nodded her head indicating the greeting party approaching from the settlement.

"Do you always have to make such a scene every time you visit?" Zeke chided her as they settled the man on the ground, "you do realize that *this* is definitely going to cut into our *catch up time...*"

Jez silenced him with a kiss before he could waste any more time, they still had a few minutes alone before the welcoming party reached them.

The tolling bamboo chimes played in time with the rustling blinds as they danced along the steady breeze which blew through the bungalow's row of large open windows. The bungalow had been built to utilize the new weather patterns so there was almost always a breeze to temper the heat, but as the morning aged the additional warmth created by the body next to him caused Zeke to rouse prematurely. With his eyes still closed he nuzzled his face into her hair and inhaled deeply, filling his lungs with her floral scent and reflexively tightening his gentle embrace with her. Slowly he opened one eye and then the other, carefully taking in the vision of the woman entwined with him. Not wanting to wake her, he allowed his fingers to just barely trace the contour of her. Yes, this was his Jez curled up next to him, it had not been just another painfully vivid dream. He lovingly brushed a wisp of hair from her face before lightly stroking her eyebrows and brushing his fingertips against her long lashes.

"Mmmm," Jez purred, "good morning." She snuggled even closer to him despite the growing heat, "Mmmm, you feel so good…"

Zeke flushed, "How long have you been awake?"

"Only just," she slowly opened her eyes.

"Oh, sorry, I didn't mean to wake you, but I couldn't help it, you're just so damn beautiful when you're asleep," he looked like an errant puppy seeking forgiveness as he hovered just above her.

Jez reached out with her free hand and pulled his face to hers so that their lips just barely touched. Slowly she whispered so that he could feel her words with his lips, "You…are…forgiven."

Zeke swiftly let his weight close the distance between them as he completed the kiss she had begun. He savored everything about her, letting his tongue guide him he planted kisses along the full of her lips and down her neck. And with each kiss he noticed that the tingling sensation she inspired spread a little farther until he was sure that every inch of his skin was shooting off sparks. Every touch, caress, and kiss was infinitely multiplied as it echoed along each nerve. He eagerly explored the soft folds of her skin and was rewarded with the sensation of being explored as much more than just their bodies merged. For a moment they existed only for each other in a place devoid of time and space, simultaneously enraptured by both their own and each others' passion. Then, slowly, their awareness of the growing heat in the bungalow returned as the holds of passion faded with their mutual release.

Zeke took a swig from the water bottle he kept next to the bed before handing it to Jez and collapsing spread eagle back on the bed. "Whew! I'm afraid to ask what other skills you've picked up since the last time I saw you," he playfully complemented her.

"I'll give you a full demonstration later," she giggled at her own attempt to sound sultry.

"Well then, we'd better go grab some breakfast. I want to be at full strength for your demonstration," he winked at her as he jumped out of bed.

Out of habit, Jez psychically scanned her surroundings as she got ready to start her day, "Oh Shit!"

"Are you okay Jez?" Zeke rushed to her side and attempted to help her sit down.

She shooed away his efforts as she rushed to dress herself, "I'm fine...I'm fine," she gave him a reassuring smile, "It's just the man I brought in last night. He's starting to come out of it and I want to be there before he comes to."

"Oh," relief washed over his face, "You definitely need to brief me on all your new skills later."

She gave him an apologetic kiss on the cheek, "I will...Promise. Now let's get moving."

Through the drawn shades, filtered sunlight gently bathed the room in a pale light and once Jez's eyes adjusted she realized that the clinic was empty except for the man resting in the cot next to the far window. She slowly made her way past the empty beds, trying to avoid disturbing the loose floorboards or make any other noise that might rouse him prematurely, she had this nagging sensation of familiarity with the man that she wanted answers to before he fully regained consciousness. Jez was sure that this sense of obligation she had towards him was somehow tied up in that familiarity because past experience had taught her the emotional ties she developed with people she encountered were never random, there was always a reason. She knew the reason here was somehow linked to her past.

Standing at his bedside, Jez searched for something that might reveal his identity. His dark hair was not quite chin length and he had a light intermittent beard. She racked her brain trying to remember the various people she had encountered in the vicinity both before and after the CAT. Could he be from one of the nearby settlements? Why did he run from her? Was somebody after him? Jez closed her eyes and slowed her breathing as she settled into the worn office chair beside his bed. She had made a connection with him before, but his thoughts were so erratic then that she couldn't focus. Perhaps if she tried again while he was still unconsciousness she could pick up on some answers to her questions.

She took another deep breath and then, as she exhaled, she slowly and methodically cleared her mind except for her focus on the man next to her, commanding her subconscious to be a blank slate. Once she had ceased all the rambling thoughts in her head Jez searched the void for some sensation of the man's consciousness to lock on to. She allowed her psyche to fill with only the presence of him until a shape began to appear in the mist of her mind's eye. As it took form Jez was able to see distinct images in a type of mental slide show. Suddenly her mind was filled with visions of fire and running, everything was covered in red. Jez gasped for breath, not in synchronicity with the running in her mind, but with the awful and instantaneous realization that this man was somehow involved in the horrors being committed by that terrorist group the NoTechs.

Abruptly, the man sat up in bed screaming, the lost connection with Jez stimulating his brain enough to allow him to break out of his repeating nightmare. His eyes shot open and he looked around to reassure himself that the visions had just been a horrible dream. Jez's gaze immediately locked on the man's distinctive blue eyes and she remembered. Despite her remarkable increase in strength – both physically and mentally – over the past months, there was a part of her that cringed with remembered fear.

"Oh my god...It's you!..." she screamed as she leapt to her feet, "Ethan!" Instantly regretting her outburst, Jez rocked in place alternating from foot to foot as she sought composure. She forced herself to speak in a controlled tone by holding her hand over her mouth as she spoke, "You're the kid who returned my pack after you helped that man beat and rob me?...you're...a...NoTech?!," she could barely get the words out as she fought to process the simultaneous disbelief, anger, and gratitude swirling around her consciousness. In a seemingly intentional contrast to Jez's heated reaction, the young man sat there silently motionless, still under the hold of her unrelenting gaze. He had made no attempt to speak or move once his initial screams had faded and Jez found herself questioning the legitimacy of her anger.

But before she could finish her thought the door swung open and slammed back against the wall, commanding her to turn and witness Zeke and Bess rushing into the room. The next moment Zeke was pulling her protectively into his arms, his stare challenging the man that had threatened his Jez.

"Wait! Miss, you don't understand," now released from Jez's mental grip Ethan found his tongue. "It's not what you think. I need to explain. Please!" desperation saturated his voice as he begged, "You have to listen to me..." Tears began to stream down his face and his lip quivered as the physical and emotional trials of the last few days threatened to catch up with him.

Jez closed her eyes and willed herself to take a deep breath from her diaphragm, focusing on the warmth of Zeke's embrace. Finally, reassured by Zeke's physical presence, she began to recover from her initial shock and her anger dissipated. Despite this young man's – no, boy's – collusion with the man that had attacked her, she owed him a great deal of gratitude. If he had not taken the risk to return her pack, there was a good chance that she would not have survived. And even though that might seem to a stranger to be a small gesture, she had always known how much courage it must have taken for him to defy the older man because, as clouded as she had been by her own fear, even then she had felt the terror the older man instilled in the boy. With her mind now clear, Jez could sense the fear rising off of Ethan with an alarming intensity that conveyed urgency more than his words ever would. She accepted that Ethan was not a willing participant in the NoTech's activities and she knew he was trustworthy. Jez settled into her acceptance of this extra sensory knowledge and her strength and confidence returned to the surface. She pulled away from Zeke's protective grasp, maintaining only the slightest touch, finger tip to finger tip, "It's okay Zeke, I just overreacted," she answered his concern as he followed her with his eyes. "So Ethan, please explain why you were running through the woods in the middle of the night. Do you know where the NoTech camp is?" she calmly requested his explanation.

Ethan was staring at his lap, watching his hands as he twisted and pulled the sheet nervously. He remembered her now and the memory flooded his mind with shame and regret in addition to the lingering terror he felt. He knew that once he looked up his eyes would announce his shame and he would be caught in her gaze. As he searched for the right words Ethan inhaled deeply and held the air in his lungs until it went stale. He slowly raised his head as he exhaled, the air as bitter as the memories he released with it, "So you don't want me to explain that night first?" Ethan questioned as he looked her directly in the eyes.

"No Ethan, I don't. Maybe we can go into that later, but right now there's obviously something more important bothering you," Jez made her peace with him and felt the last of the weight from her anger dissolve.

This time Ethan didn't feel trapped by her stare, "Okay...um...you're right," he directed his attention to the entire group as he spoke, "there is a NoTech camp around here somewhere, but I got all turned around and I'm not sure where it is anymore...I'm sorry..." he looked at Jez expecting her former anger to return.

"It's okay Ethan. We'll figure out where it is together," she took his hand and urged him along.

Relieved, Ethan tightened his grip on her hand and looked directly into her eyes, "Um...there's something else...something a lot worse that I need to warn you about first." He swallowed and blinked away the tears welling in his eyes again as he prepared to divulge the nightmare he had been living for the past few months. Ethan thought of the Doc and Tyler and for the first time since his escape, their images weren't bathed in blood.

"That will be sixteen hundred dollars, thank you very much," Becka politely demanded, her grin reaching from ear to ear, "I hope you enjoyed your stay with us."

The boy rolled his eyes and yawned, "Yes, I know...that's the third time I've landed on Boardwalk to..."

"This is Charlie Tango Niner Delta..." the radio buzzed, "Do you copy?"

Aggravated with his loosing streak, the boy seized on the interruption, "You'd better answer that Becka...Guess we'll have to put this game on hold," he volunteered the obvious.

"...Charlie Tango Niner Delta. Do you copy?" the man's voice rang out again as Becka leapt to the console oblivious to the boy's sarcasm.

"Yes, Charlie Tango Niner Delta, we copy. This is Bravo Delta Charlie Alpha," Becka responded as she logged the transmission, "How can we help you?"

"Is that you Becka? Haven't heard your lovely voice in a while. This is Jack," Becka yawned, attempting to conceal the grin that familiar name inspired, and switched the broadcast to her headphones, "I'm trying to get a message to the Mustang Jez Kyle. Remember her?"

"Yes, it's me Becka, the one and only. Good to hear from you Jack. I remember Jez, but she isn't here right now. I can take a message for her though," anxious to get past the formalities of official business, Becka quickly scribbled on a Post-It as he spoke.

> Jez 3.38
> Notech camp abandoned. What next - Alex

"Got it," she confirmed the transmission as she beckoned the boy to abandon his post by the game board, "Go post this on the message board, will ya?"

"Becka? You still there?" Jack called her attention away from the boy and her duties.

"Still here Jack, so how ya been?" she settled comfortably into her chair with the mike in her lap as soon as she heard the door click shut.

The eerie call of a lone owl drifted along the night air and was quickly answered by the shuffle of brush and the snapping of twigs. Life in the forest flourished under the darkness of the new moon, creating a picturesque night landscape that remained a stunning beauty reserved for nonhuman eyes. In stride Puk sniffed the air inquisitively before howling a greeting to a distant cousin somewhere in the night. Aside from the forest's nightlife, it was a quiet night and he and Jez led Zeke and Ethan uneventfully through the dark to the edge of the tree-line.

Zeke adjusted his night vision binoculars until the silhouette of the converted campus came into view. As he slowly panned the horizon for traces of light or movement Jez followed along his line of site.

"All quiet, it looks like everyone's probably sleeping," he whispered and passed the binoculars to Jez.

"No thanks, I can see just fine," she nudged Ethan with the binoculars in offering, "and you're right Hon, everyone's asleep." She pathed to both Zeke and Ethan, *even the mice,* she grinned as she managed to insert a mental giggle.

"Thanks Jez," Zeke ruffled her hair and gave her a quick peck on the cheek, "I'm still not used to having our own psychic surveillance system." He continued to speak aloud for Ethan since only Jez could hear his thoughts, "I still think we should make our way around to check out the other side of the campus though. Just so we're all equally familiar with the layout."

"Absolutely," Jez simultaneously spoke and pathed, "and I'm still really more like your own personal Doppler radar. I still need to see things the old fashioned way to get a complete picture."

"More like SUPER Doppler," Zeke laughed quietly at her self assessment. Somehow she always managed to lighten up even the darkest situation, at least for a moment, "So Ethan, do you know which building they're using to store the explosives and other stuff at?"

Ethan studied the campus through the binoculars for a while before pointing off into the distance, "I'm pretty sure it's that one there on the far right," he unconsciously gestured toward the building as he spoke. "Right there, where there's no windows. It was a storage room for the bookstore I think. Anyway, I'm pretty sure they burned it all," his growing disgust for Sam and the lot curled off his tongue, instantly dissolving the minor respite from the direness of the situation.

Zeke retrieved the binoculars from Ethan, "Uhm, okay, I see it," he quickly panned across the horizon to study the opposite side of the campus, "Ethan, please tell me the sleeping quarters are on the other side of the campus." He had made his peace with what had to be done in order to disarm this dangerous cult, but he still hoped they could get it done with very few casualties, or better yet, no casualties.

"They are...the blast won't reach that far anyways, right?" Ethan realized for the first time that there was a possibility that he had made the wrong decision. Could he just be substituting the murder of one group for another?

"I'm not sure Ethan," Zeke was grateful the darkness masked the doubt on his face, "I won't know that until I've seen how much and what type of explosives there are." He wrapped his arm around Jez protectively, "But I can promise you that we will do everything possible to evacuate the area. Besides, we're still hopeful that this can be done without actually having to detonate them at all."

"You really think that's possible!" Ethan buried his doubts in anger, "Sam is hoping to usher in Armageddon, do you really think he's going to walk away quietly into the sunset?"

"No one wants this to turn into another religious war Ethan," Jez automatically rubbed the lump protruding from her pack where the vials were stored, "and we're not going to allow this Sam to force us into one...You are still confident that your friend Martha can pull this off?"

Ethan focused off into the night where he knew Martha was sleeping, "You said it takes a few hours for it to take effect right?"

"Yes, that's right. And there's no taste or smell."

"Then yes, I'm sure she can get it done," Ethan answered definitively, "She'll do whatever it takes to stop that man...and so will I!"

"Well then, let's make our way back to the gear and radio Bess with our twenty," Zeke urged Jez to begin leading the way, "She's only got a couple of days to get everyone here."

The sun stretched its rays across the clear sky as it heralded the beginning of a new day. Already people were buzzing about the campus, filling the corridors and courtyards with a medley of chatter, laughter, and footsteps. A stranger would have assumed that school was back in session, but Jez knew better and made sure that she stayed within the tree-line and just out of view. She had been able to track Josh down during an earlier surveillance session thanks to Ethan's meticulous description and her previous encounter with the man. Now all she could do was sit and listen and hope to overhear something important. For once she envied Kara's ability to overhear anyone's thoughts as she sensed that there was a lot going on with Josh that he wasn't saying. So despite her growing frustration and sense of urgency, Jez continued to sit there quietly listening.

"Pastor Frank, Ah jus wanna make sure ya know what uh pleasure an honor it's been work'n with tha man that raised Sam," Josh smothered Sam's mentor in praise as thick as the syrup on their pancakes.

Frank coughed and took a sip of his tea as was his habit every time any attention was turned his way, "Speak'n uh Sam, when's he due back?"

"Umm..." Josh quickly swallowed as he mentally reviewed their schedule, "Any time now actually. We're all ready ta mobilize once he arrives an gives us tha word..."

Frank excitedly held his hand up to silence Josh. "Chirp...Chirp...Chirp..." an electronic ring sang out across the field.

"Did ya hear that beep'n Josh?" Frank cupped his hand around his ear while he turned his head to pinpoint the foreign sound's origin.

"AAAAAHHHHHHH!..." a woman's blood curdling screams nearly deafened Frank as the calm of the young morning was shattered.

"Oh!" Jez burst before biting her lip to silence herself, *SHIT!* She nearly fell over backwards as she hastily turned in retreat while awkwardly attempting to silence the errant walkie.

"Pastor, did ya hear where that come fra?" Josh rambled as he spun to face the woods and flew out of his chair, sending it flying to the pavement.

Groaning, Frank hurried to stand, "Uh...Ah thank it come from thatta ways," he began to waddle across the field toward the tree-line.

There was another scream and Josh ran off at a labored pace, screaming back over his shoulder, "Pastor, go fetch tha men...Ah'll meet ya out there!"

11

*Of peace and of blood,
They will challenge in battle,
The messenger falls, the foundation rattles...*

Sam couldn't understand why his mother refused to wake up. She had spoken to him just moments before and he thought he could hear her screaming for him now, but her eyes stayed closed and the only tears on her face were his. They had stained her face with streaks of pink flesh as they washed away the layers of dirt before dripping down into her bright red hair.

"Ma!...Please!...Please wake up now!..." he struggled to speak through his sobs.

Even though Sam could feel her going cold in his arms, he leaned down to her and focused on the mole by her brow the way he always did whenever she confided in him. He tried to will her awake, but her repeated silence caused him to retreat further into himself until he could barely see beyond the tears clouding his eyes. He couldn't hear the voices from the television anymore, even his mother's distant wails had faded away. Yet the weight of her in his arms taunted him with the fact that he wasn't just suffering though some horrible nightmare. Sam wailed and tightened his grip, he couldn't let her go, not now...

Josh could hear the screaming clearly and slowed his stride to a cautious jog so he could scan the shadows along the tree-line for the frightened woman. He was already sweating heavily and his eyes burned from the salt, making it difficult to focus beyond the leading edge of the trees, but he was reluctant to stop even though that meant running nearly blind. Instead, he did his best to navigate by following just the sound of the woman's cries, but as the screams grew more and more erratic that became nearly impossible. Finally the screaming faded to intermittent sobs and Josh decided his only option was to stop and regroup. He fished the bottom of his shirt up high enough to wipe the sweat from his eyes and dry his brow before taking a moment to carefully survey the area. Frank was no where to be seen and the sobbing was growing louder again. He couldn't wait for them any longer and reluctantly started to make his way down the trail leading into the forest. Although the change in light made it more difficult to see, he could still make out the figure of a frantic woman far down the path and began to run in her direction. As his eyes adjusted to the dimness under the canopy, he realized that the woman was Martha and without the slightest consideration, he discounted her apparent terror. Even more quickly than it had come, his current state of concern was replaced with an irritation that blended seamlessly with his natural distaste for the outspoken woman.

"Martha! What izit?" he shouted to her from the distance, his pace now barely a stroll. He made no effort to conceal his aggravation and was hoping that she would drop the whole charade before he wasted anymore time letting his breakfast get cold. To his satisfaction, she had swallowed her sobs almost immediately after he had spoken her name, although he wasn't sure if she respected him like she did Sam, he knew she at least feared him. Josh smiled as he watched her struggling to contain herself, but he quickly grew tired of waiting through the uncomfortable silence while she searched for the composure to speak, "Martha! Now what in tha tarnashuns izit woman?" he screamed at her again.

Martha pointed a quivering hand down the path as she casually clutched the other against the front of her apron pocket which was gaping open with the weight of several glass vials, "...S...am..." her voice cracked on the single syllable but it was clear enough to redirect Josh's attention past her to where the two figures sat near the fork in the path.

"Oh!...Dear Lord," Josh choked as he instantly recognized Katie's fire-engine-red streaked hair cascading over Sam's arm and realized that something must be terribly wrong for him to be caressing her in his arms. She was limp and her head and arms swayed slightly each time Sam rocked back and forth on his knees. Even over the distance Sam's anguish was clear to Josh. *What had that temptress done to Sam now?* he seethed. He had warned Sam about her, but now he genuinely regretted his accuracy. Without a moment's pause he plotted the inevitable course of action and sprinted toward Sam – with Frank and the men on his heals there was no time to waste and he hoped the old woman's hysteria might at least buy him the few extra moments he needed.

"Stay put!" he ordered Martha as he sped past, "An keep yer mouth shut!"

"Blessed Be! Thank you Goddess!" Jez quietly proclaimed as she entered the safety of their encampment. After nearly exposing her presence to the NoTechs she had trekked the entire two mile hike back in complete silence even though she had not sensed anyone following her. Focusing on maintaining her silence and scanning her surroundings thoroughly had required all of her mental resources, so now that her mind was free to relax in relative safety, she reviewed the morning's events with a level of detachment and approached the others fairly composed. *I do hope that no one was hurt,* she thought as she kissed the small goddess charm she kept around her neck for protection, *Thank you for the timing of whatever that was!* Jez casually brushed the loose hairs from her face and dusted the dirt and leaves off her clothes before finally making her presence known to the group of men and women congregated under the shade tarp.

"Uh um..." she loudly cleared her throat.

Zeke looked up from the map he had scratched in the dirt, "Oh, hey Hon," he unconsciously smiled, "So you got the message?"

"Something like that," she answered cryptically, not wanting to announce her lapse in judgment to the whole group, "So how about getting me up to speed real quick now that I'm here?"

"I don't see how you put up with her Zeke. All work and no play..." an older gentleman she recognized from town snickered and winked at Zeke.

Jez focused on jogging her memory for his name, *'A'...Alex...no...'B'...Ben...no...'C'...Chuck... That's right, Chuck, retired NAVY Seal Chuck,* "Well Chuck, someone has to keep everyone in line. After all, you obviously have no experience with self-discipline," she dished it right back, sending him into a laughing fit of mock indignation.

"Okay kids, don't make me turn this camp around," Zeke joined in as he rose to give Jez a quick hello kiss, "So did you find out anything useful?"

"Actually I did," she settled down in an empty camp chair next to him and sipped the cup of Chai he handed her, "Sam is expected back at any time and they're ready and anxious to execute their 'Mission' once he arrives and gives the word, probably today or tomorrow sometime."

Chuck scrolled through the menus on his wrist unit, "You were right Jez, they're trying to take advantage of the dark moon. My guess is that they use today and tomorrow to get in position since the moon will be at its smallest at nineteen hundred thirty-three hours the day after tomorrow," he tapped the small screen as he verified the moon's cycle.

"Chuck, do you expect the others to arrive in time to take out the armory tonight if Sam does arrive today?" Zeke briefed Jez as he continued their earlier strategizing session, "Martha's going to lace the first evening meal after Sam returns, so if we can't be ready by tonight we need to get word to her just in case...hey Jez, do you think you might be able to reach her with that telepathic trick of yours?"

"Telepathy?" Chuck raised an eyebrow as he questioned what he'd just heard, "I know a lot of weird things have become normal these days, but are you really serious?"

Yes...Chuck barely heard the thought whispered in his head...*serious*...

Jez opened her eyes, "Did you 'hear' any of that Chuck?"

"Hear what? You didn't say anything."

"I was speaking telepathically. I said 'Yes, we're serious about telepathy,'" she repeated the message aloud.

"No..." Chuck reflected as he bit his lower lip, "No...wait...I did have a thought pop into my head that was in a woman's voice so it didn't make any sense," now it was Jez's turn to raise an eyebrow, "I just heard the word 'Yes' and then a moment later the word 'Serious' popped into my head...That was you?" he nearly fell out of his chair as the light bulb went on.

"Yes, that was me," Jez felt her frustrations surfacing again, "Sorry Zeke, but I guess I haven't developed that kind of range yet. And since I've never met her, I don't have any connection with her to use as a foundation."

"Well you two, I don't think we really have anything to worry about," Chuck made a three-point shot at Zeke with a crumpled sheet of paper.

"It was just a passing thought Hon," Zeke unfolded and scanned the note, "don't beat yourself up over it. Besides, it's all working out. The Universe is looking out for us just like you're always saying it does." He could feel her frustration as he took her by the hand and passed her the wrinkled note, "The northern camp was found abandoned so the other team is on their way here as we speak."

Jez breathed out deeply and felt the weight along her shoulders melt, "Thanks, sometimes I guess I just need reminding." She laughed with relief, "For a couple of guys that couldn't light a campfire with a lighter, they turned out to be surprisingly competent...will Carl and Alex be with this backup team?"

"Yes, they asked to be here because they want to be able to identify their friends should things 'turn ugly,'" Zeke attempted to rub away the tension growing in the back of his neck at the utterance of that familiar euphemism, "Jez, do you think I was being honest with Ethan when I told him we could force Sam to walk away?"

Jez leaned over to Zeke, "Hey you," she caressed his face in her palms, "Now is not the time to loose optimism. We may not be able to order him to walk away, but we can sure as hell drag his drugged unconscious ass away before he does any more harm."

Zeke closed his eyes as he sandwiched her hands with his and savored the warmth of her against his face, "Thanks Jez..."

"Hey, hey! Get a room you two," Chuck broke into their moment, "Now that that's settled, someone needs to go relieve Ethan. The boy needs to take a break, even if he is the only one who's seen this Sam. He's been at that post over four hours straight and that's just too long..."

Adults and children sat shoulder to shoulder in the overcrowded lunch room. Every member of the camp that wasn't obligated elsewhere had arrived with the first stroke of the dinner bell since word of Sam's return had spread almost before he had emerged from the forest with Josh. With anxiety levels threatening to spill over, the gossip buzzed easily from table to table and the excited chatter bounced off the walls, filling the large cafeteria with a strangely calming white noise. Still, throughout the room eyes flickered like candles as people dared polite intermittent glances of Sam. He sat at the center of a long table which had been raised on a platform and distanced from the other tables in the front of the cafeteria. He was flanked by Josh on his left and Frank to his right and the five additional seats on either side of them were filled with various members of the camp's leadership, mostly pastors and preachers all dressed in their Sunday's best and sitting like some posed display. For their first meal together since Sam's return, Josh had carefully orchestrated the seating to insulate Sam, whom he claimed was still suffering from exhaustion and should not be bothered with idle conversation.

"Would ya care fer sum'mar bizkits? Ah baked'em up special fer th'cassion," Martha smiled widely as she flourished the basket of steaming hot garlic cheese biscuits over Sam's plate, "it bein are last hot supper fer uhwhile."

Sam didn't look up, but rather mumbled incoherently to himself and rubbed at his bloodshot eyes which seemed to water incessantly at some unknown irritation.

Josh callously pushed the basket aside and impatiently nipped any further small talk, "Thanks, but he's still work'n on the last'un."

"Sorry," Martha choked, "Ah jus...Ah...Ah werked real hard ta make enough for all'ya t'ave seconds..."

"Martha, why don't ya give me tha basket an we'll jus pass'em down tha table?" Frank stepped in with the necessary tact that Josh lacked and reached out for the basket which was visibly shaking in Martha's grip.

"Oh, sure thang," she released the basket and began to walk away but stopped in afterthought. "Make sure ta save uh couple fer Miss Katie," she watched Josh in the corner of her eye as she spoke, "they're her faverit."

"That's not supris'n. Ah thank every'en likes yer bizkits more'n pie!" Frank rubbed his belly as he complemented her in farewell.

"Why thank ya Past'r Frank," satisfied with Josh's apparent discomfort Martha curtsied and walked away, leaving the last of her special biscuits in Frank's care, "Ya'll boyz enjoy'em."

From the moment they stepped inside the dark, warm storage room they all knew they were working on borrowed time – the stagnant air reeked of fuel and chemicals. As the door quietly closed behind them the unnatural silence enveloped the explosives team in a blackness like a cold damp mist and seemed to absorb even the sound of their collective breathing while they stood there still in the dark awaiting the all-clear.

"Holy Shit!" Zeke choked under his breath as he cautiously snapped a large glow stick, "NO flashlights or lanterns! Maintain positions!" he flatly commanded before finishing his initial survey of the room.

Industrial grade shelving lined each wall and an additional row of shelving dissected the room. Automatics, rocket launchers, plastic explosives, and nearly every fathomable type of weapon were stock piled onto the shelves up to the ceiling and still more were piled up on the floor with a complete disregard of the safety risks posed by the haphazard storage. But what had caused Zeke's alarm were the large wooden crates stacked at the end of the middle row. He didn't need to decipher the faded labeling painted on the weathered wood to understand the danger. The translucent white gelatin seeping through the slits between the boards was the only warning he needed.

"Chuck, could you please verify what I am seeing?" he calmly whispered to the man next to him.

"Well Zeke, I imagine you are concerned with those three crates of dy-na-mite that appear to be seeping nitro," Chuck rattled off matter-of-factly, "as well as the high level of fumes in the air that smell quite, well, explosive. May I suggest we evacuate all unnecessary personnel in due haste."

Zeke subdued a laugh, "Yes you may Chuck. I'll even let you arm a small charge to blow this tinder box once we've got the area clear."

"Why thank you Zeke," Chuck tipped his nonexistent hat with his middle finger. "Okay people, you heard the man. Let's clear out of here," he calmly ordered as he almost casually inspected the problematic crates, "Jack, leave your case behind, I want to use our stuff for the charge. Zeke, you can evacuate with the rest of 'em. I can take care of this from here."

Zeke followed the exiting team to the door but stopped after the last person disappeared into the dark. "You know Chuck, this can be done much safer if you have an extra set of hands," he carefully shut the door but made sure Chuck heard it close, "I'll be staying. Besides, someone needs to check your work to make sure you don't blow yourself up."

Chuck grinned and snapped another glow stick, "Okay then, let's getter done!"

With the moon barely a sliver and only one small window, the room was shrouded in near complete darkness. Only the dead silence of the late night was more oppressive than the endless void of the dark. With everyone asleep there was no comforting chatter carrying down the halls or the calming rhythm of footsteps as people walked past. And there certainly were none of the modern day distractions Sam preached against, no clatter from a washing machine or dryer, no ringing of cell phones, and definitely no immoral cackles from a radio or television. By all accounts, the night should be calmly quiet with nothing aside from his own breathing to penetrate the night. Yet Sam writhed on the fold-out couch with his hands clutched over his ears and his eyes squeezed shut as if he were trying to avoid some traumatic display. And with each heartbeat he entangled himself tighter in the sweat soaked bed sheets as he continued to struggle against the unseen assailant.

"Ma! I'm trying Ma!" he sobbed in his sleep, unaware that his screams echoed down the hall.

The man gently cinched the make-shift zip-tie restraints, "I hope that's not too tight miss," he politely restrained the woman, "Now please keep quiet, otherwise I'll have to tape your mouth shut and I really don't want to."

"Ah pramiss ta kep quiet," the groggy woman complied without the slightest struggle as she was led to the holding room, "Ar ya robb'n us? Cause we got nothin. Weeze lost it all'n tha storms."

"No ma'am, we're not here to rob ya. We're just here to talk. Now you sit put and get some sleep if you can. We'll be back in a few hours to release all of you," McDowd sympathized with her as he handed the woman off to his counterpart guarding the former campus administrative offices that they had appropriated for their detention center.

"I sure hope there's not too many more, we're getting close to running out of space," he commented conversationally as he rejoined the team.

"There's not. I only sense three, maybe four, more awake down the East Hall," Jez directed the remaining members toward the hall on their left.

"Then comes the easy part of lugging a hundred plus unconscious bodies across the campus," Becka smirked, "Jez, are you sure they're not going to wake up as we're carrying them?"

"Positive. That stuff Doc gave us is regularly used to sedate horses," she lowered her tone as they approached the East Hall, "so they'll be out for hours..." Jez stopped in her tracks and instinctively shielded her temples with her hands as if the attack she felt was a physical one, "Uugh!" But her hands provided no protection against the sudden assault on her mind created by the unwanted mental presence. She had been maintaining an open connection with the people that she sensed were awake, but it had never occurred to her that someone might reverse that connection and follow it back into her mind. Now Jez could barely think with all the screaming and ranting going on in her head and the voices were all speaking at once, making it impossible for her to understand anything they said or to even identify the number of voices. To make matters worse, although she couldn't identify them, she could feel the desperate pain from a young boy and another older man. It was almost more than she could bare but she managed to focus her efforts long enough to force the voices to fade into the distance before she nearly collapsed from the resulting vertigo.

"Jez," McDowd was immediately by her side supporting her with his arm around her waist, "are you okay?"

She relaxed into his grip and concentrated all her energies on closing her mind to the intruders, pushing their remaining essences out as she exhaled. A moment later Jez took another deep breath and the anguish nearly faded from her face, "Thanks McDowd, I'm fine now."

"What was that? You looked like you were about to pass out," he challenged her reassurances as she tested her balance.

"Yeah Jez, are you sure you're fine because you don't look like it?" Becka held out the mouth piece of her Camelbak, "Here, drink some of my water. There's a Vita-Pak in it."

Jez sipped the proffered concoction as she continued to rub her temples, "Thanks, I am fine...for now anyway...So hey...could you hear anyone crying or screaming just now?"

"You mean other than you moaning in pain?" Becka urged Jez to take another sip, "No, we didn't hear anything."

"Well that's all I could hear. I can't believe it was all just in my head...it was SO loud," Jez covered her ears as if just speaking of the noise hurt, "and there seemed to be so many different voices, and then there was this boy and a man crying and sobbing...it was all so painful and I'm not sure whoever it was even realized that I was there or what they were doing to me." She took another deep breath as she continued to push away at the painful invasive thoughts, "There is definitely at least one very strong telepath in the group that's awake and we're going to have to do something about that because I don't know that I can keep them out of my head once we get closer..."

McDowd continued to hover just behind her, "Are you sure they didn't hurt you somehow Jez? Cause you still look awful pale and I don't know if you realize it, but you're shaking."

Jez held her hand up in front of her face and swallowed against her constricting throat when she realized that her hand...and the rest of her...was indeed trembling. "Probably just nerves," she quickly dismissed the anomaly, "I feel just fine, so why don't we move on."

"Okay, but you let us know the moment you sense them again and we'll take it from there," McDowd gave Becka a sideways glance.

"Yeah, I've still got plenty of that other sedative Doc gave us," Becka removed the syringes from the side pocket of her utility pants, "so you can hold back until we've sedated them. I'm not taking any chances even if you are, cause Zeke would kill me if I let anything happen to you!" She grabbed Jez by the arm as they eased their way down the dark hallway.

"Oh Ma!" Sam sobbed as he felt the warmth of her hand on his cheek.

She was caressing his face in her hands with her forehead resting against his, "You promise

Mommy you will always be that gentle when you grow up big and strong like your daddy?" her face was so close to his that he could only focus on the mole next to the bridge of her nose.

He reached out for her hand, "I'm trying Ma! I'm trying so hard!" he choked on his words. He hated to let her see him cry because he knew she would worry.

"I'm so lonely baby...I'm so lonely..." Elvis serenaded from a radio somewhere.

Sam sat up in bed as he tried to determine where the sound was coming from. There were no working radios anywhere in camp and there certainly wasn't any electricity.

"I feel so lone..." the music suddenly stopped and a moment later Sam saw a flash of light as a radio flew across the room.

"No..." his mother gasped before the radio sank beneath the suds and the circuit was complete. The shock threw her backwards and her head slammed against the edge of the dining table before she collapsed onto the cold tile floor. Sam's heart sank as he rushed to her aid.

"Okay Mommy," his hands were dwarfed by the bandage as he gently rubbed the tape into place, "Did I do a good job Mommy?"

"Yes, you did. You were very gentle," she caressed his face in her hands as she leaned her forehead against his, "You promise Mommy you will always be that gentle..."

Sam rocked back and forth on the edge of the bed, his arms wrapped tightly around himself, "I'm trying Mommy...I'm trying Mommy..." he chanted.

"I'm so lonely baby...I'm so..." Elvis answered.

"No..." his mother's cry interrupted before it was cut short.

"Stop it! Stop it!" Sam screamed and dug his fingers deeper into his ears to keep from losing his grip. His nails cut through the flesh causing his ears to bleed, but he was too overwhelmed to feel anymore pain. He laid down and curled up into a ball, seeking comfort from the closeness of his own flesh and his screams drained into sobs. Finally, his father nudged his mom with his boot as he turned to leave the kitchen.

"This never happened," his father casually walked past him without a second glance.

Sam turned and watched over his shoulder until his father disappeared into the living room and the noises of a million different voices began to trickle out, "Ma! I'm trying Ma!"

Josh reached over to the side of his head and pulled it toward his shoulder, stretching his neck until he heard it crack. He stretched the other side as well before finally feeling around in the dark for the book of matches he kept on his bedside table. The room was pitch black so he guessed that it must be sometime in the middle of the night. On the verge of their most important mission ever, the camp was wrought with apprehension and Josh felt every bit of it. He was having trouble calming his thoughts down enough to fall asleep and Sam's incessant sobbing didn't help. He couldn't risk Sam's breakdown being exposed and sending doubts rippling through camp. They had come too far to turn away now...there were expectations and plans...

Josh rubbed his eyes as he struggled to focus in the dim light of his lone candle. Yes, they had come too far.

"No!..." yet another of Sam's screams rang along the corridor, jolting the last remnants of sleep from Josh's bloodshot eyes.

Dear Lord, please help us...guide my hand... the prayer flashed through his mind as he practically flew out the door, grabbing his gun along the way.

Ethan tapped the face of his watch nervously as he stood guard by the emergency exit. "Two minutes...two minutes...they should have been here two minutes ago," he mumbled under his breath as he paced the length of the doorway, "two minutes..."

Ethan!

The woman's whisper broke into his thoughts and he nearly bit through his lip when he swallowed his startled scream before it escaped his throat, "What the...?!"

Ethan! Behind you!

The voice was loud this time, causing him to spin around and almost scream again. A lady that he didn't recognize stared back at him through the glass door. She was nearly as tall as he was and she was very pretty, he especially liked the way she had pulled her copper hair into small pigtails on either side of her neck. She waved at him and he fought the urge to run off when his face warmed in a blush.

The lady sensed his embarrassment and smiled sweetly even as she shook her head in the negative and pointed emphatically at the locked door, *I'm sorry, but we have to hurry Ethan. Jez is in trouble!* the urgency in her voice instantly dissolved his previous hesitation and he rushed to unlock the door.

"Hey, sorry I scared you but we have to hurry. Now where is the East Hall?" Kara blurted as she pushed him backward.

Ethan was surprised that her voice was the same as it had been in his head and it took him a moment to process her question, "Uhm...It's this way," he pointed the group down the hall and was nearly carried away with them as they rushed forward, "But I'm supposed to be waiting for Zeke..."

"No time!" Kara silently signaled one of her team members to take Ethan's position at the door, "He'll understand. Now pick up the pace cause Jez's life's in our hands!" She grabbed him by the arm forcing him into a jog to keep up with her, "Come on Ethan! I can't help her from here...I need to get closer!"

Sam slowly released his grip on his ears and violently shook his head like a dog shaking off fleas, but the room remained unchanged and the night remained quiet. He couldn't hear the radio or TV anymore and his mother had disappeared from his arms. He bit his lip until it bled as he fought back the terror he felt creeping up his spine. What had his father done to her? He needed to find her and explain why he hadn't helped. Sam struggled to pull himself together, he couldn't let his ma see him so emotional and unkempt. He wiped the tears from his face with his bloody hands before brushing them down his shirt to smooth out the wrinkles. Then he ran his fingers through his hair and pasted down the strays with spit until he was confident each hair was in place. He would have properly inspected his appearance in the mirror, but the room had filled with a thick fog, making it impossible to see anything beyond the length of his arm. Where was he? How was he going to find his ma in all this fog? Sam barely avoided falling into another panic as he forced himself to keep moving forward, "Ma! Which way do I go? Ma?"

Suddenly the blurry image of a woman appeared on the other side of the room and he knew it was her. Her red hair framed her face like a halo and his heart sank into his stomach.

"Ma!" he screamed as he began to run toward her. Instantly the distance between them was gone, but she remained a blur and always just beyond his reach. "Ma!...There's something wrong with me...I...I can't see right," Sam flailed his hands around in the air as he attempted to reach for her, "Ma! Why can't I touch you?"

"It's okay Sam. I'm here, just let me get closer," she reassured him, "Be a good boy and be patient."

"Yes Ma," Sam took a deep breath as he struggled to maintain his patience, "I'm waiting Ma." He could see her image taking on a more distinct shape so he closed his eyes to avoid the temptations of his impatience. Finally Sam felt her hand brush his.

"Sam, I'm here to help you. Do you want my help to get out of here?" her voice had an unearthly quality to it that Sam could feel and he knew that he didn't need to run anymore.

Sam took her hand, "Yes Ma, please help me."

"Mah Dear Lord!" Josh whispered under his breath as he rushed toward the body collapsed on the floor, "This cane't happin! Yer dead...Ah buried ya mahself!" He circled around the woman who lay on her side with her legs curled up and her hands clutched to the sides of her head. Her dark hair was strewn about her face and he struggled to make out her features in the dim light, "Yer naught real!" Afraid to touch the body, he kicked her in the ribs and nearly jumped out of his skin when she screamed in pain, "What tha hell!"

The woman shielded her belly with her arm as she tried to crawl away from her new attacker, but after only a few feet she was overwhelmed again. "Help..." she gasped as she collapsed an arm's length from the corridor her friends had taken.

Enraged, Josh easily covered the distance between them in a couple of steps. Even if this wasn't Katie, it couldn't be anyone from camp and he wouldn't be made a fool of by having some strange woman wandering the halls. In his rage he dove at the semi-conscious woman, violently grabbing her by the hair at the nape of her neck. She merely whimpered in pain, too weak to scream, so he grabbed harder.

"Who are ya an why are ya here?" he demanded.

"Huh?...What?" the woman sobbed in confusion.

"Ah said 'Who are ya?'" Josh placed the muzzle of his gun in the crook of her neck, "An why are ya here?" He tightened his grip on her hair as his anger fed on itself.

"I...I...don't know..." she cried, even more terrified as she realized she didn't have the answers to his questions.

Josh rammed the muzzle deeper into her neck, "Well, Ah say yer uh hairtic an unless ya prove me wrong Ah will send ya back ta tha hell ya come from," he cocked the gun to punctuate his point.

"Please...please...don't hurt me!" the woman begged for her life but her pleas were barely intelligible as she drifted in and out of consciousness, "Please..."

Sam sat on the edge of his bed with his head resting in his hands. He knew that it was very late and that he had been sitting there for a while, but he wasn't sure for how long. He wasn't even sure how long he'd been awake or even if he was awake. Reluctantly, he opened his eyes slowly and was relieved when he could barely see in the dark room – things were as they should be. Maybe it had all been just a bad dream. He lit the lantern by his bed and the room came into focus as he turned up the wick. He rubbed the sleep from his eyes, yes, he knew this place, at least it seemed familiar.

Sam swiftly slipped on his shoes and made his way to the door, eager to verify his circumstances with a quick walk about the church. Navigating his way down the corridor as much by memory as sight, the hallway seemed much wider than he remembered, but he was tired and it was late, so he quickly forgot the discrepancy.

"...Please..." the woman's faint sobs penetrated Sam's awareness as he turned the corner. Almost immediately his knees locked and he stood there wide-eyed and frozen. He wrapped his arms about himself as tears welled up in his eyes and he struggled to remember how to breathe. His heart was preparing to burst out of his chest and sweat trickled down his temples.

"...Please..." the woman's cries echoed in his ears so loudly that he thought his eardrums might burst, "...Please..." His breaths were now so short and fast that they burned, but he didn't care, nothing beyond her mattered, "...Please..."

"No! I will not let you hurt Ma again!" Sam launched himself at his father, determined to wrestle the gun from him and put an end to his mother's suffering.

"Sam?" the man sounded confused, dropping the woman in his grip just as Sam landed on top of him and grabbed for his gun. With his free hand the man reinforced his grip against Sam's efforts to pry the gun free, but Sam easily matched his strength. Seemingly at an impasse, the man attempted to disable Sam with a forceful blow of his head against Sam's temple. But Sam was ready for him, turning so that the man slammed into the bone of his shoulder instead, and then using the momentum to deliver a powerful thrust of his knee deep into the man's abdomen and knock the air from his lungs. Out of breath and disoriented, the man defensively clenched his fingers tighter against Sam's prying hands, forgetting the hair-pin trigger that waited at the ready.

Their cautious silence was suddenly pierced by the distinctive bang which hissed down the long hallway without losing a decibel as it easily ricocheted off the tile walls along the way.

"Oh God!" Kara screamed and clutched her abdomen as if the sound carried as much of an impact as the bullet it had originated from, "Someone's been shot!"

"Well then, let's pick up the pace! Jez might be hurt," Ethan pulled at Kara's arm as she stood transfixed, "Why is everyone just standing around?" Tears began streaking his face as he tugged nervously at Kara's arm, "Let's go!"

But Kara appeared not to hear him, like an antique porcelain doll, her face was blank and her eyes stared into nowhere as if she had been completely disconnected from her body.

"Kara!" Ethan slapped her on the cheek, "Snap out of it! We need to go!"

Tears were now welling up in her eyes and streaming down her face as she blinked, "Ethan..." she moaned, "I can't sense Jez anymore..."

Ethan steadied himself against the wall, he felt as if all the blood had just drained from his body and he couldn't breath, "No...you're wrong!" He refused to comprehend the meaning behind her words, "We have to hurry! Jez is fine!"

"Ethan... she's...gone..." Kara's voice came out in gasps as her throat threatened to close up on her.

Suddenly the dim hallway was bathed in an amber light while the walls rattled and the ground shook with the low roar of an explosion rumbling from the opposite side of the campus. Ethan glanced at his watch – half past the hour, "It's not time yet!" he tapped on the glass, "No! It's too early... it's not time yet!" he howled as he collapsed on the ground. More tears clouded his vision and his entire body shuddered with dry heaves, "it's not time yet..."

12

The mother cares not for the road,
Taken more or less,
Only for herself and her children,
The journey is the true test.

The green seedpod lazily made its way across the field as it whirled in the season's first cool breeze, but the air was crisp and invigorating and inspired the seedpod to spin faster on its journey to the fertile earth of the fresh grave. Many others had already made the pilgrimage from the forest and the grave was appropriately speckled with green sprouts. It wouldn't be long before the earth reclaimed the area and the only sign of the grave's presence would be the small wooden cross at it's head.

Kara dutifully brushed away the cobwebs and placed fresh daisies by the cross. It had been over two weeks and her belly still ached every time she approached the grave, but her intense guilt compelled her so deeply that she couldn't stay away.

"How long?" Ethan casually asked as he emerged from the forest path. He knew that she had been there for hours, but he wanted her to admit it. He had watched her slowly waste away over the past weeks and he couldn't stomach it another day, "How long, Kara?"

Kara kept her eyes fixed on the grave and pulled up a dandelion, "Not very..." she dug into the earth for the vagrant root bulb, "just wanted to put fresh flowers is all...You don't have to check up on me Ethan..."

He sat down beside her and grabbed her hand before she was able to reach for another weed, "Kara, it's not your fault. You have got to stop blaming yourself!"

She pulled her hand free and turned away to pick another weed, desperately trying to avoid the scrutiny of his deep blue eyes, "I could have done more...I was right there Ethan...I should have been able to stop it!"

"You did the best you could," he snatched her hand again and this time he held it tightly against her efforts to pull free, forcing her to face him and the guilt she refused to release, "Kara, he was going to kill Jez!"

She collapsed against him and buried her head in his chest as she finally confessed the nightmare that had consumed her, "I know!" she sobbed as the tears spilled down her face. "Ethan...I...I...

FELT him die!" she sucked in another breath before exhaling, "The bullet...the pain...the blood gushing out..." She choked on yet another breath, "I felt it all!" Kara gasped for breath as she was overcome with her grief.

Sensing her ebbing consciousness, Ethan clutched her by the shoulders and forced her to face him, "Kara...Kara...stay with me," he leaned his forehead against hers and held her gaze, "Breathe with me...In...Out...In...Out..."

She struggled to match his breaths, but she was too weak to resist him for any longer, "Ethan...he...he...he's here..." she spat out the words between breaths before she collapsed against him and everything went black.

The young woman hovered on the side of the bed near the head, her golden locks cascading down over her bare shoulders as she reached her arms out to the woman across from her, "I want you to take my hands and don't let go until I say...No matter what!"

"Do you really think we can fix it?" Jez looked longingly down at her body and back to the woman's outstretched hands.

"Positive!" there was a mischievous glint in her sea green eyes and her voice rang with certainty, "Your hands please," she turned her palms up and wiggled her fingers in a beckoning manner.

Jez reached over her comatose body, clenching the woman's wrists as she held her hands palm to palm. Immediately she felt a surge of energy that quickly traveled through her as a closed circuit was created between them and golden light as radiant as the younger woman's locks began to pulse from their joined hands, "Oh jeez! Is that coming from you?"

"No, it's coming from us because we're connected, both in this plane and," she looked down at the body beneath them, "that one. Now I need you to focus on healing that body...cell by cell...I'm not ready to sacrifice this lifetime because you're distracted!"

Jez closed her eyes and began visualizing her body healing itself, from images of her white cells absorbing infectious entities down to fortifying her very cell walls. And with each new detail she pictured, the golden orb between them grew until it engulfed them as well as the body below. They began to drift down the length of the body at visually infinitesimal increments, but Jez felt as if they were racing faster than light. Each time they reached an end of the body they started drifting back the way they had come, weaving a shroud of healing energy around Jez's motionless body. All the while Jez had no sensation of the passage of time, each moment felt simultaneously a part of the previous and a part of the next, yet she watched as her body changed and healed below her. Eventually she realized that she was looking through her outstretched arms to the body below and the shock nearly caused her to release her grip, but the woman had anticipated her reaction and tightened her hold on Jez.

"What's happening?" Jez screamed her release when she couldn't break free. Although she knew on one level that her fear was unwarranted, witnessing her own disappearance had stirred the most basic latent fear that resided in all humans, the fear of ceasing to exist.

The woman just smiled softly, returning Jez to her previous serene state as she did so, "What is happening...You are...I am..."

Jez could barely make out her hands and arms anymore but her earlier fear had been replaced by a divine understanding even as she watched her form disappear. She stopped looking with her eyes and relented to the force, which felt a thousand times heavier than gravity, pulling her down toward her body on the bed. Jez glanced back at the young woman who was fading away as well, "Thank you."

The woman wispily waved farewell and blew her a kiss as she faded away, "You're welcome...and, thank you...Mama..." her words resonated through Jez long after her mist had vanished.

"Whoa! That's good right there. Go ahead and secure it," Zeke called down to Jack as he held the massive brass crucifix in position against the wall.

Jack latched the safety on the cable wench and waved a thumbs-up, "Okay, she's secure."

With the crucifix resting steadily in place, Zeke stepped away and peered over the scaffolding,

"Thanks Jack. Now come on up and help me weld it down." He waved to the large man watching from a safe distance, "Hey Frank, last chance. Are you sure you don't want the damage repaired?"

Pastor Frank sighed and shook his head back and forth, "Nah Zeke, Ah thank its important tha'tit stay jus as it is," he took a moment to observe the battered crucifix. One arm of the cross had become detached from the figure of Christ and was bent at a downward angle while Christ's arm had been twisted nearly to his waist. And the top of the cross had bent so far forward that it now cradled Christ's scratched and tarnished face. Frank coughed against the tension constricting his throat and blotted his eyes before the tears had a chance to show, "We need tha constant remind'r how we let are fear taint are faith. Shame makes it too darn easy ta fergit the past."

"You are a good man Pastor Frank," Zeke had come to genuinely like the quirky old man as they had worked together to convert the former campus into a proper center for the ministry. Frank had stepped in and taken control over the group the morning after the explosion once he had been roused and informed of Sam's condition and the related murders of Katie and Josh. He had kept the group from exploding into violence as they awoke in confinement with strangers tending to their wounded and battling the massive blaze that still burned in the former armory. Frank had a gift when it came to communicating with the flock that he and Sam had led and Zeke was grateful for it, "and I don't see how anyone could forget that lesson with you around!"

"Uhm...Uhh..." Frank loosened his collar to dampen his sudden discomfort, "Thank ya Zeke. It means alot com'en from tha likes of ya. Specially considrin what we did. Ya walk tha walk better'en we'd ever hope ta. Ah jus want'ya ta know yer lady's in are prayers every day." He lowered his head and privately said a quick prayer for Jez as he did every time she came up in conversation.

Zeke clutched the goddess charm that dangled from his neck and gently rubbed the round black stone set in the belly. Wearing Jez's favorite necklace gave him a sense of her presence and the strength to keep going because he knew that's what she expected of him. Now, as Zeke reached the end of a project that had fostered so much cooperation and genuine respect, he took a moment to think of her. He could feel her joy and relief as strongly as his own and almost tucked it away as his personal sense of accomplishment, but something told him it was much, much more. He closed his eyes and searched for that familiar tingle down his neck that he always got just before Jez came into sight.

"Hey! Jack," Zeke bellowed as he practically flew to the ground, "can you get McDowd and finish this without me?"

"Shu..."

"Thanks!" Zeke shouted back to Jack and Frank as he ran past the bewildered men without waiting for an answer, "She's awake! Jez's awake!"

An older woman sat side saddle on the edge of the bed with her hip resting against Jez's thigh. Her blonde hair was pulled back into a tight bun at the base of her long slender neck, exposing her ears enough that with each breath her earrings flittered like faeries dancing about her face. The normally vibrant green of her deep set sea green eyes was dulled with worry and glistened only from the tears she barely kept at bay. She kept Jez's hand cradled in her lap, gently massaging it and occasionally using the tip of her own finger to trace words on Jez's palm and forearm. She had been there every day and night, making note of every change in pulse or respiration, of every twitch and eye movement. The woman knew precisely when Jez dreamt and when her mind was quiet, she could feel it. Over the past hour she had noticed a constant rise in Jez's breathing and heart rate, but more than that, she sensed there was something going on at that moment and she prayed for it to be good.

A moment later Jez's eyes began to drift slowly from side-to-side under her closed lids. The woman stopped massaging Jez's hand and held still, afraid to even dare a breath, waiting, waiting for a sign her daughter was still there. And then she knew. It was just the faintest twitch, but she knew.

"Jez...Jez, its okay to wake up honey. Mama's here," she leaned over and cooed in her daughter's ear, the warm breath of her words trailing over her daughter's face. As she looked over Sylvia noticed Jez's eyelids flicker in response and then she felt

Jez's fingers wiggle against her palm. "Al!...Al!...Hurry, she's waking up," she shouted out the door at the top of her lungs, "Someone get Zeke!"

Jez's eyes opened and she struggled to focus her vision against the swirling room, "Ma?...Al?" her voice was scratchy at best, just barely a whisper. Her mother gently squeezed her hand and Jez burst into tears with the physical confirmation that her long journey was over. She beckoned with her free hand for Al to join them and the tall woman gladly abandoned her post by the door, revealing Puk, who quickly leapt up onto the bed and covered Jez in sweet doggie kisses all over her face before anyone could intervene. Apparently satisfied with Jez's recovery, Puk settled down and curled up by her side. With the end to her K-9 assault, Jez cautiously opened her eyes only to fall into another round of joyous sobs, "Oh! Zeke!..."

The dial crept its way along the edge of the gage, steadily closing the distance to the awaiting green field. Further down the panel another display blinked "100" and yet more dials all wobbled among fields of green. And over it all, the old familiar hum of technology filled the pristine control room.

"I've got all green here," Derek zipped down the twelve foot length of the control panel with a quick thrust of his foot as he leaned on the arm of his swivel chair, "How are things on your end?"

Kit simultaneously flipped a series of switches and typed in the desired response codes, her long slender fingers appearing to dance along the monitoring station. She chewed on her lower lip as she pondered a questionable readout, then tapped a few more keys before pushing away from her workstation.

"We're good to go Babe!" she held her thumb up as she spoke so that the good omen was visible through the observation window above the control panel.

"We're ready Betsy! Just say the word!" Derek radioed their status to the anxious councilwoman even as the rumble of applause made its way into the control room.

"Thanks Derek," Betsy's elated response was nearly drowned out by the accompanying shouts of celebration, "Stand by."

Betsy patted down the air with her hands – her various bangles jingling with the exaggerated motions – until the wave of anxious silence made its way through the crowd gathered on the electrical plant's main floor. The open maintenance bay was ordinarily used to store the facility's mobile lifts and other heavy equipment, but today it looked more like a lecture hall at a convention center. Row upon row of folding chairs had been artfully arranged in a semi-circle around a small stage built just for the occasion. Someone had even adorned the end of each row of chairs as well as the stage with a variety of potted plants and candles. The media section to the right of the stage was also surrounded by greenery which did little to draw attention away from the handful of photographers and former reporters who were dutifully recording the event for posterity while another group was broadcasting it as breaking news over the shortwave radio network in place.

A loud knocking sound echoed through the solid concrete building and all eyes turned to Betsy as she tapped the microphone positioned at the front of the stage. "Good eve'nin ya'll," she paused until the chatter subsided, "Just'in case yer not familiar with me, I'm Bessie an I'm on the townsh'ps council. Now, I'm not goin ta go off on any long speech," she smiled as a good natured laugh erupted from the crowd. "Okay, quiet down now or Ah'll hafta change my mind about tha speech," she snickered. "Okay, as Ah was say'n...We all know what uh mon-u-mental day this is. An we certainly all know tha sacrifices it took taggit this done right," she locked eyes with Jez before passing a smile over Zeke, Ethan, Kara, and the group surrounding them, "So let's jus get'on with it, shall we?" She held out her hand in a beckoning manner, "Jez, please come'n up here an do tha honors."

Another round of applause and cat calls echoed off the walls, compelling Jez's compliance. With Zeke's arm wrapped protectively around her waist and her mother attached to the other side, Jez gingerly made her way up the platform to the awaiting mike. As if on cue, the crowd went silent just before she opened her mouth.

"Thank you all for this honor. I really don't deserve it alone," her voice cracked as she fought back the tears and impending sobs. She took a deep breath and held it, ransoming her composure for additional oxygen, "In fact, I wouldn't be alive today had it not been for the grace of many of you," she exhaled and directed a smile and a mental hug toward her family, Ethan, Kara, and Zeke, "so I must insist that we all share in the honor. On three...ONE...TWO..."

"POWER ON," the words rang through the building and the countryside as hundreds of voices in the plant and every radio control room along the coast shouted the command in unison. Their collective energy combined with the power emerging from the plant so that all present felt the initial surge, their skin tingling and their body hair standing erect long enough to initiate a cacophony of "Oo's" and "Ah's". Some even began to sway as the tingle continued throughout their body and brain, creating a euphoric sensation. Jez herself struggled against gravity as the tingle enveloped her belly and challenged her stability, but Zeke had been waiting for the moment and easily scooped her up into his arms. Eventually the sensation faded away and the murmurs faded in as the crowd waited for official notice that the ceremony was over.

"Excuse me," Zeke commanded the crowd's attention while keeping his eyes locked on Jez,

"But there's one more event that needs your attention." He paused a moment as he struggled for self-control and the crowd resumed its silence in response. "Jezzelle Aurora Kyle," he gently eased her into a chair draped in white that someone had sneaked onto the middle of the stage, "You are truly the light of my life. You are the part of my soul that was missing...the part that inspires me to do more, to be more..."

Jez sank into the chair, grateful for its support since she was quivering so violently that she doubted her ability to stay upright on her own. Only a fool couldn't predict where Zeke was leading, and not only was Jez no fool, she was a telepath. She tried her best to wait for him to speak, but his thoughts couldn't have been clearer to her if he had spelled them out in electroluminescent wire about his head. Fighting the nervous energy that threatened her composure she fanned her face with her hands to stem off the blush she knew would soon consume her cheeks, but Zeke grabbed her hand as he knelt down on one knee and unwittingly released her controls. Tears immediately burst from her eyes as she lost all restraint, "Yes! Yes! Yes!" she gushed, "I will marry you right now, right here, forever!"

I knew you wouldn't be able to let me finish, Zeke's voice chuckled in her head, triggering an even more all encompassing smile as Jez realized that he had intentionally directed the silent message to her.

Jez eagerly presented her ring finger to Zeke, *You've been holding out on me,* she pathed the playful challenge.

"In more ways than one, my love," he crooned and pathed simultaneously as he retrieved an intricately carved antique silver band and tenderly slipped it onto her proffered finger.

In an instant the black night subsided as a wave of light burst from the heart of the power plant and quickly spread across the distance like luminescent dominoes toppling across the landscape. Shouts and applause followed in a second wave like thunder after lightning. And not the least bit frightened by the sudden influx of light and sound, Tyler clapped his hands and jumped up and down with pure innocent excitement like only a child could, "Ma, it's just like fireworks!" he cheered.

Evie picked him up in her arms and spun quickly around in circles, "Yes Tyler! The most beautiful fireworks ever!" The rooftop of the hospital had afforded them a panoramic view which was now speckled with lights that continued to circle around them even after Evie had stopped spinning.

"Thanks Ma! That was great!" Tyler loosened himself from her grip and started spinning on his own with his arms outstretched.

"Okay, whose next?" Evie prepared herself for a marathon session of spinning as her other two children raced toward her for the privilege of being next.

"Next...Naxed Frank!" Martha held the last key down as she waited for Frank to flip her sheet music to the next page, "Its hard enough read'en by candlelit without ya messin up my timen..."

"Oh, sorry," Frank apologized as he quickly turned the page, "Ah was jus caught up'en tha bee-u-tiful organ music yer makin."

"Now Frank, iffen yer gonna sweet talk me yer gonna hafta lie better'en that," Martha hit the keys extra hard so that the plastic tapping was clearly audible, "There ain't nuttin com'en from this here organ but clickin till tha power gets back on."

"Oh, well..." Frank cleared his throat, "Ah musta bin day dream'en..."

"Ya certainly were...Now here comes tha chorus. It'll be mighty beaut'ful once tha organs work'en," as Martha's fingers danced along the keyboard the sound of French horns suddenly filled the room, sending her screaming into the air before she realized what had happened.

Frank clutched his large belly as he rolled with laughter, "Yeah, kinda like that...Ah'll go fetch tha choir whiles ya compose yerself...It's about time we had ourself uh real rehearsal!"

Martha straightened her skirt and righted the stool she had flung over in her escape, "Yew...yew...Ya plann'd this all along ya rascal!... 'Ya need the practice'... 'Yaren't afraid ta practice by candlelit are ya,'" Martha mumbled in mockery under her breath as she seated herself back at the electric organ.

Undeterred by her scowling, Frank practically skipped out of the room he was so delighted with his prank. "Ah'll jus turn the lights on fer ya," he snickered his warning as he closed the door behind him.

The door opened and radiant white light flooded into the dark room as the woman slowly glided across the floor to Sam's bedside. He was sleeping curled up on his side with his arms wrapped around his knees. His brows were knotted tight and his lips were stretched thin across his cinched shut mouth, making him appear quite troubled. The woman gently shook him by the shoulder to wake him and he jumped violently out of bed before cowering against the wall.

"Ma!" he cried, "You're dead! You're not real! You're not real! This is a dream...this is a dream..." he chanted as he closed his eyes and buried his head between his knees.

His mother knelt before him and grabbed his head, forcing him to look at her by holding his forehead against hers, "Sam Brown, you open your eyes and look at your mother! I need you to listen to me, there's not much time!" she lovingly commanded his obedience as she had often done during her short period of motherhood.

Sam obediently opened his eyes and nodded his acquiescence.

"Sam, you are correct. I am dead and this is a dream. I don't have time to explain, but what I'm about to tell you IS real," she paused a moment to emphasize the importance of her words, "Sam, Josh is very, very angry..."

"Josh is dead!" Sam cut her off.

His mother tightened her grip and her eyes cut into him, "Sam, I know that! Now be quiet and let me finish! Josh is very angry and he's very strong over here. He's coming for revenge, Sam! Now I want you to say it back to me...you must remember this when you wake up!"

Sam swallowed as he struggled to speak, "I'm sorry Ma," he whimpered while she watched a shadow pass over his face.

"Say it back to me!" she pled and glanced over her shoulder, "Quickly, he's coming!"

Sam fought back the tears, "Josh is angry and he's coming ba..."

"Sam, can you hear me? Sam, it's Kara," Kara held Sam tightly by the shoulders and shook him as she spoke.

"Kara?" Sam startled awake.

"Yes Sam," relief filled her voice, "it's me Kara. You've been very sick and got trapped in your dreams again." She spoke reassuringly as she locked eyes with him, "I'm going to come visit you in your mind so you can show me what's got you so scared, okay?"

Confused, Sam broke eye contact with Kara long enough to recognize Josh standing behind her. The next moment Josh's finger was perched across his lips as if to silence Sam.

"Kara, No! Josh..." Sam blurted but Kara couldn't hear him.

"It's okay Sam. Here I come," she cooed as she took a deep breath and naively rushed to open her mind, forgetting to establish the blocks that Jez had tried to drill into her. And with her next breath, like a cartoon character being sucked into a vacuum, Sam watched in horror as Josh disappeared into the back of Kara's head. Entranced, Sam sat on the edge of his bed as she tightened her grip with an unearthly strength and dislocated his shoulder while she perched the finger of her other hand across her lips, "Ssh...it's okay Sam. Ah'm savin ya fer last," she cooed in his ear.

Before he realized what had happened Kara had made her way to the nurse standing watch in the doorway. "Nurse, please inform tha Doc that Sam has suffered a regression an needs ta be put back on his meds immediately before he hurts himself, or worse, someone else..." she hissed as the nurse locked the door.

Personal Affects

The following documents are graciously on loan
from the historical archives of the
Kyle Development & Preservation Institute.

Hey Al,   May 29th

Congratulations on the new job Sis! I'm so ooper dooper proud of you! I can't believe my little sis is going to be designing pest resistant crops... sounds so sci-fi! Isn't it funny how when things are looking their bleakest you suddenly get everything you wanted all along? Glad I could help out and that the timing of it all worked out like we'd hoped, even on my end.... we'll be wrapping up this big mural project early, which means I'll be getting my bonus and have some moola to travel with! Looks like I'll make it to the housewarming after all (I miss you guys soooo much!)

Anyway, new job, new house, I'd say things are really starting to fall into place for you — well aside from the fact that you'll be living close to Mom & Dad...just glad it's you and not me :) (bad joke I know, but I couldn't help myself...he he he)

Well I gotta run to work...

Hugs and flowers,

    Jez

October 16th

Hey Sis! I really enjoyed our visit, just wish it could have been longer. There was so much that I wanted to talk to you about but there just wasn't any time for us to talk alone and I know Dad would have just made a fuss if I brought it up in front of him. Anyway, what I wanted to talk to you about was this "feeling" I've been having lately... I just know that something's going to happen, but I don't know when. You know my gut feelings are usually right on... remember how I picked out the plant strains to discuss during your job interview and it worked out just like I said :) So I can't really describe the feeling I've been having, maybe it's like a deja vous kind of thing, but everytime there's a story on the news about another earthquake or hurricane I get this weird "tingle" in my head. Give me a call when you've got time because I really would like to talk this over with you. Sometimes I just need reminding that I'm not completely crazy!

Hugs & Kisses! XXOO

Jez

December 23rd

Al, Mom & I ran out to grab a bite cause we figured you and Dad wouldn't be back for hours. I sure hope you were able to convince him to get a cell phone because I really worry about him driving without one. If he didn't listen give me a call 733.555.7170 and I'll buy one for him for xmas.

XXOO
Jez

Hey All!   July 1st

Thanks for listening and the advice. Like I said, I can't explain it, but I just know that something weird is going on with the earth and that "feeling" I have keeps getting stronger and stronger. The stuff I read about a cataclysmic shift of the different earth crusts is starting to sound and "feel" like a real possibility!

I just can't get over this feeling that there is something really BIG that is waiting for me down the line and I sometimes wonder if it doesn't have something to do with this. Just in case I've started taking a bunch of "free" wilderness courses that the big outdoor supply store down the street from me was offering (of course I had to buy a bunch of their stuff to get the free courses, but it was all camping gear I needed anyway, plus it was all on sale and you know me and my bargain shopping!) I'm learning some really cool stuff too, like how to preserve meat and tan leather. It's pretty funny cause they're even teaching us to make soap, you should see all the guys in class struggling with that and trying to make "macho" soap! Cracks me up! I figure if I do turn out to be wrong about this cataclysm thing, I'll at least be the most skilled camper you know! :)

Oh, and I followed your advice... I'm sending you guys "hurricane" survival packs... just promise to hold on to them and keep them handy so I can stop worrying about you. I made packs to keep in the house and some smaller ones to go in your cars. I also got you each a photovoltaic cell phone charger, so you'll be able to use your cell phones even if the power's off for a while. (BTW, has Dad even taken his out of the box, he never uses any minutes, so I'm getting suspicious.)

Well, here's a list of what both packs will have:

- Batteryless flashlight & radio

- Several butane lighters and some matches (just in case)

- Water purification tablets

- Large Camelbak (you can probably put the purification tablets right in the Camelbak if you don't have a water jug handy)

- 1 case of power bars (got your favorite: oatmeal raison!)

- Emergency thermal foil blankets

- Travel wet naps (great way to freshen up when there's no running water or soap available)

- Sharpies (always handy to have around)

- Duct tape (can fix absolutely anything :)

- A spiral notebook and pen (can at least be used to play hangman or doodle)

- 2 decks of cards (you know how much Mom love solitaire!)

For the car packs, I've added a few extra travel type things and packed it all in a nice hiking backpack...just in case you can't make it back to the house. There's a small roll up mat to sleep on and an inflatable travel pillow, but feel free to include a regular pillow if you like

Call me when you get this so I know that all the boxes made it there in tact.

Give Mom & Dad my love.

Life is Flowers!

Jez XXOOXXOO

ABOUT THE AUTHOR

From her mother, who was an artist who colorized black and white photographic portraits, PATRICIA GRIFFIN received the gifts of the eyes, hands, and heart of an artist. From her father, who was a college professor and textbook author, she received the powers of a strong intellect and reason. She has long felt that the purpose of this lifetime seems to be to find a balance between those two strong callings. With GAIA'S REVOLT, Patricia has indeed found that balance.